LEAF

AND

THE RUSHING WATERS

BY JO MARSHALL

ILLUSTRATED BY D.W. MURRAY

ISBN: 1461135788
ISBN-13: 9781461135784

Twig Stories are environmental fantasies
with family values for young readers

Twig Stories royalties are shared with nonprofit
organizations concerned
with protection of wildlife,
climate change research,
nature conservancy,
and forest preservation.

"With her *Twig* tales, Jo Marshall has done something amazing – tie a story of epic adventure to a naturally anchored account of environmental awareness – all tailored to the fresh, engaging mind of the youngster. Since beavers are already being reintroduced globally to combat the effects of climate change, I am certain the story's heroes are completely fitting. Our earth is unfortunate in that it currently lacks goliath beavers – so it's just going to have to make do with lots and lots of regular-sized ones.

With unexpected grace, Jo's charming fantasy helps make the daunting world of beavers and climate change more accessible."

Heidi Perryman, Ph.D.
President and Founder
Worth A Dam
www.martinezbeavers.org

"Leaf & the Rushing Waters is an engaging, evocative and fast-moving adventure story. Author Jo Marshall's Twig "people" come alive in an exciting, wild world where glaciers are melting. But Twigs recruit beavers to face the challenge. This new work is relevant to today's major challenge of climate change, and, simultaneously, is a delightful read for young people or anyone who enjoys nature."

Sharon T. Brown, M.A.
Director and Wildlife Biologist
Beavers: Wetlands & Wildlife
www.BeaversWW.org

Acknowledgements

I owe so much to my intuitive daughter, Ali, for her storyline designs and strategy. My loving thanks to my meticulous son, John, who insisted on sensible structure. My sincere gratitude goes to David Murray whose beautiful art continues to astonish and inspire us. Thanks to my editor, Bridget Rongner, for her cheerful pursuit of excellence. And to my husband and lifetime engineer, Tim, thanks for the reinforcement!

LEAF AND THE RUSHING WATERS

To Harvey & Reve
Stick to your dreams!
So Marshall

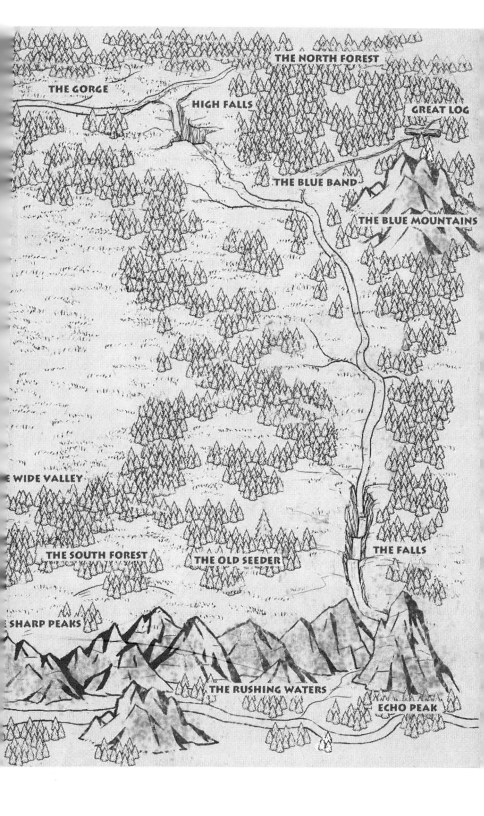

For John,

who kept my sense of humor

A TWIG NAMED LEAF

The soft, two-toed hooves of the mountain goat kid stubbornly gripped the granite slab. He bowed his head against the shrieking wind and brutal onslaught of the unusual storm. Ice clung to his eyelashes. Streams of sleet soaked his powder-white hair. His legs trembled uncontrollably. Slashes of lightening crackled and sizzled all around him. Yet, still the tiny kid refused to move.

Desperate to save him, his mum nudged her kid toward their only escape—a slippery, treacherous trail across an enormous ice dam. The dam spanned a sickeningly deep canyon, and barricaded a lake the color of turquoise.

We must cross over!

A vast ice pack—an ancient glacier—pressed against the lake, and embraced its shore. A soaring ridge cradled the glacier, and a track along its rim had led the mum and kid to the dam.

Cross over! You must!

Just then a heart-stopping *BOOM! BOOM! BOOM!* rolled over the frozen peak. A jagged bolt stabbed the ice! Crystals exploded! Gigantic slabs broke away, and plunged into the lake. The water heaved. As if gasping for air, the slabs rolled over and over until they gave up struggling, grew still, and spread out like white lilies floating on the frigid water. They drifted toward the ice dam, bombarded by the relentless, abnormally warm rain.

A sudden, ferocious slap of hail and wind-whipped sleet punished the remaining glacier.

Panicked, the older mountain goats abandoned the high trail, and skidded down the cliffs. They leapt from slick crags to reach the ledge where the kid trembled, and blocked their way. Frantic bleats battled the deafening thunder. Their wails urged the terrified kid to step from the granite, and onto the icy barrier that held the lake back from the chasm.

Cross over! Cross over!

The kid took a tentative step. Then, another. The herd grew silent. One nimble, cloven hoof after another proved its skill. In the midst of the screaming storm, the mountain goat herd crossed the dam, and fled from the frozen volcano to the dark forest below Thunder Peak.

In the distance, and across a wide, grassy valley, which was far away from Thunder Peak, the soaring tip of an old cedar tree poked up through a wandering, thin mist, and swayed.

Leaf looked up. His knotty, stick fingers grasped the spindly branch just above his leafy, green hair. He tested the limb's strength. Cautiously, he pulled himself up higher, and then crouched among fernlike fronds. Still damp from the dawn mist, the pale green needles sparkled in the early morning sun. Leaf was near the highest tip of the gigantic cedar tree called the Old Seeder—his home.

Far below, twisted roots curled across the forest floor, and buried themselves deep in the earth. More like gnarled fingers than roots, they clutched granite boulders and anchored the tree's incredible height. Through

3

long seasons and many storms the Old Seeder grew ever taller.

Leaf peeked through the feathery fronds and wispy strands of fog at the brilliantly blue sky. Only a few more slender limbs to climb and he would reach the top of this enormous, towering tree. He knew he must be very careful at so great a height.

Leaf's emerald colored eyes were the same shade as his leafy hair. Teeny leaves sprouted here and there from his arms and legs. He was skinny, strong, daring, and a Twig—an impish stick creature no taller than a robin. Leaf was an excellent climber, too. So he pulled himself up to the next limb confidently. *Just a little higher!*

"Wait! Wait for me!" chirped an irritating voice.

Leaf glanced down and frowned. He stepped hastily over stubby stems jutting out at odd angles along the branch, and pressed his stick body against the trunk. He knew he would blend perfectly into the bark. Slyly, he peeked from his hiding spot at the impish Twig yelling at him.

Far below Leaf, in the curling mist and among golden-tipped sprays, two orange eyes appeared and blinked. It was his little sister, Fern. Her golden, leafy hair sprouted in disarray. Unlike Leaf's, hers drooped in sloppy, neglected tangles.

"Wait for me!" cried Fern again. She stared straight into Leaf's eyes. "You can't hide from me, you know!"

"Go away!" shouted Leaf, annoyed with her persistence. He quickly grabbed hold of a branch, intending to climb up even faster, but a sharp *PLOCK! PLOCK!* and a blast of chattering teeth stopped him. Alarmed, he looked down.

Fern was grinning as she threw cappynuts at a gray squirrel.

Bristling and furious, the squirrel barked at her from a lower branch. Its whiskers stuck out like porcupine quills. It waved its sharp claws, rolled its eyes wildly, and stared pointedly at the moss bag Fern gripped in her fist.

"Go away, you chatter!" Fern demanded. Her voice was as nerve-shattering as the chatter's bark. She clutched her bag fiercely, and glared at the squirrel.

Leaf frowned, and yelled, "You better give it back its cappynuts, Fern!"

The gray squirrel was much bigger than Fern. It knew she had stolen its secret stash. Frantic, it hopped back and forth snapping its teeth like popping hail—a serious warning. Its claws scratched the air as if to swirl the breeze into a whirlwind, and its barks crackled like lightening.

Leaf covered his ears at the grating noise. *What a silly thing to do! It's gonna push her right off the limb!* "Give'em back, you nuthead!" yelled Leaf impatiently.

Fern ignored him. Instead she glowered stubbornly at the chatter. She yanked another nut out of the moss bag, took careful aim, and whirled it with all her might. It thumped the pointy head of the squirrel right between its eyes. Then it bounced high into the air, and spun off through the branches.

For a moment, the squirrel's eyes glazed over and its ears drooped.

Fern grinned, "Gotcha!"

But in the next instant, the chatter's tail bristled like sharp needles, and its eyes blazed in fury!

Frightened, Fern sucked in her breath, stumbled backwards, and grabbed hold of a spindly stem. She tried to hide behind a cluster of tiny cones.

Right away Leaf ripped a piece of bark from the trunk, and lifted it above his head, ready to hurl it if the chatter charged Fern.

But instead, it screeched *CHRLIRRRP!* The ear-splitting blast rushed at Fern so fast her leafy hair blew straight up.

Fern let the moss bag slip from her trembling hand. It bounced off a branch, and spiraled to the forest floor.

The squirrel sneered with satisfaction. At once it flung itself into the sky, and with outstretched arms, embraced the crisp air. Gracefully, it floated down to where the nuts lay scattered over the moss. Casting an occasional smirk at Fern, the chatter hopped around like a whirlwind. It gathered it cappynuts, and buried them as fast as possible beneath the cedar's roots.

Fern gave an embarrassed half-grin to Leaf and shrugged.

Leaf frowned back. He was twice his sister's age, twice her size, and knew more about chatters than she ever would.

"Go back!" Leaf yelled irritably. "You aren't supposed to climb so high anyway. You'll get us both in trouble! Go back to the knothole!"

Fern scowled at him, hurt and disappointed.

"Slimerspit!" Leaf suddenly cried out. He hopped backwards, held up a foot, and shook it. Brown globs were mashed in between his toes.

A confused wooly caterpillar crawled out of a deep furrow in the bark. Its black and brown striped, fuzzy hair blended perfectly with the colors of the cedar.

"Well, you can sure hide better than I do!" Leaf muttered sourly to the crawly.

Flustered, the caterpillar bunched up its body, gathered together its teeny legs, and tucked them protectively into its belly. Its eyes shimmered with alarm for it had nearly been squashed.

Leaf grinned mischievously. Stooping over, he spoke softly to the wooly caterpillar, "Here you go, little crawly. Climb on here now. I won't hurt you." Good-naturedly the caterpillar crawled onto Leaf's outstretched finger.

Right away Fern asked, "Whatcha' got?"

"Oh, wait 'til you see this!" exclaimed Leaf slyly. All the while the caterpillar squirmed from one finger of Leaf's hand to the next. He held his hand out above Fern's upturned face as if he were going to offer his sister a pretty blossom.

Immediately Fern's expression changed to suspicion. "*What is it?*"

"It's for you, Fern! Catch!" Leaf giggled. He dropped the caterpillar on her nose.

Stunned for a moment, Fern crossed her eyes as she tried to focus on the crawly, which crossed its eyes, too, trying to focus on Fern's.

Abruptly, the caterpillar sat up, whirled its antennae, and crawled on to Fern's eyebrows, which happily resembled food!

"Ugh!" screamed Fern. Hastily she flung the poor creature into the air. "Leaf, I'm telling Mumma!" she shouted angrily.

Leaf laughed disdainfully. "Go on, then, you jay-jay-tell!" He leapt skillfully up and caught a higher branch. He was determined to get as far away from his little sister as quickly as possible. So higher and higher he climbed.

Fern crouched far below. She kept an anxious watch as Leaf disappeared into the thin fronds and mist.

Finally Leaf reached the tree's highest tip. The slender stem swayed with the weight of his stick body as if testing its own strength. Pale green fronds spread out wide and sparkled in the early light of day. Leaf closed his eyes, felt the rhythm of the breeze, and enjoyed the icy air on his warm face.

When he opened his eyes, he immediately noticed the dark clouds above Thunder Peak. Although it was far in the north, the storm was ominous and threatening. *Scary!* Leaf flinched as bright flashes ripped apart the morning sky. Even from so far away, he could hear the rippling crackles.

A few moments more brought a throbbing *BOOM! BOOM! BOOM!* across the grassy valley that stretched between Thunder Peak and Leaf. The booming rolled past Leaf until it struck another glacier-covered volcano behind him, Echo Peak. Then the thunder bounced back and forth, endlessly echoing between the frozen peaks. In awe, Leaf swayed in the treetop, and listened to the storm rage.

The Old Seeder's tip was the most excellent lookout in the forest. From this high up, the Sharp Peaks were only a dark, murky silhouette in the west. At the foot of this dark ridge lay a vast, grassy plain that gently rolled away into the hazy slopes of the Blue Mountains in the east. From Leaf's lookout he could see it all, except for the canyon that sliced the Sharp Peaks in half. Through this deep canyon rushed a violent river that Twigs called the Rushing Waters.

Leaf wriggled further into the gold-tipped needles, and narrowed his eyes to thin slits. Now they looked like fluttering leaves. A red-capped woodpecker chased a fat beetle up a slim limb. Leaf peered intently at it, daring the bird to see him. Even though the woodpecker was taller than him, Leaf was unafraid. He thought about plucking a few of its tail feathers. *I could use them to sweep away the spider webs in my hollow!*

As if sensing Leaf's intentions, the woodpecker nervously glanced around, scooped up the beetle, and hastily flew away. It disappeared into the glare of the sparkling glaciers on Echo Peak.

A red-tailed hawk circled above the grassy valley on a lazy hunt. Its stiff, outstretched wings caught a warm current of air, and it soared higher and higher. Leaf felt jealous. He wished he could leap into the sky, and soar off, too. *I want to go somewhere—anywhere—just fly away from this old tree!*

"Leaf, you're too high! Come down!" Fern shouted up plaintively.

"Oh, fine," grumbled Leaf. Lately he felt like he was being stalked by Fern. *She's such a jay-jay-tell!*

Leaf dropped swiftly from limb to limb. He paused to hang for a moment above Fern, grabbed hold of a cluster of needles, and gleefully thrashed them from their stems. The sap-filled needles fell into Fern's hair, and stuck out at all angles.

"I'm tellin' Mumma!" Fern whined. "Ouch, ouch!" she glared at Leaf. With exaggerated pain she plucked the sticky needles from her leafy head.

"Come on, you chitterbug," Leaf retorted. "Mumma made sapsuckers!" He dropped to a limb below Fern. "Hurry up before Buddy and Burba get their pudgy fingers on them! And you sure won't get any sapsuckers if you crawl around on your hands and knees like a slimer!" he teased her.

Fern crept like a slug along the branch. She blinked nervously, tested each grip and toehold on the bark twice, and anxiously watched the earth far below. Yet, with a flip of a leafy strand, which had fallen over her eyes, she tossed off her brother's challenge. "Oh, don't worry about me!" she answered casually. "I'll be right behind you!"

"Right!" Leaf replied in a voice dripping with sarcasm.

Fern was frightened of heights, and because of her fear, she always climbed as slow as a slug in the mud. With hesitant, jerky movements, she slid down the trunk. She kept her toes buried deep in the furrows of the bark all the way.

Halfway down the Old Seeder, Leaf's head disappeared into the shadow of a gnarled lump, which was actually a very large knothole. It stuck out from the trunk of the Old Seeder like the face of a grizzly bear.

Fern dropped onto their porch-branch outside the knothole, stepped into their haven, and with a sigh of relief, closed the round door behind her.

Leaf was chattering excitedly. "Mumma, a really creepy-looking storm is hanging right over Thunder Peak! It's all dark and billowy, and I think it's coming this way!"

Immediately fearful, Fern's eyes grew huge. The worst of storms often torched tall trees like the Old Seeder. *Especially* tall trees like the Old Seeder.

Leaf's tiny brothers, Buddy and Burba, who had been cooing and playing happily with sunlit, dust balls, now grew silent. They pulled their sloppy, wet fingers from their mouths, and stared intently at Leaf. They had recognized the "storm" word.

With a brisk rustle of her aspen-leaf apron Mumma abruptly spiraled around. Her orange eyes flashed at Leaf angrily. She pushed back a stray, gold leaf from her eyes.

Leaf flinched.

Fern grinned.

"Really, Leaf! I'm going to give you to the chompers so they can stuff you in their dam! You're so thoughtless!" Mumma declared. "You're scaring the babes!"

The twins stared at Mumma, the storm forgotten. Now they were horrified that their big brother might be given to chompers.

Mumma always tied up her leafy hair with several swirls of ivy vines. The bunch of knotted leaves seemed to sprout right out of the top of her head, which made her seem taller. When she was upset, her topknot quivered with unspoken threats.

The twins' eyes were as wide as daisies.

Leaf cringed at the thought of being shredded to pieces by a chomper and stuffed in its dam. Still he shrugged, rolled his eyes, and grinned weakly at Buddy and Burba to reassure them Mumma wouldn't really toss him to the chompers.

Fern caught Leaf's eye and smirked. Her eyes lit up with possible revenge. *Just wait until I tell Mumma what you did to me!*

Suddenly Leaf felt very uncomfortable. He scowled at Fern, warning her to not tell on him.

Mumma ignored them both. She smiled and blew kisses to the twins. Reassured, they drooled all over their feet. Round, light-green bumps sprouted on Buddy and Burba's heads, but their sprouts were all they had in common. Buddy's eyes were golden, and Burba's, orange. Buddy was sweet. Burba...well, Burba was...*Burba!* Mumma turned back to stirring puffy seeds in a smooth wooden bowl. She mixed them with mashed berries, and skillfully folded the patties between sweet leaves.

"But Mumma," Leaf blurted out again, "it's really a bad storm. It's black and huge."

Mumma whirled around, and curled a knobby finger over Leaf's head as if she intended to give it a hard *THUMP!*

Leaf's ducked. Even though Mumma had never thumped him before, Leaf knew there was always a first time. He considered the possibility anxiously.

With her finger poised over Leaf's head, Mumma's silently warned him to keep quiet. Her golden topknot quivered, her orange eyes narrowed, and her russet lips became a terse, straight line.

Reluctantly, Leaf backed away, and waved his hands in surrender. He mumbled loudly to himself, "Well, anyway, Pappo will wanna' know."

"Here, Leaf," Mumma said, her voice sharp, "do something useful. Give your little brothers these sapsuckers and berry cakes. Pappo and I must hunt before the morning flows away. He hopes to find pine nuts, and we need some cherry blossoms to stuff in our pillows."

Leaf hid the treats behind his back, and wondered whether or not to eat the sapsuckers and berry cakes himself.

Mumma stuck her head out of the knothole and examined the sky. "Look!" she exclaimed. "The pretty pink colors are already rushing away. The sky's growing bluer so I must go now. Pappo's waiting for me in the roots."

Leaf and Fern glanced at each other and frowned, unhappy with the thought of being stuck with each other's company all morning. Burba and Buddy crawled around behind Leaf. They wobbled on their pudgy legs, and reached for the sapsuckers.

Mumma's tone was sharp. "No nonsense!" She waggled her finger in the air to hush their protests. At once she hopped through the knothole onto the porch-branch.

"Hurry up, Ivy," Pappo called impatiently from the roots. His voice boomed like a giant woodpecker drumming on the trunk. "The day isn't flowing any slower!"

"I'm on my way, Needles!" replied Mumma cheerfully. She left the door standing open. Swiftly and gracefully she swung from limb to limb all the way down to the mossy forest floor. At once, her patch-work dress blended into the spotty, sunlit shadows of the forest path, and she disappeared.

Leaf stuck his head from the knothole, and jealously watched her and Pappo leave.

Mumma's voice floated back to the knothole, "Mind Leaf," she reminded Fern, Buddy, and Burba. But her words only hovered in the air, and like weightless hummingbirds, fluttered away, unheeded.

CHAPTER TWO

RUSTLE ON THE RIDGE

Further west of the Old Seeder, where the Sharp Peaks butted up against the edge of the wide valley, and where the rubble of long-ago avalanches spilled into the forest, an overly confident young Twig stood perched on a jutting slab of granite. He stood as he usually did— his legs braced and planted apart, and his hands on his hips—a rather arrogant stance. Absentmindedly he tugged at the strap over his shoulder. In its back loop it held a long walking stick that lay slanted across his back. A large, flat gemstone with a golden hue was stuffed in the stick's top knothole. A braided rope twisted around his waist, and was tossed carelessly over his shoulder opposite the strap.

He was Rustle, and he called himself a Ridge Twig.

Rustle was well-outfitted with one exception. The only hunting tool he didn't carry was a whistletube. He didn't feel he needed one. When he whistled, it was extraordinarily shrill and annoying, and louder than any other Twig's in the forest.

Like a leaping frog, Rustle sprang off of the dagger-like boulder. He crouched over a mound of pine nuts, yanked a few more nuts from a pouch slung over his shoulder, and dribbled them onto the stack. Then he molded the pile into a sloppy cone. Rustle glanced up at the overhanging limb of a whitebark pine tree. Like a fast, four-legged spider he scaled the twisted trunk, and scrambled along a long branch. He squatted in the middle of a cluster of purple pine cones directly above the pine nut mound. He watched the nuts with keen eyes, almost as if he thought they might scatter in all directions at once.

Rustle concentrated on being invisible, yet his smug grin was hard to hide. His copper-colored eyes narrowed like Twig's eyes do when peeking through leaves. But Rustle's eyes looked more like glittery beetles. His leafy hair bristled like a pine cone, yet it also glowed with a bronze luster rather than a cone's dull shade.

He crouched over to look like a stem growing out of the branch. But he forgot that he was brown, and the whitebark limb was white. He waited impatiently on the branch, and tried not to wriggle around.

Soon a blue-gray nutcracker fluttered down to inspect the weird pine nut stump. Warily it darted glances back and forth, ruffled its wings, and fluffed up its feathers. It marched around the pine nuts with curious interest. But the pile also made the nutcracker uneasy. It usually had to attack whitebark cones to wrestle the nuts from their tough hold. The nutcracker cocked its head suspiciously to one side, and then to the other as it calculated the risk of attacking the stack.

Rustle held his breath.

At last the nutcracker snatched a nut. A moment later it dipped its head to seize another.

"Gotcha' now!" Rustle whispered. He slid off the branch, and fell with his legs and arms stretched out wide like a bizarre spider dropping down from its web.

Instantly the nutcracker skittered sideways. With an unpleasant crow-like *CAWK!* it whipped its tail at the clumsy Twig's nose, and swiftly flew up to the branch from which Rustle had just slipped. The nutcracker squinted at him with a scornful expression.

Rustle belly-flopped on the stack. The nuts exploded in a burst around him. With his nose stinging and buried in the dirt, he lay on his belly, humiliated. After a moment, he groaned and rolled over. In his hand Rustle grasped one tiny gray, tail feather plucked from the nutcracker.

KRAAK! KRAAK! echoed off the cliffs.

"Look what I got!" Rustle yelled. "Why don't you come back and get it?" He stood up and waved the feather above his head.

The nutcracker pranced disdainfully on the limb above him.

In a pathetic attempt to hit the bird, Rustle threw a large nut at it, but the nut only bounced harmlessly off of the branch.

With a dismissive tilt of its bill and twitch of its tail, the nutcracker soared away into a cloudless, blue sky.

"Next time, you nutty bird," Rustle shouted. "You better watch out! I'll catch you next time!" Rustle stuck the feather in his belt, and ruffled his leafy hair with both hands. A billowing cloud of dust filled the air, for Rustle rarely brushed any dirt from his hair at all. "Fine," he grumbled, "who needs a bird to fly anyway? I have the best flyers in the world."

Rustle quickly turned his attention to a new challenge. Not far away a huge cappynut tree twisted its limbs over a pretty clearing. Rustle strolled over and examined the roots of the old tree. Warily he pushed aside some dead leaves with his foot. His eyes lit up. He leaned over, and grasped hold of a long, skinny stem. With extraordinary patience, Rustle tugged out an enormous, red maple leaf. Once it was free of the debris, he laid it out in the sun. After a while he gingerly stepped on it with one foot. At once the leaf split in half.

"Oh, that's great, just great!" Rustle exclaimed, disgusted. "Now I hav'ta find another one." He stared at tree limbs above, and studied the new buds, which were just sprouting.

A sparkling blue butterfly fluttered busily around Rustle's head. Its wings left dusty traces on his coppery hair tips.

Since there was no one around to talk to, Rustle confided in the pretty creature. "Hmmm, not many big leaves up there yet. Too early in the season, eh? So I'll just hav'ta find one somewhere else, don't cha' think?" He rubbed his chin. The butterfly floated in the dust above Rustle's head.

The rock-strewed ground was lit by slanted, early morning sunbeams. Most of last season's dead leaves had been blown into tree roots. Their soggy, moldy clumps now teemed with all sorts of scurrying crawlies. Still, Rustle knew many large leaves had been protected through the cold season at the bottom of these slimy mats, and he needed a leaf large enough to carry him through the thin air of the high cliffs—the cliffs of the ridge that was his haven.

"Got it!" Rustle snapped his fingers smartly. He nodded to the startled butterfly, and then pointed at a particular, jumbled-up heap.

Muddy clods, splintered sticks, dead moss, dried-up mushrooms, and dry leaves were stuffed into the cleft of a large, cracked boulder. Smaller rocks had tumbled from the ridge above it, and partially blocked the mysterious-looking rubble.

"There'll be one in there for sure," Rustle stated as if it were a fact.

Disinterested, the butterfly zigzagged away.

Now very cautious, Rustle pulled out the long walking stick from his shoulder strap's back loop. Standing at the ready, as if he were on guard against a vicious beast, Rustle jabbed at the pile, ready to scramble backwards at the first sign of danger. Nothing but tiny tufts of moss billowed up. Still not satisfied, Rustle pushed apart the top layers with his stick, and poked it into the mold underneath. Black beetles, earwigs, roaches, and centipedes rushed away. Now confident that the crawlies had fled, he reached down, and tossed stinky mats of stuck-together leaves over his shoulder.

"Whew, this stinks!" Rustle complained as he dug through the mold. "Stinky, stinky, stinks a lot!" At last he declared, "Ah, ha!" In slow motion, he tugged out a huge red leaf from the bottom of the pile. "All I need to do is dry you out, add a few spider webs, and pull you up there!" Rustle pointed at an outcrop halfway up the cliff. He spoke earnestly to the slimy leaf. "I bet you could fly me clear over the grassy flatland to the other side of the valley from here, don't 'cha think, eh?"

A strange expression flickered over Rustle's face. He appeared confused for a moment, and then sad. He put his hands on his hips, and stared at the limp leaf at his feet, suddenly lost in thought. With an oddly defiant tone in his voice, he muttered, "Not that we'd ever want ta' fly over the valley, eh? We don't ever want to go that far. Aren't any Twigs left in *that* forest, eh? It's all burned up!" Rustle took a deep breath.

A white butterfly floated onto his eyelashes.

"So we'll never go there, right, dodger?" Rustle crossed his eyes as he spoke to the butterfly. In the next breath he answered himself, "Right!" He nodded sharply. At once he dismissed his random, troubling memories.

All of a sudden, the musty pile rustled and the mold shifted sideways. A large spider with a fat, fuzzy body and bristly legs poked its head out. It had been hidden in its funnel-shaped web, which had been disturbed.

"Hang on there, eightlegs!" screamed Rustle fiercely. He pointed his stick like a spear at the spider's head as if he were ready to pierce it. The spider squatted on its torn web, confused by the unexpected sunlight.

The gold stone that was stuck in the stick reflected in the spider's three rows of eight eyes. With an anxious expression, the creature stared at the Twig. It seemed more worried about its damaged web than being at the point of Rustle's spear. It set about repairing its funnel web.

"Don't even move!" warned Rustle loudly. An unpleasant thought crept up on him. "You're not a *jumping* eightlegs, are you?" he asked as if the spider heard and might actually answer him.

The pile of slimy leaves rustled again. To Rustle's horror hundreds of teeny, white, dot-like spider babes swarmed from the stinky pile, and surrounded their spider mum's legs! They bunched together for a moment, and then scurried from under her belly as if excited to be free at last of their egg sac. Like crazed tufts of dandelions, many wriggled onto their mum's web, and stuck to its dewy strands.

Many others gathered in a tangled mob, and rolled toward Rustle!

"Back, back into your hole!" ordered Rustle, although his voice sounded more feeble than commanding. He jabbed frantically at the hundreds of sunlit-sparkling legs.

But the torrent of spider babes flooded right over Rustle's feet and surged up to his knees.

"Ahhh!" Rustle shrieked. He lost his balance, fell backwards, and tripped over his own stick in a desperate attempt to escape the teeny spiders. "Eeeeaahhh!" Rustle bolted for the nearest tree, which he climbed quicker than the nutcracker had skittered sideways.

With a gasp of relief, Rustle perched in the limbs of a giant fir. He watched the teeny spiders scurry away into the forest. There they would grow fat, weave their secret funnel webs, and gobble up crawlies.

"Great, just great," complained Rustle to a wooly caterpillar on a pine cone near his head, "looks like I won't be flying anywhere for a while." He shrugged. "Oh well. I hav'ta wait until that soggy, old leaf dries out anyway." He grinned. "It's a perfect leaf, though, isn't it? Perfect for a leaf-flyer, eh?"

From the tree limb, Rustle watched the red leaf being trampled by even more spider babes. Hundreds of teeny feet left faint traces in the reddish colored slime. The tracks merged into the same pattern as the dark veins of the leaf.

The caterpillar crawled near Rustle's ear.

As if he were passing along a great secret, Rustle whispered to the curious creature, "Well, that old red leaf is gonna make the best leaf-flyer yet, don't cha think? The very best one ever!"

A teeny, white spider scurried over his nose headed for his hair. Rustle swiftly plucked the nutcracker feather from his belt, and brushed the spider babe into the air.

"I thought this might come in handy," he praised his own cleverness.

The spider babe floated away on a breeze that rushed down the cliffs from Echo Peak.

Rustle leaned back, crossed his arms under his head, and with a huge sigh, he closed his eyes. He dreamt of soaring on an enormous red leaf between swirling, puffy clouds.

CHAPTER THREE

A GOLIATH CHOMPER

Far across the wide valley from where the Old Seeder cast its shadow over the forest, and from where the granite cracked into jagged slabs on Rustle's ridge, an unusually gigantic beaver with an enormous, flat, egg-shaped tail balanced atop his dam. He threw back his massive head, and sucked in the air with his immense, black, twitching nose. The blood-red splashes of dawn streaked his brown fur as if it were slashed by the claws of an enraged beast. The goliath beaver's huge shadow fell onto the surface of the pond behind him, and stretched into a contorted, freakish-looking silhouette.

He was Slapper—an awesome beaver and powerful. He was the leader of his colony. Even so, he could not balance on his huge, webbed feet for very long. His legs were deformed—crippled by a reckless act long ago. Slapper dropped clumsily to his hands. He was uneasy, which was a troubling mood for a leader of a colony.

The air smelled dusty, and its swirling currents whispered to Slapper that a storm was near. That was strange for so early in the morning. A warm ribbon of air twisted within a crisp, chilly breeze. Sudden, sinister gusts blew in one direction, rushed back, and then whirled away in another.

Yet the center of the pond lay smooth and calm as if it held its breath. It reflected the peaceful, rolling foothills. White trunks of birch trees crowded the slopes, and floated on the water's surface in a soft blur. If Slapper's eyes were sharper, he might have seen that behind the gentle hills, an enormous, white peak soared up abruptly, a frozen cone blanketed by black, whirling clouds. But Slapper could only see his pond. Still, the warm, muggy air bothered him.

The woven stick-roof of the beavers' mud-packed lodge peeked above the surface in the center of the pond where the water was deepest. Slapper's mate, Patty, scurried busily about inside. Using her broad nose she pushed shredded willow sticks against the walls, and shoved marshy grass into a large mound. Patty was preparing a nest for her new kits, soon to arrive. Patty was actually larger than Slapper, and usually the more bossy of the two. But lately she was distracted with nesting. It was difficult to supervise the dam, her daughters, and prepare for kits, so for now she left the management of the colony to Slapper.

Outside the lodge, Slapper and Patty's two daughters, Splash and Splatter, played silly games in the pond, yet soon they would be ready for their own mates. They were now yearlings, and nearly as large as Patty. Slapper knew they would help Patty, and gently care for the new kits. When the kits were older, their big sisters would teach them their silly games, and show them all their secret pathways in the pond.

Splash and Splatter had a nickname for their large, watery home—the Spreading Pond. Each season the beavers gnawed more and more trees along its banks. So each season they dug longer and longer canals to float the aspen and birch logs to the massive dam. Not all of the trees helped strengthen and enlarge the dam. Many of the tender saplings were simply stored underwater for the cold season's food.

Fondly, Slapper watched his daughters play. Splash and Splatter had been such tiny kits when they were first born. But they grew so fast. Now they were enormous yearlings, almost full grown. Soon they would be goliath beavers like Slapper and Patty. And they had already proved themselves to be shrewd and clever engineers.

With a crooked, jerky shuffle, Slapper padded around to survey the dam. The mighty barricade rose up high between two bluffs. There was a deep gulch on one side. Long arms of interlaced logs embraced a serene pond on the other side. From the base of the dam a thin ribbon of water trickled into the gulch. This well-designed spillway relieved the tremendous pressure of the water that pushed constantly against the dam. Rocks, mud, grass, and sticks were stuffed in all the gaps between the logs. Being ever vigilant, Slapper examined this huge structure for leaks all the time.

It had been a long night's work gathering more young saplings for their food stores. They were stashed under the water near their lodge since it was much safer to sneak out for a quick snack than to pop up by the pond's banks. That's where hunters prowled.

Warily, Slapper glanced at the steep bluff that curved over one end of the dam. Not long ago strangers had arrived. Two goliath beavers had dug burrows in the high mud embankment. Being a fierce, protective leader of his colony, Slapper would have chased them away—maybe even attacked them—but he hesitated. They were enormous beavers, too. From the smell of them, they had travelled very far up the gulley, probably from the grasslands in the wide valley. Slapper recognized them as weary bachelors who were searching for mates. Most likely, they had been chased from colony to colony. In an odd way, Slapper felt sorry for them, for the same journey had also brought him to this very place long ago.

The bachelors kept a respectful distance from Slapper, yet Splash had touched her nose to one, and Splatter had sniffed the other's muzzle. With hopeful snorts, his daughters had told Slapper the strangers' names—Birchbite and Clacker.

Slapper frowned. Out of the corner of his eye, he suspiciously watched the bachelors. He considered whether or not Birchbite and Clacker were good enough for his daughters.

Birchbite and Clacker sat at the edge of the pond— closer to Slapper than ever before—and groomed their oily, slick fur. Splash and Splatter paddled onto the bank from the water. The two daughters sat near the bachelors. Their fur sparkled in the early sunlight. Bashfully they blinked their long eyelashes, and blew breathy, welcoming puffs of mist. Apart, yet together, the four young beavers groomed their already shiny fur, and kept one eye on their prospective mates.

Slapper sighed. *Yes, it's time—but not just yet. I will signal the bachelors at dusk when we all wake up. They may join the colony then. That will be soon enough. There is something else, something more important, I must do first.*

Slapper needed to investigate the musty smell that swirled in the breeze. It came from the ravine across the pond where the cool mountain creek met the warmer water. A strange trickling sound now came from there, too—a sound which had grown louder over the past few days, and distorted the pretty splashing noise of the creek in the ravine. And just yesterday, an unusually frigid stream of water started to flow into the pond.

Slapper glanced at his lodge. Soft mist rose up from the breathing holes he had punched through the roof. Lately, Patty was always fussing over her nest. Slapper sighed wearily. Yes, it was time to signal to Birchbite and Clacker they could leave their burrows, if they wished. Together with Splash and Splatter, they could build their own lodges in the pond.

For a moment more, Slapper lingered on top of the dam. Vibrantly colored wood ducks paddled back and forth in the center of the pond, and stirred the still water into splashy ripples. They didn't notice the ominous breeze, or simply didn't care. Instead, they cried *OOEEK! OOEEK!* over and over, fussing about one thing or another. They urged their teeny, fuzzy chicks to paddle away from the tall cattails. Foxes hid there. The cattail's heavy, brown heads bobbed in a friendly nod in reedy rows along the muddy bank. But sometimes they hid dangerous hunters.

In slow motion, a lanky blue heron with long, stick-like legs stepped delicately and silently among the reeds. But it was difficult to hide the blood-red color of its spear-like bill. The heron deftly stabbed a sleepy frog with a quick stroke, lifted its meal to the sky, and swallowed it in one gulp.

Proud white swans floated gracefully in the middle of the pond. They watched the heron with amusement. It was better to use a long neck underwater for scooping up minnows than a long bill to stab their meal.

The swans leaned their heads near to one another to create a drifting shadow below their bellies. The minnows, which mistook the shade for shelter, gathered below. The swans easily scooped up them up.

Splash and Splatter slipped back into the pond. They slapped the water hard with their flat tails and then dove underway to practice warning one another of danger. The huge splashes that erupted from their smacks nearly drowned the helpless ducklings nearby.

Immediately, the duck mums flapped and quivered their wings angrily. But it was a futile display for the daughters simply continued to slap the water and shower the ducklings. The mums *OOOEEEK!* furiously, and beat their wings until their bellies were lifted above the water. They hovered there for a moment like mad, tubby hawks, and then they flew in fury at Splash and Splatter, warning them to stop or be beaten with their wings and stabbed with their beaks!

With innocent expressions, Splash and Splatter simply rolled away, dove underwater, and blew rude bubbles. After a while, the yearlings swam to the bottom of the pond near the lodge where a snack of leafy boughs was stashed.

Birchbite and Clacker sat motionless in the mud, and sadly watched them leave. They blinked hopeful eyes at Slapper.

But Slapper just ignored them. *Perhaps, Birchbite and Clacker could be useful,* he brooded. *I may need to build a new dam to block the ravine's creek if it is flowing too fast into the pond. The bachelors could then prove their skills.*

Thunder rolled across the water. The pond, which stretched away into the foothills, darkened. On its banks, the tips of water-logged grass, which usually swayed, now shivered with the trembling currents. Sparkling, silver minnows, which fed on the grassy roots, vanished. Dark lilies, which spotted frogs used as stepping stones across the pond, were pushed into bouncing clumps along its muddy embankments.

From atop the dam, Slapper gazed down at the Spreading Pond. A gently curled swan feather floated by, and was caught in the whirlpool swirling above the spillway. It was abruptly sucked under, and then spit into the creek that spilled out from under the dam. The feather floated off on shimmering ripples toward the grassy valley.

Slapper dove into the murky water. He swam swiftly to the lodge. His twisted legs were still powerful. When he reached the underwater entrance, he limped through the tunnel to his sweet-smelling mate, Patty. She welcomed him with a sloppy kiss on his nose. Splash and Splatter waddled up the tunnel into the lodge past Slapper. They snuggled into shallow hollows to nap for the day. Patty was busy arranging the sweet-smelling marsh grass into smooth curls along the den walls.

As Slapper eased himself into his favorite sleeping hollow, his aching bones reminded him of his old injuries. Once again Slapper told himself to wake earlier than the others, when the first faint stars appeared before twilight. He would swim to the ravine that cradled the creek flowing into his pond, and then decide what must be done.

Yes, he thought sleepily, *it would be good to have the bachelors' help building a new dam. It is time to welcome Birchbite and Clacker to my colony.*

High above where the beavers slept, and far up the ravine, the glacier lake stirred. The whale-like slabs of ice, which had fallen from the glacier, drifted silently, one after the other. They floated to the ice dam until they bumped against the thick, frozen barrier.

The storm's unusually warm rain beat down upon the ancient dam that had held the lake back for so long. A frozen crystal splintered, and fell into the Rushing Waters that flowed from the base of the dam.

The great wall of ice cracked.

CHAPTER FOUR

A SILVER LEAF TWIG

"Look at me, Speckles! I'm so pretty!" exclaimed Feather.

The young Twig leaned over the rippling pool to scrutinize her reflection. She tugged impatiently at the ivy-braided headband that bound the thick leaves sprouting from her head. Her leafy hair was so unruly her headband could not tame her bronze-colored leaves.

"Just look how rosy my eyes are today!"

Feather blinked and tilted her woody face to study each angle of her cheeks and nose.

"So what'cha think, Speckles?" She sat back on her heels, and stared expectantly at a chipmunk, who squatted in a nearby clump of clover. Two stripes ran down his back, and both were covered with so many spots that they blurred into a dazzle in the morning sunrays.

Speckles ripped off the soft, sweet leaves of the clover tips, and greedily stuffed them in his cheeks. But he paused munching long enough to stare blankly at his insistent friend. Four leaves of clover hung forgotten out of the side of his mouth as he tried to figure out what she wanted. He did not understand Feather's words, but she usually expected something from him. So he blinked his warm, brown eyes, and twitched his tiny nose.

"So you agree?" Feather asked, smiling brightly.

Puzzled, Speckles twitched his whiskers.

"Wonderful!" Feather laughed.

A white swan feather floated down the creek, and into the pool. The stream flowed all the way from Thunder Peak to reach this steep gulley where Feather now knelt and admired her reflection. The swan feather swirled and spun around in lazy, slow circles.

"Oh, look, Speckles," Feather cried out, "a new feather for my braid!" She grabbed a long stick lying nearby, and poked at the feather until she was able to lift it, dripping and limp, from the cool water. She shook it briskly— and sprinkled Speckles—until the feather puffed into a fuzzy hook.

Irritated by the unexpected shower, Speckles ducked and covered his face. Then, with his legs as stiff as sticks and his tail bristling like a pine cone, he hopped behind a tall, fat mushroom.

"I think this must have floated all the way down from the chomper dam!" Feather declared. She shivered at the thought of the scary creatures, which ripped apart the trees she loved. Feather remembered a faint voice from long ago warning her to stay far away from chompers, or she might end up stuck in their dam!

"Well, never mind," Feather said as she dismissed the dreary thought, "it's a lovely feather. A little limp, but..." her voice trailed away. She frowned as she stared at her reflection again. At once, she stuck the feather into her headband, yanked it out, and stuck it in again at a different angle. She did this repeatedly until finally she was satisfied with her image. Her smug smile reflected back and rippled across the pool.

"Well, I think that will do." Feather stated. "What do you think, Speckles?"

Too disgruntled to respond, Speckles frowned, and bounded up the creek bank to a huckleberry bush.

"Fine, then, you old grump." Feather yelled after him.

After a moment, she sighed and pulled herself away from the pool. She climbed up the embankment, and strolled over to Speckles.

"Let's go see what's up in the grassy meadow, shall we?" With a quick, skillful leap, she landed on Speckles' back, and grabbed a flaxen braid that encircled his neck. She leaned forward and whispered in his ear, "Come on sweet-buds. Let's go!"

At once cheerful again, Speckles burst into a swift, bouncing jog. He bounced through eerie woods of young, pine trees and huge, ashen stumps. He darted in and out of thickets, which grew as tall as the saplings. Patchy white flowers thrived in tangles everywhere. They covered the traces of a not-so-long-ago fire. A thin layer of needles covered cooled cinders, left by a horrific inferno that had destroyed Feather's forest in just a day.

Excited by the speed, Feather laughed. Like Speckles, she loved to run fast—fast enough so that the burnt stumps around her became a ghostly blur! Suddenly Speckles skidded sideways and slid into a burrow at the edge of a grassy field.

"Watch out, Speckles!" yelled Feather as the chipmunk dug in his heels to avoid the smashing the burrow completely. "You silly chippie! Remember, the poppers are coming out of their burrows now," she reminded him sharply. "They'll come after us if we're anywhere near their pups!"

Speckles nodded contritely.

After giving his neck a reassuring pat, Feather slid from Speckle's back. With a couple of skips, she jumped on top of a boulder near the edge of the grasslands. Once there, she stood on tiptoe, and held her hand over her eyes to block the early morning glare. She strained to her tallest height to see past the tips of the prairie grass. She was nearly as tall as a robin.

"Oh, the grass is growing up too high in the middle of the valley to see anything," she complained. "I can just barely see the black ridge and the two white peaks over there. Soon all we'll see is grass." Discouraged, Feather sat down on the boulder, put her elbows on her knees, cradled her chin, and gazed at her companion. She felt bored.

Speckles stuck his head in a prickly thicket, and nibbled on a few huckleberries, ignoring Feather's glum, one-sided conversation.

"Well, one day, Speckles, we're gonna' ride right through this grass and past all those poppers, and find out if there's any other Twigs on the other side of this valley." Feather stared at the tip of the frozen volcano, Echo Peak. She gazed at it nearly every day, although she did not know its name. "All the Twigs can't have died in the fire!" she declared. "I'm sure I'm not the only Twig left!"

Speckles scowled at her. Pink berry juice stained his nose. He wasn't sure what she said, but he sensed it involved something dangerous, and he didn't like the tone of her voice, or her staring off into the grasslands with that odd expression. He chirped a warning.

Feather glanced over and laughed. "Oh, don't worry, you silly old chippie. We're not going yet." She gazed wistfully at the grass tips. "Not this season anyway. Too many poppers already." Feather frowned and peered into the grass at the many prairie dog burrows spread out before her. "There seems to be more of them every season!"

A fuzzy, brown body stirred the blades. A prairie dog mum popped her head out of a well-packed burrow. She blinked rapidly in the bright morning sun, ducked back down, and then reappeared. She pushed two tiny pups up until they somersaulted over the burrow's edge, and into the grass. At once, she scampered over to the nearby burrows to greet other popper mums. With friendly chirps, she stretched up on tiptoe and planted a quick kiss on their muzzles. Gracious and polite, each kissed her back.

With slow movements, Feather slid down from the boulder, and crouched behind it. She kept a wary eye on the poppers. If the mums spotted her, she knew there would be no friendly kiss. Poppers attacked furiously when they believed their pups were in danger. Feather waited for the popper families to wander away. After a while there were no more rustlings in the grass.

Then noisy squeaks erupted from the other side of the boulder, accompanied by wild flapping and teeny chirps! Startled by the commotion, Speckles and Feather stared at each other, afraid to move. Feather put a finger to her lips, warning Speckles to be still and quiet.

With wide eyes, Speckles froze at once even though he had three huge huckleberries stuffed in his mouth.

Slowly, Feather crawled on her hands and knees, and peeked around the boulder.

Near an old, abandoned popper burrow surrounded by short grass, four burrowing owl chicks clumsily tumbled after a frightened grasshopper. The chicks were only a little larger than the hopper itself.

Feather's eyes grew huge with delight. She turned to Speckles and whispered, "Bobos!"

Speckles nodded and gulped the berries. At once disinterested, he returned to scouring the bush for more treats.

Feather giggled. Quickly she clapped a hand over her mouth. After she checked to be sure the popper families had all left, she crawled on top of the boulder again. It was always fun to spy on bobo chicks.

Very near Feather, the bobo mum watched over her brood. Her skinny, gangly legs were surprisingly long for an owl of any sort. They propped up her squat body as if she walked on stilts. Even though she stood ramrod straight, she was not much taller than Feather. Still, the bobo mum had the moonlike, golden eyes of larger owls, which always appeared alarmed and glaring. Wisely, the mum hid her teeny chicks in a burrow at night. But during the day, she pushed them out so they could learn how to hunt crawlies. But today's lesson wasn't going well. The chicks tumbled over their own long legs more than they hopped.

Feather laughed. Hastily she slid behind the boulder, hunched over and shook with silent giggles.

The bobo mum spun her head around backwards, and glared suspiciously at the boulder, sensing a trespasser. She scrutinized the large rock, but seeing nothing, spun her head back around and glared at the grass as if to warn each quivering blade to stay far away from her chicks.

Feather peeked around the boulder, and again clasped her hands over her mouth.

One by one, more bobo chicks popped out of the burrow. Most of them pressed together in a fuzzy bunch, and stood rigid and intense. With huge solemn eyes, they glared at the first four chicks, which clumsily chased grasshoppers.

Unexpectedly the smallest chick broke away from the grasshopper pursuit, and dashed after a black beetle. Another chick darted after the first. But when the beetle flared its wings, the chicks awkwardly bumped into each other, and somersaulted over its head. With a twitch of its butt, the beetle scurried into the grass and escaped.

Sensing movement, one of the largest chicks turned its head around backwards. Horrified, it fixed its eyes on a praying mantis clinging to a tall blade of grass. The mantis swung back and forth unafraid for it was nearly as tall as the teeny bobo itself. Panicked at the sight of the giant crawly, the chick broke from the cluster of bobo chicks. In a futile attempt to fly, it feebly flapped its scrawny wings. Chirping like a cricket, it rushed around the boulder where Feather hid, and stumbled over its own too-long legs. Right away the chick spotted Feather atop the boulder, but it had no idea what a Twig was. To the chick, Feather looked like a weird stick-bird with leaves sprouting all over it. Only this creature had large, rosy-colored eyes and a shimmery white feather poking out of its head. The chick turned its head upside-down to get a better view of the giant, white feather. Curious about this strange bird, it examined Feather with keen, wondering eyes.

Feather blinked. Gently, she smiled.

Startled, the chick fluffed up its feathers and chirped in alarm.

Suddenly the bobo mum rushed over after her chick. She stared aghast at Feather perched on top of the boulder. She flapped her wings protectively. Alarmed, the chicks bounced off each other as they tried to be the first back in the burrow.

Once they stuffed themselves inside, a sinister warning erupted. It was a creepy noise, *Rssst! Rssst! Rssst!* It sounded more like rattlesnakes rattling their tails than the chatters of harmless bobos. With this noisy bravado, the chicks made sure no beast would dare approach their haven.

Feather sighed with disappointment. Her bobo watching was over for the day. In any case, she had something very important to do. She jumped off of the boulder, and hopped onto Speckles' back. At once he bolted away into the woods.

They raced past the ashen stumps that were suffocated by lichen and moss. Pretty, blue periwinkles smothered their dead roots. Splintered trunks stabbed the sky, and limbs stretched out like spooky skeletons.

Yet, skinny saplings grew fast, too. The young trees reached up to the sun from the ash-covered earth. Their leafy boughs spread out further every day, and their trunks, grew thicker.

For many seasons, the ghostly shapes had reminded Feather of the devastating firestorm that swept the Twigs from their havens. But the seasons crawled by, and now the memories of her family and the terrible fire grew fainter. She barely noticed the scarred landscape anymore.

Speckles bounced past a cappynut sapling. Feather glanced at it. *One day one of these cappynuts will have a deep knothole, and I will finally have a haven again,* she assured herself.

Memories of her family drifted into her thoughts— her paps, her mum, her two little sisters, Lark and Swift. *What was it her mum used to sing?*

A deep sadness overwhelmed Feather. But it was not sadness from having lost her family. It was because she was losing them all over again. Their memories were fading away just like the burnt limbs, which fell to the forest floor and crumbled into ash. She was afraid that soon she would not remember them at all. Feather wrapped her arms around Speckles, and buried her nose in his soft, warm fur.

Feeling tears on his neck, Speckles chirped sweetly to cheer his best friend. At once he vaulted over puffy, flat-topped mushrooms, and darted through swinging vines to a sparkling creek. Mercilessly, he jiggled Feather back and forth from bank to bank in the narrow gulch until Feather was forced to sit up.

"Oh, Speckles," Feather giggled, "can't you let a Twig feel sorry for herself just once?"

Speckles tickled her cheek with his tail.

Feather's joyful laugh echoed all the way up the steep gulch to the foothills of Thunder Peak.

CHAPTER FIVE

WHISTLE IN THE FOREST

Leaf glared at his brothers and thrust the sweet, sticky treats at them.

Delighted, Buddy and Burba clapped their hands. Greedily they grabbed the berry cakes and the sapsuckers with stubby, fat fingers. Not sure which to stuff in their mouths first, they shoved both of them in together. Their eyes squeezed shut, and their cheeks bulged out like a bullfrog's throat when it burps.

Alarmed, Fern protested, "Leaf, don't give it to them all at once!" She rushed over, and yanked the slobbery sapsuckers from Buddy and Burba's mouths. Then she grabbed a large, feathery fern, dipped it in a bowl of cool water, and wiped the twins' messy hands and faces.

"Really, Leaf! Just because *you* don't get to go hunting, you don't need to be so careless!"

Irritated with them all, Leaf shrugged and turned away. He had to watch his little sister and brothers every day while his Mumma and Pappo hunted in the forest. *Oh, slimerspit! I'm old enough to go hunting, but they won't take me cause of them!* Leaf glanced back at his sister and brothers, and scowled at them with resentment. Then he sighed and leaned against the doorway's edge. He stared out of the knothole at the forest below.

Not that Leaf had any hunting tools anyway. Sometimes Mumma let him practice hunting in the Old Seeder with hers. She had promised Leaf that one day he could use her tools to hunt in the forest. But he didn't want hers. Her old tools were useless! Her rope was limp and soft like an ivy vine. Her saver didn't even look like a walking stick anymore—more like a twisted, knotted cattail. And its carvings that Pappo had scratched into it were nearly rubbed completely away. The blue gemstone stuck in the knothole at the top of Mumma's saver barely glowed in the sun! When he blew on the whistletube Pappo made for her from a softeye's antler, he sounded more like a jay-jay screaming than a Twig whistling. But Mumma still told him that no other Twig ever played a whistletube prettier than her little Leaf.

Dismally Leaf stared out of the haven's knothole. *Little Leaf? Slugs and slimers! I'm no sprout anymore! Forget those old tools. My tools will be better than any Twig's in the forest!* Leaf imagined what his saver would be like. *His* saver would be unbreakable and twice as tall as Pappo! A gold gemstone would be tied into the knothole at its top! *His* rope would be woven from goldenrods! And *his* whistletube would be a fang!

Fern was used to Leaf brooding. She ignored him. Instead she winked at Buddy, lifted a bundle of thin birch bark out of a woven basket, and plopped down near him. A shaft of sunlight pierced a small knothole above their heads, and made Fern's leafy hair glow even more golden. Buddy and Fern could sit together all day, and gaze at forest creatures they had drawn with berry juice on the soft birch bark. As they intently studied their own sketches, Buddy and Fern's gold and orange eyes reflected the colorful figures. They were lost at once in the stories they created.

"Play with me!" whined Burba as he tugged at a leaf that sprouted from Leaf's knee.

Leaf considered Burba with despair. If only Burba would sit quietly with Fern too. But the evil twin showed a remarkable ability to mangle whatever was within reach, plus he shoved everything in his mouth.

Burba crawled between Leaf's legs, plopped on his bottom, and peeked out of the knothole.

A large, indigo-colored blue jay with a black hood pecked for crawlies on the porch-branch. It's long, stiff tail swished across the soft bark right before Burba's eyes, and unfortunately, right before his fingers, too.

Immediately, Burba giggled and reached for the blue jay's tail. He wriggled his fingers wildly in a clumsy attempt to grab a feather. The blue jay's tail flicked back and forth just beyond Burba's reach.

An instant later the jay sensed the weird movements behind it. With a whish of its feathers, it spun around and hopped backwards in surprise. The large bird was taller than Leaf, who stared warily at the blue jay's beak. The jay tilted its head, and peered intently at Burba's stubby fingers. They looked like fat, tasty worms only these wiggled in the air. The jay cocked its head sideways to the left, and then to the right. Greedily it studied Burba's flailing fingers.

"Burba, stop!" ordered Leaf. He jerked Burba's hand back inside, safely out of reach of the jay's spear-like beak. Then he waved both arms at the blue jay, and yelled, "Go dig around on another branch, you nutty jay-jay!"

The jay complained with a loud, scratchy *WAAWAAH!* and hopped to a higher limb.

Leaf pushed Burba away from the knothole. He wondered whether the jay-jay nearly lost a tail feather, or Burba nearly lost a finger. "Burba, just find something to do with yourself!" said Leaf, impatiently. "Go play with your own feathers, you dandydum head!"

Fern glanced up. Her eyes flashed at Leaf. "Don't call names," she said flatly, and returned at once to her birch bark stories.

Leaf grabbed a soft, brown pouch from a crooked shelf, loosened its string, and knelt beside Burba. As if he were revealing a great mystery, he dangled the pouch in front of Burba's nose. "Look here, Burba, sparkle stones!" Leaf emptied the pouch of its treasures. Shimmering gemstones of many different colors tumbled onto the dusty floor.

Instead of being awed by the colorful gemstones, Burba eyed Leaf's head, which was now within reach.

He balanced on his wobbly legs, and stretched up to grab a tiny leaf sprouting from his big brother's ear. At once, he lost his balance and tumbled backwards, but had captured his prize! He stuck the leaf in his mouth, rolled around in the dust, and giggled.

"Ow!" Leaf cried. "That hurt!" He stood up out of his brother's reach, and pushed the gems toward Burba with his foot. His voice dripped with fake sweetness as he urged his brother to play with the gemstones, "Here, Burba, play with the shiny sparkles!"

Dozens of sun rays streamed in from the knotholes, which poked through the thick trunk from high in the hollow. The beams struck the translucent stones. A bright rainbow flashed across the haven's walls. Unimpressed with the flashy display, Burba shoved one of the gems in his mouth. Quickly, he spit it out in disgust.

Leaf chuckled. Involuntarily he smiled fondly at Burba. He looked around, and then, from another shelf, grabbed a bundle of short sticks tied with twine, and tossed them on the floor.

Fern looked up briefly, and smiled gently at Leaf. At least Burba *sometimes* minded Leaf. He never minded her at all.

A neat flaxen bow tied the sticks together, but it quickly became a slobbery knot once Burba drooled all over it. So Burba beat the bundle on the floor until it burst apart. The sticks scattered around the hollow. At once Burba became absorbed with the odd patterns they had created when mixed up with the gemstones.

For all his worrisome ways, Burba had a weird ability to build complicated traps and elaborate puzzles. Caught up in his own intense imagination, he began to build a miniature chomper dam. The sparkling gems became water, and the sticks became logs. Burba rolled the stones over and over the dam, each time rearranging the sticks as he investigated his tiny dam's weaknesses and strengths.

"Ova' dama! Ova' dama," muttered Burba as he rolled the gems over the interwoven sticks. "Dama! Dama! Wata' here. Wata' there." As Burba rearranged his project his drool hung suspended over the sticks. "Dama! Dama!"

Buddy looked up from the birch bark to watch his brother. He giggled and tugged his toes with delight. "Burba's say'in dama!" he gurgled in his funny garbled way of speaking.

Buddy always spoke so softly that Leaf and Fern usually had to tilt their heads to understand his words. But he usually repeated himself anyway.

"Burba's say'in dama!" He burbled again. His drool dripped slowly over his toes. Buddy stared in fascination at the slimy strands.

"Yes, Buddy," whispered Fern as if they shared a special secret. "Burba's building a huge chomper dam."

Leaf rolled his eyes at Fern who grinned back. At least Burba was busy for a while. Leaf still felt unhappy. Once again, he stared dismally out of the half-opened door of the haven's knothole. *When will I get to hunt?*

At that exact moment, an ear-splitting shriek echoed from the depths of the forest. There was a moment's silence followed by frantic screeching much more intense than the first cry. It pierced the calm morning and terrified the birds. In a frenzy to escape, they flew blindly into branches, clawed their way through the leaves, and left a cloud of shredded feathers floating in the air behind them.

Horrified, Leaf and Fern stared at each other, speechless. The twins crawled hastily across the floor, huddled together in a ball, and hugged one another. Pale and trembling, they pulled the birch bark over their heads, and cowered under it.

"Is that Pappo's whistletube?" whispered Fern, her voice low and shaky.

Grimfaced, Leaf nodded solemnly.

They both knew the peculiar, urgent whistle meant only one thing. *A Twig is in danger!*

Not knowing what else to do, Leaf and Fern patted the heads of the frightened babes.

After a while, they heard snapping and crashing noises. Something was moving fast as it climbed up the Old Seeder. It broke branches and grunted as it came nearer.

Leaf darted over to close the knothole's door, but just then—in one breathless, tumbling crash—Pappo somersaulted wildly through the knothole, and sprawled on the haven's floor. The few gray leaves, which stuck from his head, lay limp and tangled. His golden eyes flickered from Leaf to Fern to the babes, then back again to Leaf. He sucked in gulps of air, struggling to breathe. He shook his balding head as if buzzing bees hovered around his ears.

Fern tucked Buddy and Burba close beside her. She tugged the birch bark over their eyes to shield them from Pappo's frightened face.

Pappo suddenly sprang to his feet, and stammered, "Stay back from the door! They're climbing up with Mumma! She's in a carry-cradle, and they're bringing her now. Fern, you must gather warm wraps and mint tea! Leaf, we need more moss. They're here!"

Stunned, Leaf and Fern pressed their backs to the wall, afraid to move.

In the next moment, two crooked, old Twigs backed through the knothole door. Two more Twigs, who carried the other ends of a pair of long sticks, stepped into the haven. Between them they carried a cradle made of moss, fern, sticks, and ivy vines. In the middle of this soft bed, lay Mumma. She was pale and seemingly lifeless. All four Twigs grasped the cradle's sticks firmly yet gently, balancing Mumma securely between them. They paused just inside the door, and gazed around the large hollow, seeking a place to lay their fragile bundle.

"Here, now!" said Pappo with a surprisingly commanding tone of voice. He waved at a large chair in the corner that was stuffed with fluffy moss. A small, flat stool sat before it. "I'll get a blanket!" exclaimed Pappo. He noticed Leaf and Fern still stood motionless against the wall, so he clapped his hands sharply.

"Fern, the tea and wraps at once! Leaf, find moss! Buddy, Burba, into your hollow, now." Pappo's voice softened. "Don't worry little ones. We'll take care of Mumma. Off you go now. Take your stories and stones."

Burba crawled around hastily, and gathered up the sticks and stones. He clutched them in his tiny fists, and waddled to a narrow tunnel that led to his and Buddy's small hollow. Right behind him, Buddy dragged the birch bark. Fern gave them an encouraging smile, and tugged at a limp leaf, which fell from a hook and neatly closed their hollow tunnel.

The carriers lifted Mumma from the cradle, and gingerly sat her into the overstuffed chair.

As Leaf brought an armful of moss from his own bed, a loud clattering near the door made him jump. An elderly, grizzled-faced Twig had stepped into their haven, and carelessly tossed Mumma's old hunting tools on the floor. Even though he was very old, the grizzly Twig moved swiftly to Mumma's side. Leaf hesitated, unsure now whether or not to stuff more moss in her chair.

Pappo grasped the hands of each of the Twigs who had carried Mumma. He thanked them profusely, but at the same time shoved them toward the door. One by one, they murmured kind words to Mumma, and then reluctantly left.

Leaf could not bear to see Mumma's tools trampled by the Twigs as they shuffled out, so he gathered them up. Hastily he slid the strap over his head, tucked the saver in the back loop, wound the rope around his waist, and tied the whistletube's braid around his neck. The string was so long the whistle dangled just above his knees. He watched the healer bend over Mumma, lay his hand on her head, and gently touch her arms and legs.

Mumma's eyes fluttered and opened slightly. Leaf heard her murmur softly, "Don't worry. . ." Then she fainted.

Pappo groaned, leaned over her, and pressed his palm to her forehead. Mumma lay still, pale, and limp as if in a deep sleep.

The grizzled Twig motioned to Pappo to step outside. Reluctantly, Pappo allowed himself to be tugged through the knothole. He and Pappo stood close together on the porch-branch just beyond the round, wooden door. The old healer spoke earnestly to Pappo.

Fern tiptoed over to Mumma. Anxiously, she watched her breathe. Feeling that she must do something more to help, she wrapped a bunch of feathery ferns around Mumma's head. She patted her hand nervously, and murmured, "It will be alright."

Silently, Leaf crept near the knothole, and deliberately eavesdropped.

With one hand on Pappo's shoulder, the healer muttered words no more distinct than that of petals fluttering in the wind. Yet Leaf heard him.

Ivy's arm and leg have snapped. They will heal, but very slowly. Be patient. Don't worry. Ivy's wounds will knot together, and then her knots will make her stronger. The old Twig gave a brief nod, patted the top of Pappo's head a few times as if to reassure him, and at once sprang from the branch straight to the mossy roots below.

Sadly Pappo returned to Mumma's side, and sat on a low stool beside her. He still wore his hunting strap although it was twisted and lopsided. Blossoms that had been tucked into its pockets now lay scattered around Pappo's feet. His whistletube bumped against his walking stick, which hung upside-down and crossways on his back. The saver's gnarled knothole, which was usually upright, now traced puzzling patterns in the dust on the floor. The loops of his flaxen rope, which normally wound around his waist and over his shoulder, were now twisted into tangled knots. Pappo hung his head as though Mumma's fall was entirely his fault.

Leaf and Fern exchanged glances. It was obvious that Pappo felt helpless.

Sympathetically, Fern patted his hand, and then returned to her tasks. She laid moist ferns on Mumma's arm, and propped her feet up with puffy pillows.

Unexpectedly, Mumma's orange-speckled eyes opened and fluttered a few times like confused butterflies. She struggled to sit up straighter, smiled feebly, and with a weak voice murmured, "I'll be fine, dear ones. Now stop sprouting worries. Please don't fuss so, Fern. I'm much better."

Pappo smiled at her hopefully.

Buddy and Burba peeked out of their hollow.

Fern simply tightened her mouth, and continued to stack ferns and moss on top of, and around, Mumma's head, arms, and legs. She seemed determined to smother all Mumma's injuries.

Leaf stepped over and smiled at Mumma. He blurted out, "You're gonna' be just fine! You just got snapped a little, and you need time to grow back together. Soon you'll be all knotted up!"

Fern, Burba, Buddy, Pappo, and Mumma stared blankly at Leaf for a moment, startled at his outburst. Then they burst into laughter. The twins rushed over, but were blocked by Fern's arm. She scowled a silent warning to them that they better keep their distance. They plopped on their bottoms and watched with great interest.

Leaf blushed. "Well, the healer said so! I heard him!" He tossed a few strands of leafy hair over his eyes, fidgeted with the strap across his chest, and stared at the floor. Painfully self-conscious now, he planted his feet stubbornly and crossed his arms. He tried to look confident, but he suspected he only appeared silly. Embarrassed, he peeked at Mumma from under his leafy hair.

But Mumma's face gazed at him with an expression Leaf had never seen before. "Pappo, look at Leaf," she murmured.

Pappo stared at Leaf. Clearly, he did not understand why he was supposed to.

"Pappo," she urged, "look!"

Instantly, a sharp breath caught in Pappo's throat. His expression changed to the same mysterious one as Mumma's.

Even Fern stopped fussing with the moss packs, and stared at Leaf. Her face had an odd look, but hers was more like disbelief.

Leaf felt even more uncomfortable now. *Why are they all staring at me?*

Mumma spoke softly, "Leaf looks like a hunter!"

"Yes, yes he does," agreed Pappo in a wondering tone.

"Leaf!" gasped Fern with a giggle, "You look like Mumma!"

Taken aback, Leaf suddenly remembered that he wore Mumma's wrinkled strap and frayed, old rope. Her worn-out cappynut saver was stuck sideways into the strap's back loop. Her whistletube dangled from his neck, and slapped against his knees.

"Come here," said Mumma with a no-nonsense tone of voice.

Leaf moved reluctantly to her side, worried he was in trouble. He knelt and patted her hand nervously.

Mumma winced. Still, she reached up, untied the whistletube's braid from around Leaf's neck. Quickly she retied the knot, and lifted it back over Leaf's head. Now it hung near his elbows rather than his knees.

"Oh no, Mumma," said Leaf, startled. "I don't want it. I was just keeping it from being trampled by the Twigs! It's your whistletube, not mine."

"Shhhh," she hushed his protests as she weakly patted his hand. "It's yours for now until I'm well again." She leaned close to Leaf's ear, and whispered, "Maybe one day, it will be yours, little Leaf."

Leaf stared at his toes to hide his disappointment. *I want my own tools!* But he didn't want to appear ungrateful, so he gave Mumma a big hug. Immediately, she groaned. Aghast, Leaf cried out in distress, "I'm so sorry! Are you all right?"

"No, of course she's not all right, you cappynuthead!" Fern growled at him as she shoved him aside. "You're crushing her! Move out of the way!" She briskly adjusted the ferns that had slipped from Mumma's head.

Leaf frowned at Fern. She sounded so bossy, even more bossy than she had before. *Well*, he considered as he quickly stepped out of his sister's way, *at least Fern will be too busy now to follow me around.*

Pappo watched Leaf stumble over the rope he had clumsily wrapped around his waist. Mumma's saver was so long it bumped the floor, and knocked Leaf in the back of his head.

Leaf tried to see his reflection in the tea water, which was gently steaming, warmed by a sunbeam that pierced a small knothole. He frowned because it was too blurry to see.

Pappo smiled and turned away.

"Well," Mumma said, "Pappo, I think you should take Leaf out for his first hunt."

Pappo appeared startled. Thoughtfully, he rubbed his chin.

"I'm fine now," Mumma said matter-of-factly. "Fern is here." She held out her thin hand, and encircled Fern's with hers. Fern looked proud and not worried at all about suddenly being in charge of Mumma, the twins, and their haven. Being the boss for once was fine with her.

"But is Leaf ready to hunt?" Pappo's voice faltered at Mumma's sharp glance.

"It's time," Mumma insisted. She smiled lovingly at Leaf. "Pappo, look at him. He's almost a full-grown Twig."

Pappo stood up to study Leaf closely. His eyes squinted nearly shut. He scratched his chin, tilted his head from side to side, and shuffled around Leaf, examining him from his green, leafy head to his curly, knotty toes with exaggerated skepticism.

Leaf stood ramrod straight. Anxiously, he held his breath, and puffed up his chest.

After many long moments, during which Pappo grunted and muttered vague words under his breath, he finally declared, "Well, I guess you're right, Mumma!"

Leaf gasped for air.

Pappo chuckled. "Leaf, put some eats in those pockets on that strap. Let's finish the day's hunting." He shifted his own strap, and tugged it to better balance his saver. Carefully, Pappo tucked his whistletube in a pocket, so it would be out of the way when he swung through the branches. At last, he pulled his rope into a neat coil around his waist and shoulders. Briskly, he helped Leaf re-wind his rope around his waist, and checked to be sure his strap held his saver properly. He nodded his approval.

Leaf grinned broadly.

Pappo softly brushed Mumma's cheek with his own. "We'll be home before nightfall," he whispered, and squeezed her hand tenderly. He turned, stepped across the hollow, and jumped through the knothole to the broad porch-branch beyond. The bark had grown warm with the rays of the early morning sun.

Leaf had only enough time to grab a couple of sapsuckers. Quickly, he stuffed them in a pocket on his strap.

Mumma and Fern smiled at him.

"Uh, see you later!" Leaf stuttered as he leapt through the knothole. Pappo's shadow was already far below. Leaf flung himself down through the tangle of limbs at once, although for some reason he felt disappointed. He had always expected that there would be some sort of celebration on his first hunting day.

Oh well.

Leaf easily caught hold of one limb after another as he slipped through the branches. At last he dropped onto the soft moss. Pappo's skinny silhouette faded into a huckleberry thicket. Leaf vaulted over a mushroom, and sprinted through some dew-covered periwinkles. He slipped in between twisted huckleberry stems, popped out through a bush to a wide clearing, and raced to catch up. At last he jogged alongside Pappo, awkwardly trying to match his father's pace.

Pappo glanced sideways at Leaf, who now trotted breathlessly beside him. Mumma's long saver slapped his butt as he ran, and her rope threatened to slide off his shoulder, and slip from his waist. With one hand, Leaf gripped her whistletube to stop it bouncing up and hitting his nose. With the other hand, he batted at his leafy hair to keep it out of his eyes.

Pappo smiled, and jogged a little faster. Suddenly he darted ahead of Leaf. With a chuckle, he called over his shoulder merrily, "Better keep up, Leaf! The day isn't flowing any slower!"

CHAPTER SIX

THE HUNTER

"D on't move!" whispered Pappo.

Leaf froze. He held the saver in front of him with both hands as if to defend himself. He hardly dared take a breath.

"Good!" Pappo praised him. "Uh . . . you *can* breathe, you know."

In the bright, sunny glade Pappo was teaching Leaf hunting skills. Leaf's green hair sparkled in the morning sun. It was so shimmery it attracted the curious affection of a ladybug. It had spotted Leaf's hair ruffling in the morning breeze, flew sluggishly over, and plopped among the leaves sprouting from Leaf's head. The sweet crawly fluttered its red and black-spotted wings affectionately. Right away it crawled under a leaf sticking out from the top of Leaf's ear. Its black eyes glistened with joy.

"Hey, go away, spottie" shouted Leaf. He swung his saver in a wide circle, and clumsily whacked the back of his own head.

Startled, the ladybug only gripped hold of its cherished leaf tighter.

In disgust, Leaf threw the saver on the grass, and waved his arms above his head. He shouted, "Go on, you creepy crawly! Find someplace else to sit! Oh, slimerspit!"

Pappo chuckled. He strolled over, blew on the ladybugs' face, and waved it away. It flew off—a little confused—yet already searching for more sparkles in the peaceful glade.

In a low voice Pappo suddenly exclaimed, "Look, Leaf! A bellycrawler! Why don't you try a sleep song with the whistletube?"

Pappo signaled silently to Leaf to look under a nearby blackberry bush. Below its spiky stems lay a beautifully striped, blue meadow snake. Pappo quickly yanked out his own whistletube, and blew a few soft notes, which sounded surprisingly like the low moans of a mourning dove. The snake's head sank onto the dirt, and its body fell limp. Pappo grinned and winked at Leaf. Right afterwards, Pappo suddenly hooted. The hoot sounded very creepy, almost like a screecher owl on the hunt. The meadow snake sleepily lifted its head up until abruptly it recognized Pappo's hoot. It buried its head in the earth, and in an instant it blended into the thicket's roots, invisible in the shadows.

That's just dumb, thought Leaf. *Why can't we just go hunting?* Reluctantly he lifted the whistletube to his lips. Instead of a mourning dove's coo, though, he blasted the crackling warning of a coopers hawk. Spooked, the snake slithered immediately into a crevice in a rock pile covered with moss. It had suffered enough dangers for the day.

With a pleased expression, Leaf watched the snake's tail flick away. He grinned at Pappo.

Pappo frowned. "Leaf, sky hunters kill bellycrawlers, don't you know? Don't you think a dreamsleep coo would have worked better?"

Leaf just shrugged. *Chitterbugs! Blowing coo coo songs is for sprouts! I want to trap something!*

"Don't worry," Pappo said encouragingly, "you'll get it." Pappo put his arm over Leaf's shoulders. "Tell you what, how about you try roping a quilla!" He pointed at a funny-looking creature shuffling into the sunny clearing.

A porcupine cub waddled near a fallen tree at the edge of the glade. Its silvery bristles bunched up around its dark, fuzzy face. It looked like a bouncing ball spiked with needles. It also wore a broad stripe of darker quills down its back, and dragged them behind in the grass. With dark, velvety hands it scratched at the moist bark of the old tree. Happily, it chewed the tender wood beneath, crunching and flashing its orange teeth. The cub gazed contentedly at the pretty, pink daisies nearby, since it couldn't see much further than that anyway.

"Sure!" Leaf answered enthusiastically. *Finally,* he thought smugly, *this catch will be easy! That silly quilla is too busy grubbing around for treats to notice me!*

Pappo motioned that they both should keep quiet. He loosened his own rope from his waist. Patiently he fashioned a loop at one end of the rope, which once finished, was twice as wide as his outstretched arms.

Still silent, Pappo slowly twirled the loop around and around until it became a stiff, spinning circle. Then he casually tossed the loop over a pointy rock jutting up from the earth nearby. He pulled the loop tight, and neatly snagged the rock. The rock was captured! With a wink and a grin at Leaf, Pappo nodded.

Leaf nodded back. *Got it!* He unwound his rope from his waist, and laid a sloppy-looking loop on the ground beside his feet. He tried to swirl it around beside him, but it collapsed again and again, and lay tangled in the grass. But he didn't give up. Over and over Leaf tried to spin a loop half as well as Pappo's. Finally a wobbly oval spun just above the grass. *Whew!* Leaf thought. *Thank the stars! My arm is about to drop off!*

"Good," whispered Pappo. "Well done. Now, move very quietly up behind the quilla cub, and toss the rope over its head. It's busy searching for crawlies, and won't notice you coming."

Leaf tiptoed up behind the quilla's tail. The cub rustled its long quills back and forth, and waddled from blossom to blossom. Leaf kept a wary eye on the shifting barbed needles as he struggled with his rope. At last, he managed to spin a shaky loop and keep it hovering just above the grass.

"Leaf," Pappo suddenly cried out.

Unnerved, Leaf glanced back at Pappo. Somehow he kept his loop spinning. "What?" he whispered nervously.

"Be sure to let go if it runs!"

Right! Leaf nodded, although he had no intention of releasing the cub. *Let go? Why would I let go? I wanna take it home and show Fern!*

The rear end of the quilla cub wiggled and jiggled about as it dug up the roots of blue periwinkles where the juiciest worms lived.

Stealthily Leaf crept closer to the quilla's tail. All at once, with an awkward stumble, he threw the rope high up in the air. It fell perfectly over the quilla cub's head!

Startled, the clumsy cub bolted!

Leaf gripped tight, braced his legs, and stubbornly leaned back against the sudden tension of the rope.

"Let go!" yelled Pappo. "Let go, let it go!"

But Leaf wouldn't. *I caught it! I'm gonna keep it!*

Frightened by the tightening noose, the porcupine cub pulled Leaf around and around the clearing, too afraid to look back. Leaf's heels dug two ruts into the soft earth. Yet the cub pulled him faster and faster until with a heavy thud, Leaf rammed into a clover clump. He was yanked forward. He fell headfirst into a patch of flowers. Leaf twisted over and over, but still hung on as he ploughed through the daisies. The flowers burst all around him. He was covered with so many stems he looked like a weird quilla cub himself! Moss stuck out of his hair, and his emerald eyes blinked through pink and yellow petals. Yet, still he hung on!

"Let go, Leaf!" Pappo shouted as he raced after him. Frantic to help, he tried in vain to catch hold of Leaf's twirling feet. "You must let go! Leaf, let go!"

The poor quilla caught a glimpse of the wild-looking Twigs racing after it, and panic stricken, it scurried even faster!

Finally Leaf could hold on no longer. His hands hurt. The dirt filled his nose, ears, and eyes. His knees were scratched and sappy. Exhausted, Leaf let go of the rope. It slid through his hands. Leaf watched the quilla cub waddle away with his rope.

But as quickly as it had bolted away, the quilla cub stopped running. The rope relaxed its strangle-hold on its neck. With a shake of the noose, the quilla cub stepped backwards. Almost effortlessly, it slipped its head out of the loop, and the rope fell on the ground. At once, the cub waddled off again, the strange scare completely forgotten. Once more it snuffled contently for crawlies in a nearby log.

Leaf stared at it in astonishment. "You knew it would do that!" he cried out.

Pappo laughed merrily, and said, "Of course, Leaf. Maybe next time, you'll do what I tell you! Go get your rope, young Twig. Let's try out your skills in the forest."

Leaf dusted the dirt off his arms and knees, plucked the daisy petals from his hair, and retrieved his saver from under a holly bush, where it had been kicked. Impatiently, he wrapped Mumma's rope around his waist. It hung sloppy and tangled. Already tired of the day, and his failures as a hunter, Leaf gripped the bottom of the saver, and dragged it behind him into the shade of the forest. The blue gemstone, which had been stuck into its top knot, thumped over the rocks. The rope trailed along beside him, and twisted around the long stick. His whistletube bounced awkwardly against his elbow.

When Leaf reached the shadows of the forest, he smelled the musty scent of cedar bark, and it reminded him of the Old Seeder. He suddenly stopped walking.

Mumma had been so proud of me! he remembered. *What would she think now?*

With a deep sigh, Leaf held up the saver with both hands across his chest like Pappo had tried to teach him to do. The blue stone at its top twinkled in a ray of sun that had pierced the thick canopy above his head. Leaf caught his own reflection in the polished gem. Startled, he stared at himself. *I look like a babe!* he thought dismally.

For the first time, Leaf noticed how complex the figures were that Pappo had carved on the saver. The forest creatures' eyes nearly blinked. Their ears nearly wiggled. Many looked as if they might race off the long stick at any moment.

Leaf ran his hands over the saver's worn surface. The carvings were faded but the stick felt sturdy. He unwound the rope that hung in a tangle from his waist, and carefully rewound it. For the first time, he noticed the rope's elaborate, yet strongly woven quality. The whistle, which dangled too long on its string, has bruised his elbow. So he re-tied it to hang below his shoulder at just the right length. He felt the shoulder strap's soft, smooth texture, and realized it fit him perfectly. *I can do this,* he told himself. *I will learn the skills of a hunter, no matter how many mistakes I make!* Leaf jabbed his saver into the strap's back loop, and hurried to catch up to Pappo.

After a long, silent jog on dark, trampled paths, Pappo and Leaf paused by a slow running stream. It was wider and deeper than the one near their home.

"Let's rest here a moment," Pappo said. "It's a fine spot to gather treats. But watch out for those." He motioned toward the creeper vines that wound around the tree trunks along the creek's embankments. Holding his saver in one hand, Pappo began searching the banks of the creek for fallen pine nuts, which might have floated down the waterway from the high, steep cliffs that bordered their forest. Pine nuts were especially tasty and were also Mumma's favorite treat.

Leaf searched the bushes along the creek. He wanted to do well today. He hoped to impress Pappo and Mumma. He concentrated on finding every tiny seed that had fallen from the pine cones and every ripe berry on the huckleberry bushes. He intended to return to their haven with his pockets full.

Leaf avoided the edge of the forest. The twisted, tangled-up creeper vines clung to the limbs of the old cappynut trees lining the creek bank. The vines were vicious. They crept up the tree trunks, and wove deadly patterns in the bark. Twigs knew to steer clear of creepers. Their choking vines squeezed anything caught in their grasp. The only way to escape was to slash the thick vines, which wasn't easy. The vines were tough. Eventually a creeper vine smothered any tree caught in its grasp, and the tree endured an anguished, suffocating death.

A strange, ruffling noise suddenly alarmed Pappo and Leaf. An oddly-shaped shadow swept over their heads.

Pappo froze, crouched down, and whispered loudly to Leaf, "Something sounds wrong." He looked slowly around, and then up at the topmost branches of the trees. Carefully, he searched the sky.

Frightened and wary, Leaf crouched low and tried to blend into the mud.

"There's odd movement up high in the trees where there should be none," Pappo explained in a low murmur to Leaf.

Leaf concentrated, straining to hear the weird noise again. It had sounded like a flat flapping—like stiff wings beating against the fronds of a cedar tree. "What was it?" he wondered aloud.

Pappo just shook his head. "Stay here," he ordered in a no-nonsense tone. Without another word, he crept into a prickly bush on the edge of a sloping ditch, and disappeared.

Leaf froze as he had been taught to do. *Like a fawn,* Pappo had told him, *which lays motionless in the tall grass when it's left all alone, and danger approaches.*

Only he wasn't a fawn in the grass. Leaf suddenly realized he was crouching in mud with only sky above him. He scooted over to the embankment, and crawled into a holly bush growing beneath a dying cappynut tree covered with creeper vines. *At least here I can be invisible.* Leaf stuck his leafy head among the twisted branches, shoved his long fingers into the soft earth like roots, and closed his eyes until they looked like leaves fluttering in the breeze.

He blended so well into his surroundings that a grosbeak fluttered down onto the moss nearby. It pecked and tugged at some scraggly tufts of moss, searching for a few juicy worms.

A wicked grin crept over Leaf's face as he contemplated plucking a few feathers from the bird's tail. He was so near the grosbeak's white-speckled wings that he could have blown a soft breath to ruffle its feathers, and the bird would have felt only an unexpected breeze. But Leaf knew he must remain invisible, and not startle the bird. It would reveal his hiding place.

After a while the fat grosbeak grew disappointed with its search, and skidded awkwardly down the embankment to the creek, leaving bizarre claw marks in the mud. With its fat, blunt beak it scooped up a cool drink of water.

At that very moment, chaos erupted above Leaf! The grosbeak screeched and took flight. Something bizarre plummeted through the cappynut's tree limbs. As it fell, branches snapped, cracked, and splintered. Furious sounding cries echoed in the forest as it thrashed its way down from the treetop directly toward Leaf's head!

Without thinking Leaf somersaulted out of the holly bush, rolled down the bank, and into the middle of the creek. Soaked and shivering, he crouched in the water, and searched the cappynut tree's creeper-covered branches for the beast. Shredded leaves floated down, stripped from the thick vines.

"Slimerslicks and spiderbellies!" an angry voice shouted from a tangled clump of creepers. In its midst, a young Twig with copper-colored hair hung upside-down. He twisted around trying to free himself.

Leaf stared in horror! The Twig was caught in the death grip of the suffocating creeper vines!

CHAPTER SEVEN

THE SAVER

"Chitterbugs!" cried Leaf.

At once the hanging Twig stopped moving. He twirled slowly around and around, nearly invisible now that he had quit struggling in the ever tightening creeper vines. Large copper eyes gazed calmly at Leaf for a brief moment each time the Twig twisted past. His hair stuck out at all angles—the same coppery color as his eyes. His spin slowed as the vines twisted to their limit, and then suddenly he began spinning around in the opposite direction, faster at first, then slower and slower.

Leaf was astonished, yet in the same moment he realized, the creepers had probably saved the Twig's life. He had fallen from such a great height. If the creepers had not caught him, he would have been broken into pieces in the tree roots.

The upside-down Twig serenely folded his arms across his chest. Each time he spun around, he gazed with cool and steady eyes at Leaf, just as if this sort of thing happened every day!

Finally, as the spin slowed once more, a soft, sure voice spoke from the cluster of vines, "Well? Gonna' help me, then?" All at once he spun swiftly around in the opposite direction again. "Hmmm, maybe you're going to just sit staring at me the rest of the day?" His voice rushed by as he whirled. "Or do you enjoy sitting in the water, eh?"

Startled beyond words, Leaf simply blinked.

"Well?" the Twig asked again, now with a mocking tone as he twirled. "You do move, don't you? Climb up here and untangle my feet will you?"

"What, er . . . who are you?" stammered Leaf.

"Who are *you*?" the Twig grumbled impatiently. He frowned, twirled, and grunted, obviously irritated.

"Uh, oh, I'm Leaf. My branch is the Old Seeder Twigs," answered Leaf. He lifted a dripping hand from the water in a polite salute-like wave.

The hanging Twig's face softened. "Oh, Leaf. I didn't recognize you. It's been a while since you sprouted." he murmured. The vines twisted to their limit, paused, and then quickly spun the Twig around in the opposite direction again. As his face blurred past, he looked wistful. Once the vines slowed, he abruptly declared, "Well, Leaf, most likely you don't remember me, but I'm Rustle of the Ridge Twigs. Good to see you! Now, jump up here and see if you can untangle my feet, while I cut loose these vines." His voice sounded much friendlier now.

Impatiently Rustle twisted his arms, and tugged on the vines that constricted his movements. The weight of his body stretched the vines. That made it impossible for Rustle to free himself, even if he had stopped spinning.

Cautiously, Leaf studied the creepers. He would need to climb out on the branch, cut away the vines, and be extra careful to not get tangled up himself, or they both would hang there until Pappo found them!

All of a sudden Leaf felt an unexpected chill. A red-tailed hawk—a deadly sky hunter—soared swiftly over the top of the cappynut.

Immediately Leaf crouched down in the creek, hoping to look like a stone in the water. Warily he watched the wavy shadow of the hawk's powerful wings glide upstream. After a moment, the sky hunter tilted its wings, and soared back toward the tree. The hawk was searching for prey along the ribbon-like stream. The shadow swept over them once again, and continued downstream.

Leaf relaxed.

Rustle twirled around and winked.

But in the next instant, the cappynut leaves shivered as a bloodcurdling shriek shook its limbs.

The hawk had spotted them!

Panicked, Leaf leapt from the water at once, and threw himself under a holly bush below Rustle. The sky hunter circled around, in an ever tighter spiral, to take a closer look. It appeared to the hawk that a helpless creature was caught in the vines. Once again, the creepers offered the hawk an easy meal. It narrowed its black, marble-like eyes on the very spot where Rustle spun and hung!

"Hide, Leaf, hide!" Rustle hissed sharply. "Hide well!"

Scrambling for safety, Leaf crawled deeper into the holly thicket, and squatted in its shadows. Immediately afterwards, Leaf felt ashamed of himself for deserting Rustle. He crawled out of the holly bush, determined to help somehow. Leaf suspected that once the hawk realized the Twig wasn't food, it would tear Rustle apart, carry his pieces to a high cliff nest, and stuff him in it.

"Hide!" hissed Rustle.

Grim-faced, Leaf shook his head, and yanked out the saver from his strap's back loop. With trembling hands he pointed the long stick at the sky hunter like he was ready to whack it.

The hawk spiraled closer and closer. It was obviously not afraid of Leaf or his saver.

"Run away, Leaf! Hide!" Rustle cried out. "I can take care of myself!"

The hawk fixed an eager gaze on the unusual movements in the creepers. Its wings stretched out like arms embracing the wind. Their feathers spread open, and stiffened at their tips as if dozens of fingers scraped the sky. The hawk's tail abruptly tilted down, flat and wide, which stopped its flight midair. At once the sky hunter banked into a pinpoint turn, which Leaf knew would soon become a steep dive.

In a frenzy Leaf jabbed the sky over and over, hoping he looked like a fierce beast. "Go away!" he screamed.

"No, Leaf, hide!" Rustle yelled. He struggled frantically, but the creepers only squeezed him tighter.

The hawk folded back its wings, prepared to strike.

Leaf realized he had but a moment to think of something that might protect Rustle. He scanned the creek bed and bushes around him. There were no weapons better than the saver he held!

"It's too late!" screamed Rustle. "Run! Run! It's diving!"

The hawk dove.

At that moment, the blue gemstone stuck in the saver's top knothole flashed in the sunlight.

Of course, Leaf thought. *The stone!*

Faster than the hawk could reach them, Leaf rammed the saver into the earth between his feet, and slanted it until the gemstone caught a ray of sun. At once, a blue beam burst from the gem, crossed the creek, and scorched the bark of birch tree! In the time its takes to breathe once, Leaf swung the beam at the diving hawk. The pinpoint of heat burned one of the hawk's eyes, and blinded it!

Shocked, the hawk screamed in pain. It scrambled backwards midair, and beat its wings frantically to avoid the exploding stab of light. The hawk was so close to them, Leaf and Rustle felt the wind rush from its whipping wings. Again, it screamed furiously! Confused and in pain, the wounded sky hunter whirled away, just a blur of flapping feathers.

Leaf gasped in disbelief. *It worked!*

"Well done!" a familiar voice cried out breathlessly from a blackberry bush across the stream. An excited Pappo thrashed his way through its thorny stems, splashed through the creek, and rushed over to Leaf. Thrilled, he hugged Leaf tightly. "That was close! Quick thinking, Leaf!"

"I'll say!" declared Rustle. He grinned and laughed with relief. "Whew!"

"Rustle? Is that Rustle?" Pappo asked with an incredulous tone of voice. He peered into the tangle of creeper vines. "Why, it *is* Rustle!" he exclaimed joyfully as if he had just discovered a rare treasure. "How did *you* ever get trapped in creepers?"

Pappo paced back and forth beneath the twisting, upside-down Twig. Fascinated, he scratched his chin, peered into the twirling cluster of vines, and chuckled. But Pappo made no attempt to free Rustle. "Hmmm, had a little trouble with your leaf flyer?" he asked innocently.

"Oh, my flyers aren't the problem," Rustle answered nonchalantly. He snorted. The creepers twisted tighter around his feet as he continued to spin, one direction and then the other. "It's those pesky pokers! They keep poking holes in my leaves!"

Pappo's eyes grew wide with disbelief and amusement. "Pokers? Really? Didn't I teach you better than that? You only need to toss a few crawlies on a tree trunk, and they'll leave you alone!"

Leaf stared from Rustle to Pappo. He wondered when Pappo had taught Rustle anything.

Rustle hung silent for a moment, spun around again, and then wryly commented, "Well now, that's a good trick indeed, but I don't remember *you* ever telling me that. So tell me now, what's the trick to getting out of creepers, eh?"

Pappo chuckled, "Well, Rustle, that's one trick I don't know." He grinned broadly. "Maybe you just need a hawk to yank you out!" Pappo slapped Leaf's back, and laughed heartily at his own joke, but as he did he pulled out a sharpened rock shard, and reached up on tiptoe to cut away the creeper vines.

With extreme care, Leaf climbed over the vines that suffocated the cappynut's trunk until he could tug

Rustle's feet free. Just as Pappo cut loose the vines around his arms, Leaf freed Rustle's feet. In an instant Rustle plopped down on his head. He grunted, stretched out his arms gratefully, and rubbed his throbbing legs.

"Thank you, Leaf" said Rustle as soon as he was able to stand up. "You most likely saved my life, you know. Falling from a flyer like that. It was unlucky to fall into creepers."

"A flyer? Uh, you fly?" asked Leaf. He couldn't help sounding completely bewildered. *How could a Twig fly?*

Rustle burst out laughing. It was more like a hoot. It sounded so much like the call of an owl at midnight, an alarmed frog hopped from the creek into muddy hole.

Pappo chuckled like he knew a secret.

"Oh sure, Leaf, I fly," Rustle replied casually. "I fly all the time! I make the best flyers, too! Today I was trying out my new design," he said proudly. "Quite a sky flyer, eh?" He waved to a tattered red maple leaf stuck on top of the holly bush. Gobs of spider webs dripped from its stem. Still, Rustle glowed as he surveyed the leaf's damage. "But, ya' know, it couldn't catch the up-thrusters like I thought it would! It wouldn't slide into the down drifts, either. Twisted like a whirly seed on the breezy-drops, too." Rustle paused and commented more to himself than Leaf or Pappo, "Actually, it didn't do anything I wanted it to do!" He sounded a little embarrassed— but just a little.

"You fly on leaves?" spluttered Leaf.

"Now, now, Leaf," warned Pappo as if he could read Leaf's mind, "it takes great skill to handle leaves on the wind. Flyers are very unpredictable. And fragile, too! They are only made from leaves and spider webs."

Leaf felt more interested, not less.

A twinkle in Pappo's eyes betrayed the fact that he obviously admired Rustle's abilities. He could not help adding, "Rustle's flyers truly are amazing! And he flies as fast as a sky hunter! Well, *usually* he can fly like a sky hunter anyway," Pappo paused, considering what had just happened, "Guess he flew more like a pine cone today!"

Leaf grinned. Eagerly, he stepped over to examine Rustle's crumpled flyer.

Rustle exclaimed, "Needles, you didn't tell me Leaf was as quick-witted as Ivy! Not like you at all!" he joked.

Leaf glanced at the brash, young Twig, surprised that he was teasing Pappo with such a familiar manner. Rustle stood with both hands on his hips, grinning at

Leaf. He had the arrogance of blue jay, although he had just been rescued from creepers. He acted like a Twig who thought he knew a great deal about the forest, yet he'd just dropped from the sky, and crashed into creepers. *Still,* Leaf thought, *Pappo sounds very pleased to see him.*

"Ah, Rustle, you must visit us more often!" Pappo exclaimed. "It's not been so very long ago that you saved my life, remember?"

Startled, Leaf blurted out, "What? Rustle saved your life?"

Pappo nodded, and answered "Leaf, don't you remember those old stories about a Twig who can sound like forest creatures?"

"Oh, sure. Those dumb, old stories? Those are just made up!" declared Leaf.

"I suppose they do sound made-up," laughed Pappo, "but they aren't! Remember the story about me being trapped in a log? A sly sniffer had me trapped, and I thought I'd be stuck there for days. But to my good fortune, a horrible scream scared that sniffer so bad that it took off into the forest. All I saw was its tail disappearing in the shadows." Pappo's eyes twinkled with the memory of the fox's tail whipping away when the blood-curdling shriek of a mad badger shattered the air. "Well, Leaf, that horrible scream was Rustle's!"

Leaf looked confused. "Rustle's?"

Pappo gently shook his shoulder and explained, "Leaf, Rustle can sound like almost any creature in the forest. If you ever hear him snarl like a stalker, you'll never know it's only Rustle!"

A frightening vision popped into Leaf's mind of the lynx, which stalks its prey from limb to limb. Their screams were horrifying when they fought over their kill.

"Oh, and you should hear his screecher!" Pappo added, "Rustle will make your knees weak with that one!"

Leaf shivered thinking of the round, golden eyes a screecher swooping in the night sky. When a screecher shrieked at night, a Twig was known to faint straight-away!

Gleefully, Rustle added, "But that's nothing to my *whoosh!*" Rustle blurted a rude noise through vibrating lips.

Right away Leaf recognized the sound a skunk makes when it shoots its horrible stench.

Rustle chuckled, "Sounds just like a stinker when it sprays, eh?"

Pappo grinned, and urged Rustle again, "Please come visit! Ivy wants to see you!"

"Sorry, Needles. It must be another day." Rustle sounded genuinely disappointed. "When my new flyer lifted off from the ridge, it almost left without me, and I lost hold of my hunting tools. They scattered all over the crest. I must get to them before a masked-marauder thinks it's found some treasures to drag off to its den. But please tell Ivy all about our adventure today—especially about Leaf. He kept a cool head, and was very brave and clever. I owe him my life!"

Pappo's eyes shone with pride.

Leaf felt awkward. Rustle's praise made him sound like he was brave or something. He had been scared the whole time.

Rustle's eyes twinkled, and he winked at Leaf. "I'll see you soon, I promise."

"Of course, Rustle," said Pappo. "Thank you for the kind words about Leaf. Although, I'm sure you would have thought of something to save yourself!" He added, "By the way, Ivy took a tumble. She'll need to rest for awhile."

At once, Rustle's faced clouded over with concern.

Pappo reassured him at once. "She'll grow together again, Rustle. Don't worry. Just needs to mend her sticks a little. She'll be herself in no time at all. Remember, you must visit soon."

Rustle nodded, gave Pappo a slight salute wave, and turned to examine his mangled flyer, which had slid off the bush, and was now crumpled in the mud near the creek.

"Come now, Leaf," called Pappo as he jumped over the mossy embankment. "It's time to take our treats home. He trotted into the forest's shadows. "Fare well, Rustle!" His voice faded away.

Leaf hesitated. He had so many questions to ask Rustle. He hated to leave just yet.

Rustle sensed Leaf standing behind him. He turned around, and gazed at the younger Twig seriously. "Leaf, I really do owe you. If you ever need me, go to the high ridge, and call from the crest. I'll hear you anywhere in the forest from there. Now, young Twig, catch up to Pappo! Hurry!"

Thinking of nothing more he could say, Leaf nodded. He quickly climbed over the creek bank, and sprinted into the forest. He glanced back at Rustle, who now knelt beside the sad, mangled maple leaf and spider webs that had been his leaf-flyer.

Leaf hurried into the shadows to catch up to Pappo. *When will I see the amazing flying Rustle again?* He wondered, and smiled.

A hummingbird, which glowed with brilliant colors in the speckled sunlight, flittered for an instant beside him. In the wink of an eye, it swiftly zigzagged away just above a sunlit path.

Flying! Leaf watched the teeny hummer with envy. *Maybe one day.* He grinned as he sprinted on the mossy trail.

Before long, he caught up to Pappo, and trotted along behind him, matching his stride. He watched Pappo's gray, barely-leafed head bounce ahead of him. Pappo's bald spots gleamed in the sun. Leaf puzzled over the friendship between Rustle, Mumma, and Pappo. He realized he knew so little about any of them.

As Leaf jumped over a squatty mushroom, the saver slid across his back. He paused to adjust the strap that secured it, and also tightened the braided rope around his waist. He patted Mumma's whistletube to be sure it was stuffed safely under his strap. Leaf smiled to himself.

My tools! My saver! And I actually used a hunting skill today! Unexpectedly a feeling of pride made him flush. *Maybe I had been brave...just a little. And these old tools...well, they really aren't so bad at all!*

Then Leaf remembered roping the quilla cub. He sighed. There was still so much to learn! With a resolute grunt, he bolted past Pappo.

"The day isn't flowing any slower!" Leaf shouted over his shoulder. "Better keep up!"

CHAPTER EIGHT

OUTBURST

Pink colors in an evening sky shimmered on the surface of the pond. Slapper woke to the tree frogs' cheerful *chirp, chirp, chirp.* He rolled his huge body over, and pushed himself up with care so as not to disturb Patty. It was time to investigate the strange, trickling noise at the far end of the pond. He limped into the tunnel, and slid over the hard-packed dirt into the cool, green water of the pond.

The water would only be clear for a little while. Soon Splash and Splatter would slip into the shallow pond, too. They would rip up the grassy plants on the bottom, and stir the mud with their huge, webbed feet. Tonight their muddy clouds would be lit by a brilliant full moon.

Slapper swam fast. His strokes were powerful. In the water, his legs did not feel crooked. His kicks were strong, and he paddled swiftly. His flat tail pushed against the water as he steered himself to the far end. There, a thin stream tumbled down a ravine, and spilled into the pond.

Slapper peeked above the water at the steep ravine. Unexpectedly, nightmarish memories overwhelmed him. He stopped paddling, floated in the water, and drifted with the swirling eddies. His feet hung limp just above the bottom, and the tips of the grass tickled his toes. But he didn't notice.

I was so young, and so reckless. I should have died. How did I survive? he thought.

The nightmare began many seasons ago on a sweet-scented morning when he was very young. Instead of sleeping as usual during the day in his mum's burrow with all his brothers and sisters, the smell of flowers lured Slapper upstream. He was restless and unhappy because his old pond just had too many beavers. So once he was out of sight of his colony's dam, he decided to leave altogether.

Slapper went searching for a perfect place to engineer his *own* dam and begin his *own* colony. He wandered upstream into the foothills of the icy, cone-shaped mountain peak. Soon he found a spot where the creek ran through a narrow gulley. On one side lay a pretty meadow. Blocking the creek at this spot would create a deep pool. The pond would then overflow the gulley and swallow up the nearby tree roots. It would be a perfect pond.

Slapper set to work. He gnawed through a willow and the four, thin trunks of a river birch. He stripped them of their limbs and leaves, dragged the skinny logs to the gulley, and toppled them over the edge. He scrambled down into the creek, and stacked the logs on top of each other. The creek spilled in between the trunks, so he shoved mud, grass, and stones into the cracks. The water began to well up behind the squatty-looking dam. Slapper had never built his own dam, but he felt sure this was the way to begin. He sat back and admired his clever work.

It was then that Slapper was attacked! Dozens of cappynuts whizzed by his head! He tried to dive into the creek, but the water was too shallow. He crouched behind a round stone, and peeked over the top. On the embankment above him, five Twigs hung from a long branch of a red leaf tree. They laughed gleefully, swung flaxen slings loaded with cappynuts, and continued to pelt him with stones. Slapper tried to dig his way deep into the creek bed.

The Twigs jumped onto his dam, and arrogantly paced back and forth. They laughed at his tiny pond. Slapper lay still, but the Twigs spotted his shiny fur. They balanced heavy, sharpened quilla needles on their shoulders, and aimed the spears right at Slapper. Altogether with a shout, the five Twigs threw the quills as hard as they could.

Slapper was astonished how much the needles hurt for they really weren't very big. Still they stung like poisoned nettles. Slapper twisted and thrashed in the water, and tried desperately to yank the barbs out with his teeth, but many were stuck in his back and out of his reach.

The Twigs vanished.

Right away, Slapper heard weird noises. It sounded like scraping and digging from the creek bed on the other side of his dam. Slapper listened intently. Then he spotted flaxen braids that had been twisted around the slender trunks. All at once the saplings were pried from the mud and grass! The little pond rushed out in one big gush. All of Slapper's hard work was destroyed in an instant.

Too shocked to paddle against the flow of the rushing water, Slapper slipped past the Twigs and his broken dam. Stunned with the sudden turn of his fortune, he slid downstream over the smooth stones. He was carried along with the tumbling creek until finally he smashed into a mud bank. For a long time he lay stuck there until at last he was able to tug himself free. The sticky mud yanked out the last of the quilla barbs from his back.

Downhearted and sad, Slapper waddled to a clear pool of water. Anxiously he groomed himself, taking great care to wash away all the mud until at last his sleek fur once again reflected the sunlight.

But soon Slapper grew angry with the destructive Twigs. He padded back upstream along the edge of the creek, determined to find another place for his dam. He climbed over the willow and birch logs that he had so perfectly crafted into a dam. Now they lay useless on the banks of the creek.

The five heartless Twigs laughed as Slapper waddled past their red leaf tree. They hurled countless blueberries at him that stained his beautiful, sleek fur. They chanted a mean song, too. Slapper felt glad he did not understand Twig songs. He hurried further upstream.

Slapper decided to travel all the way to the end of the creek, and escape the land of Twigs, if possible. So he followed the stream through the foothills and into a narrow canyon. As he padded along, he daydreamed about building his perfect dam, living in his perfect pond, and meeting his perfect mate. On the way, Slapper ran across the remains of a weary-looking, neglected beaver dam, but he didn't stop there. He didn't want to repair an old, crumbling dam. He wanted his own.

Slapper followed the creek into a steep ravine. He climbed up, higher and higher, until he heard the roar of fast-flowing water. At last he reached the end of the stream. It trickled from a wide crack in the granite. When Slapper waddled through the crack he stood on a ledge above a deep canyon. He peeked over, blinked a few times, and squinted. Below him a powerful river rushed by. Further upriver, a shimmering wall rose up nearly to the height of the cliffs. The river spilled out from its base. It took some time for Slapper to understand what he was seeing, but after a while he recognized it. He gazed in awe at the massive dam made of ice!

So this is where the creek comes from!

Being an engineer, Slapper wanted to scrutinize the flow of the river and the strength of the dam. He wondered if a better dam might be built at this spot. He looked around. There were many pine trees growing everywhere, enormous ones that seemed to sprout right out of granite boulders. The trees leaned oddly, this way and that, shoved by old avalanches.

One enormous yellow cedar had been pushed into a weird angle, and now stretched out over the river. It hovered there at a precarious slant. Its roots clung stubbornly to gigantic boulders. Spray-soaked fronds hung just above the curling rapids. The tree's tip brushed the white caps of the river.

Lost in fantastic dreams of building a mighty dam at this very spot, Slapper scrambled over the rocks, and crept out onto the trunk of the yellow cedar. He looked up at the waterfall, and the cliffs. *What a great pond this would make!*

But in one terrifying moment Slapper's fantasy was shattered. He slipped, and fell into the river. That was the beginning of his nightmare.

Slapper remembered choking, coughing, and being slammed against boulders again and again. He fought against the current until he was exhausted. Suddenly there was an overpowering roar, and a great granite slab in the middle of the river. He hit it with such force his legs were crushed instantly. Then, for a long time, all was black. Slapper drifted from dark to light and back to dark again. Whenever he struggled to reach the light, he felt terrible, stabbing pain, so he fled back into his dark dreams—his nightmares.

At last there was a scent of cedar, a twinkle of sunlight, and less pain. Slapper had the sensation that many days were flowing by until one morning he became fully conscious. He was alone, and lay on a pad of moss in between the roots of a huge cappynut tree. A thin waterfall fell from a high cliff, and splashed into a pool nearby.

What frightened him at once was that his legs were tightly bound with flax and sticks! Fighting back a rising panic, Slapper chewed through the wrappings, and pulled himself from the roots. Terrified of the towering trees, and although his legs hurt with each movement, Slapper crawled away. Refusing to give in to the pain, he struggled toward the drifting scent of the valley grass, and its rain-washed dirt. Slapper's instincts led him around the wide valley and its popper burrows until he found the very same stream, which flowed from the ravine and back to his colony.

Slapper's family made a great fuss over his return. It took a long time for his legs to heal. Even though he was crippled, his crooked legs worked, and he became very strong, even more powerful. For some reason, Slapper knew he was also wiser.

So he decided to travel back upstream to the old, neglected dam in the foothills—the crumbling dam he had so arrogantly bypassed long ago. Slapper made his home there. He engineered the dam he always dreamed of building. It took many long seasons of hard work, but finally he created a pond full of beauty and life. His mate, Patty, came to him one day, and not long afterwards, his daughters were born. Slapper had built his perfect dam.

But he sometimes wondered about that dark time. *How did he survive? What had happened?*

Slapper shook the troubling memories away. It was time to find the reason for the odd, trickling sound, and the cold current seeping into his pond. He paddled toward the ravine.

Far away on Thunder Peak the storm had drifted away. But the turquoise lake was now so swollen it spilled over the top of the ice dam, and into the canyon. The great chunks of ice that had fallen from the glacier into the lake bumped against the ice dam again and again.

Then horribly—in one screaming, shattering moment—shrieks echoed off the cliffs! Rippling cracks that looked like flashes of lightening raced through the dam, and pierced its thick wall.

POP! POP! POP! Instantly the dam fractured into a thousand pieces! With an enormous gasp, the glacier lake exploded into the canyon, and the mighty dam burst!

Slapper never made it up the ravine. A deep throb pulsed through the pond. He felt the water shudder as if an enormous fist had slammed it. With a powerful thrust of his webbed feet, Slapper shoved himself up halfway out of the water. He squinted to focus on what was happening. He heard a loud, crunching, grinding noise, and then he saw it! A massive log jam filled the gulley, and was sliding right at him!

Shredded trees and bushes, rocks, mud, and boulders filled up the ravine and moved toward Slapper like a battering ram!

With his heart pounding, Slapper twisted around and paddled as fast as he could toward the lodge. *Patty! Splash! Splatter!*

The ugly surge sucked everything in the ravine into its whirlpool of debris. The mudflow rose higher and higher up the steep bluffs. Then it struck the pond!

The pond's water heaved up into a sickening, lurching curl. At once Slapper was launched up on the huge wave, and out of control. He somersaulted backwards over and over! Then the log jam, which followed the wave, overtook him. Instinctively, Slapper grasped on to a tree, and clawed at the bark until he sat on top of the twisted, half-shredded trunk. Terrified, he rode the debris flow toward his lodge. The mangled trees rushed even faster now as they slid across the surface of the Spreading Pond. Slapper spotted his lodge.

I must save Patty, Splash, and Splatter!

Slapper crouched down, ready to jump, and hoped his crippled legs had strength enough to push him to the lodge before it was crushed.

But just then, a piercing whistle sliced through the air.

Slapper searched for the whistler.

High on the bluff that braced the south end of his dam Slapper spotted Patty's goliath silhouette. She was rigid with fear. Beside her squatted Splash, Splatter, Birchbite, and Clacker.

The log jam crushed the lodge, and flowed on toward the dam, moving faster as the logs broke apart in the pond. In a moment, the flood would smash into the dam, and flood the gulley below!

Slapper leapt from one rolling log to another, desperate to reach the bluff before the flood surged over the dam. One giant tree slammed into the embankment. Slapper leapt onto it, and with all the strength he had left, jumped to the bluff, where Patty stood. At last he clung to a clump of grass overhanging the bluff's edge.

At once Patty was there. She gripped his neck with her teeth and yanked him onto the bluff. Slapper lay there gasping beside her. Splash and Splatter whined anxiously, and waddled back and forth, clasping their hands.

Insistently Patty nudged Slapper, forcing him to sit up. *Look at our pond!*

As if in a nightmare, Slapper watched trees, mud, and boulders roll over the top of the dam. The flood's debris roared by the chompers, crashed into the gulch, and smashed the creek bed below. Then it crushed everything in the gulley as it made it way on toward the grassy valley.

Somehow, in spite of the horrific onslaught, Slapper's dam held together. When the wave hit the wall of logs, much of it swirled back upon itself. The dam was spared complete destruction, and the gulley was protected from an even greater flood.

After a while, the dirty water calmed. The flood was over. But giant splinters interlaced the embankments. The wide, marshy meadow was filled with thick mud. The lush reeds and clumps of lilies had vanished, and in their place lay weird twisted tree trunks with contorted limbs. The canals, which Slapper had so painstakingly engineered, were smothered in sludge.

The Spreading Pond was gone.

Shocked, Patty pressed against her mate, and stared in disbelief at the destruction. Splash and Splatter whined, murmured breathy worries, and nuzzled her. Patty turned to comfort them, and Slapper grunted his reassurance.

Birchbite and Clacker shuffled near. With a piercing stare, Slapper focused on the two bachelors. He understood that they must have spotted the onrushing flood from their burrows on the bluff, and that they must have alerted his family. Their warning signal gave Patty, Splash, and Splatter time to escape.

Slapper nodded in gratitude.

The bachelors puffed up their cheeks, and blew softly in and out a few times to show their respect.

Slapper touched his nose to their heads, and grunted a welcome to Birchbite and Clacker. It was an invitation to join his colony.

With shining eyes, the bachelors grunted back. They wasted no time shuffling over to help calm Splash and Splatter. Splash touched her nose to Birchbite's, and Splatter rubbed her muzzle against Clacker's.

Slapper turned and stared sadly at his pond. The others slipped from the bluff, and began to tug at the tangle of logs, but Slapper knew the Spreading Pond would never again be their home. They might remain here another day or two, but soon he would lead them all away to find another meadow, another creek, and to build another dam. Grim and subdued, Slapper decided that this time, it would not be just one dam. He must build two, or more. He had learned another painful lesson.

In the distance the sound of splintering trees echoed up from the gulley as the flood smashed its way toward the grasslands.

Slapper sniffed the air. He will remember the musty scent that hung in the air this morning. He will remember the strange, trickling sound and the creeping, frigid stream that spilled into his warm pond. He will not forget them, for it was not long after these warnings that the flood came.

Patty crept along the edge of the pond looking for clean water to drink. But her search was hopeless.

Abruptly Slapper clucked a command to his colony to return to the burrows in the bluff. The pond was too dangerous now to be near it.

In despair, Patty gazed up at her mate. Her eyes seemed to ask only one question. *Where can I build my kits' nest now?*

CHAPTER NINE

A FEATHER BED

Far down the gulch, and much further away from Slapper's dam, Feather fussed with a braided hammock strung from a slender birch tree on one side of the gulley to a willow on the other. Dark green ivy and golden honeysuckle strands with orange-colored blossoms fell in disarray from the cocoon-like sack that hung just above the creek. The smooth, green trunk of the willow oozed a soothing scent in the air. Its branches bounced and swayed with the jiggles of Feather's maneuvers. She hung upside-down from one of the thicker branches of the willow, and yanked a flaxen knot tighter.

Across the creek, at the other end of the hammock, the pale, cracked bark of the birch tree glowed even whiter in the pink colors of twilight. The tree leaned away from the creek, and tugged the hammock with it. The willow strands brushed their tips over the creek stones and soothed the water, while the birch leaves rustled in the evening breeze.

Feather loved to sleep above the creek. The cheerful splashes helped her to feel safe at night. As she slept, the gentle sway of the hammock rocked with the rhythm of her restless kicking, which was more like running away from nightmares.

Feather finished tightening the knot. She dropped to the ground just as a wild-eyed chipmunk vaulted over the embankment, and zigzagged toward her through the shallow creek.

"Oh, watch out!" cried Feather.

But it was too late. The chipmunk made a clumsy attempt to leap over Feather's head, but instead knocked her backwards and into the water. The chipmunk sailed on past her and was caught by the willow strands. He swung back and forth, forlorn and helpless. His toes trembled and his tail twitched in jerky snaps. He stared in horror at Feather sitting in the middle of the creek.

In disgust, Feather stared back, soaked and dripping. Then all at once she reached out and searched the creek bed. "Oh! My stone, my rock-slicer! Where did it go?" She felt the smooth pebbles around her for the sharpened piece of granite she always carried. Soon her hand closed over the tool. Relieved, she stood up, blew her wet swan feather from her nose, and tucked the slicer into her belt. She glared impatiently at the chipmunk, still swinging in the tangle of willow branches. His whiskers quivered.

"Claws, why can't you watch where you're bouncing?" muttered Feather crossly. Her rosy eyes flashed.

Claws blinked innocently, wiggled his toes, and tried to look sweet.

Feather shook her finger right before his nose. "Really, Claws! I think you ate a bunch of bad nuts when you were a chippie." Feather frowned, yet nonetheless she swiftly cut away the willow strands with her granite shard. She helped the chipmunk to gently drop onto the creek bank.

A wavering shadow fell upon the ground beside them. Feather glanced over her shoulder, and murmured softly, "Oh, allo, Whisper. Have you been watching out for your nutty friend?"

A very gentle chipmunk, Whisper, stepped gracefully up, and blinked sweetly at Feather. She sat down and waited patiently, yet watched Claws with great concern. Her dark brown stripes were covered with freckles just like Speckles' fuzzy coat.

Feather didn't know for certain, but she was pretty sure that Speckles and Whisper were brother and sister. Both looked so similar, and were so alike—courageous and smart. And they were fiercely loyal to each other. But Speckles and Whisper were also loyal to Claws, and Feather was certain they were *not* related to him. Feather wondered why Speckles and Whisper cared so much about Claws. He was so bizarre. The most absurd, awkward chippie she had ever known. Perhaps they cared about him just because no other chippies would.

Completely chastised, Claws squatted in the mud. In a futile attempt to appear responsible he licked his hands and wiped his whiskers. He used the claws on his back feet to comb the tufts of hair in each of his ears. Then he tried to catch his tail to groom it too, but only spun around in a circle until he grew dizzy and fell into the creek.

Feather sighed. From the moment she rescued Claws, she knew he was very lucky to be alive. She had found him only a few days after the fire. He was just a tiny pup. Abandoned, discarded, stuck in a burnt out log. Terribly weak and feeble, his pathetic chirps sounded more like a bird's than a chippie's. Even so, Claws fought against his own rescue—biting, struggling, and scratching her again and again until she pulled him from the log in spite of himself. He earned his name right away.

Claws needed so much care, and there was so little to eat after the fire. Feather searched for cappynuts buried by squirrels. She discovered many stashes untouched by the fire, which had ripe nuts, and so she was able to save Claws, Whisper, Speckles, and herself, too.

Over time Feather gained Claws' trust slowly, and after a long while he allowed her to wash away the ash from his burnt fur. The stripes that ran down his back were so crooked that it made her smile for the first time after the firestorm.

Still, even with Feather's gentle care, Claws never calmed down. Jumpy and nervous, he hopped all over the place all the time. He'd whirl his head around as if he suspected some horrible threat would rush up on him. Sometimes he'd make an unexpected, sideways leap to outwit an imaginary beast. More often than not, Claws would race off, and because he was so busy looking behind him, he'd crash right into a tree. And his eyes! They never seemed to stop twitching back and forth. Feather could only shake her head in despair.

"You need to watch where you're going, Claws, instead of where you've been!" Feather shook her finger at him as she scolded Claws again. Under her breath she added, "If you can see anything at all, that is."

Embarrassed, Claws stared at his toes. His whiskers quivered uncontrollably.

Feather's irritation melted away. "Oh Claws, you nuthead," she whispered, "I'm so sorry I can't fix you!" She clasped her arms around Claws' trembling shoulders, and gave him a long, tight hug. She sweetened her words with a light kiss on his cheek.

At once, Claws' eyes sparkled with joy. He bounced away from Feather's embrace, bit off a piece of a puffy mushroom, and spit it at her just to show he accepted her apology. Then he raced up the birch tree to tuck himself into a leafy nest for the night.

"Thanks, Claws," said Feather sarcastically. She rolled her eyes at Whisper who kissed Feather's cheek with a wet nose to apologize for her odd friend. Then Whisper scampered to a branch near Claws.

Feather brushed the slobbery clumps of mushroom from her leafy hair, and sighed. "Now let me make sure this knot will hold," she mumbled. She pulled the hammock until it was stretched tight, and let go. It bounced furiously back and forth, but the vines did not break. "That should do it!"

Feather balanced on a large stone, which jutted up above the water in the middle of the creek. She jumped into her hammock, stretched her skinny arms out wide, and folded them behind her head. With a satisfied grunt she crossed one leg over the over, and stared up through the fluttering willow leaves at the faint stars. They had just begun to blink in the pale blue twilight.

Speckles curled up in an old bird's nest in the birch tree. Sleepily he opened one eye to check on Feather, and then he draped his tail over his head.

"This is lovely!" exclaimed Feather to the leaves that dangled just above her nose. She gazed at her dozing friend. "Seriously, Speckles! This vine-bed is best I've ever woven! It's as soft as dandydum fluff! You should come and sleep with me! I made it extra wide! Just for you!"

Speckles opened one eye again. He didn't understand Feather's words but he understood her invitation well enough. He refused to crawl into that flimsy, swinging nest she had made. Speckles curled his fluffy tail over his ears so he could pretend not to hear her.

"Oh fine then," declared Feather. "Nuts!" She rolled over, grunted, and then rolled over again. She bounced her feet against the hammock restlessly. Finally she lay flat with her arms outstretched, hanging out over the hammock's edges. The swan feather stuck out crookedly from her headband, and hovered above her nose. Absentmindedly, Feather blew its tip up again and again, and studied its wispy wiggles. Then, with a long heavy sigh, she asked the chippies, "So how about a story?"

Speckles let his tail slide from his ears until it curled neatly against his furry white belly. He loved Feather's murmurs at twilight. It was as if she were singing. Sometimes she sang until the stars melted into a wide, glittering stream in the black sky. Other times, she sang for only a little while—her voice softly drifting off with the evening breeze.

Sometimes, Feather would abruptly stop murmuring altogether. Those nights were the longest—filled with her restless thrashing and mutters. It was on those nights that Speckles sometimes heard her weeping, and it was then that Speckles crawled into her hammock, covered her with his tail, and sadly swung beside her until dawn.

But now Feather's voice sounded happy and sweet. Speckles felt sure she would sing a lovely sleep-song tonight. He snuggled further into his nest, closed his eyes, and listened. Feather's voice seemed to sway back and forth with the hammock's rhythm as she swung one leg lazily over its edge. The creek splashed beneath her, and added its own cheery notes to her song.

Feather told her chippie friends a story.

"Long ago in a beautiful green forest, there were great, big trees everywhere you looked. There were also so many branches of Valley Twigs no one knew all their names! They all lived in knotholes of many different kinds of trees—some were huge, some old, some twisted and white, some with enormous leaves, and some with needles.

"But there was one Twig family that was the best of all! They were called the Silver Leaf Twigs. They had a papps, a mum, and three tiny little Twigs named Lark, Swift, and Feather. And the oldest and smartest Twig of the Silver Leaf sisters was Feather!

"Feather was also the prettiest, smartest, and bravest Twig of any other Twig in the valley! She ran faster than any other Twig. She climbed higher than any other Twig. And she chipped off the best slicer ever from a broken piece of sparkling granite! She sharpened it until it was extra sharp! When she sliced with her rock-slicer, things were really sliced! In fact, hers was the sharpest in the valley!"

Feather tugged her sharpened granite shard from her belt, tossed it carelessly up in the air, caught it expertly, and promptly sliced the willow leaves hanging just above her nose to prove her point. With a furious flurry, the pieces of leaves fluttered down to the water, and floated away.

Skeptically, Speckles opened one eye, and peeked over the edge of his nest as if to question her fanciful story.

"Well, she could!" Feather stated flatly in response to his dubious expression. Reluctantly, Feather tucked her rock shard back in her belt, crossed her arms under her head again, crossed one leg over the other, and continued with her story-song.

"The Silver Leaf Twigs lived in a giant tree whose branches grew straight up like they were reaching for the clouds. The leaves were green on top but silver underneath so when the wind blew, the whole tree looked like a hundred shimmering icicles!"

Speckles peeked at her again. His nose wrinkled up in disbelief.

"Now, *that's* true!" Feather waggled her finger at him. "Anyway, the Silver Leaf Twigs were all very happy in their knothole."

Feather lowered her voice as if she were sharing a secret. "Now, not very far away from the perfect Silver Leaf tree was a tremendous, sprawling old Red Leaf tree full of Red Leaf Twigs. They had lots of irritating little Twigs running around shouting and yelling all the time. They had ridiculous names like Pounce, Jumpfrog, Rustle, Twitter, Wrinkle, and Spinner.

"They loved to scream and jump from their tree branches and chase bellycrawlers and chatters and even jay-jays. They'd throw anything they could find at any creature. They were just horrible Twigs! I had to rescue creatures from them all the time. They were just awful, dreadful, dandydumhead Twigs!"

Claws snored loudly.

Speckles snored gently.

Whisper laid her nose on the edge of her nest, and blinked her almond-shaped, brown eyes at Feather to let her know that she was still listening. Feather smiled back fondly.

"So anyway," Feather continued, "Those Twigs just couldn't stay put anywhere. They were always jumping from their own tree to the giant furry tree beside it. They'd climb up to the furry tree's highest tip, jump off, and float away on their giant red leaves! Can you imagine that? What nonsense! I don't know why they didn't just stay in their own tree!"

Whisper gave a huge yawn, and jerked her head up to stay awake a little longer.

Surprised, Feather blinked at the chippie, and exclaimed, "Whisper! Listen! This is the best part of the story! That Red Leaf Twigs' papps didn't even like his own Twig babes 'cause one day, I saw him throwing the littlest one—the youngest one named Rustle—off the tip top of that giant furry tree! I guess he just had one too many of his own little stinkers! He rolled that tiny Twig up in a big, red leaf, and threw him as hard as he could!"

Whisper flicked her tail doubtfully.

"Really!" exclaimed Feather. "He just threw him away!"

Feather's story-song had lasted too long even for Whisper. With a sigh, she nodded sleepily, slid deep into her nest, and tucked her head into her soft, white belly.

"But really, he did!" Feather protested to the trio of snoring chipmunks. She struggled to remember a night long ago. When she spoke her voice blended into the trickling of the creek.

"Well, maybe his papps threw him off that branch 'cause of the fire." Confused and sleepy, Feather murmured to herself, "Wasn't that when the fire came, Whisper? Wasn't that the same night the red leaf tree and the giant furry tree caught fire? Yes, I think that was the same night. Remember how Rustle was thrown away, but then a blast of hot wind whipped him up so high that he flew right over the trees? He just floated away into the dark sky, right up to the stars. I wonder what ever happened to him."

Feather's voice grew faint. Sleep and time clouded her memories. She yawned, rolled over, but continued to whisper more to herself than the chippies.

"Remember, Speckles, when I ran to the river and got lost in the smoke? But then you and Whisper found me. And I hung onto your back, Speckles, all the way to the river. And we hid in a burrow in the bank, and we were safe from the fire. Remember? We were safe, safe in a burrow." Feather's voice finally trickled away like the water beneath her hammock. She dreamed of floating on ripples in the creek like a leaf floating in the sky.

It was then that a terrifying nightmare gripped her. Feather felt claws ripping apart her hammock, and attacking her. Teeth sunk into her belt, and shook her violently. Feather felt herself being viciously wrenched into cold water, and dragged across hard, wet stones. She suddenly woke up, panic-stricken, and whacked wildly at the crazed chipmunk that had seized hold of her.

But Speckles only gripped her belt tighter as he jerked her up the bank of the steep gulch, and scrambled backwards up over its slippery rim.

In the next instant Feather realized she was awake, and a horrible howl echoed all around. There was a screech of granite against granite, the roar of an unnatural, vicious beast, and a sickening noise like the splintering scream of trees being ripped from the earth. The noise hurt her ears.

Horror-struck, Feather felt the earth shudder. In the brilliant moonlight she witnessed a massive wave of ugly brown water bursting from the gulley. The wave angrily shoved a tangle of logs and boulders before it.

With a violent crunch, they buried her hammock, and sucked in the trembling trees.

Panic-stricken, Feather threw herself on Speckles' back. Through a blur of blackened, scarred trees, they fled for their lives. Feather sensed that Whisper and Claws ran alongside them, but she did not look beyond her clenched fists. Feather thought only of holding on.

The flood surged on through the ravine until it reached a cliff at the edge of a great chasm. The gash in the earth was so deep that when the debris-filled water spilled over the cliff's edge it fell silently for a long time until the chasm swallowed the flood up in one gulp.

CHAPTER TEN

THE WATERFALL

Leaf and Pappo slipped into their warm haven with their bounty. The twins' tiny faces glowed with the fading sun. Its rosy streaks poked through the scattered knotholes of the Old Seeder's massive, hollow trunk. The two hunters spread out their treasures on the floor. Berries, blossoms, prickly cones, and pine nuts blanketed the tree's swirling rings that decorated the haven's wood.

"Dewdrops!" Fern cried out with delight. She picked out the juiciest berries from the pile, and stuffed them into a bark box for safekeeping. Burba and Buddy giggled as they rolled a large pine cone that was stuffed with tiny seeds back and forth between them.

"And here," whispered Pappo softly. He pulled a pink starflower from his strap pocket, stepped over to Mumma, and laid it on her lap.

She breathed in the musky scent of the flower mingled with grass and dirt, and smiled. "Wherever did you find it, Needles?"

Pappo murmured, "It blew onto a stream bank from the valley just for you, dear Ivy."

"It's perfect!" exclaimed Mumma. She lifted the little flower into a sunbeam, and admired each tiny petal.

Fern, Leaf, and the twins watched this embarrassing display of affection, and rolled their eyes at one another.

In a more matter-of-fact tone Pappo asked, "How are you doing?"

"I'm about the same as a newborn fawn," Mumma reassured him. "I move slowly, but I've taken a few steps."

Pappo looked greatly relieved.

Leaf stepped back, and took a hunter's stance by the knothole door—legs planted apart and arms crossed over his chest, but no one noticed him there.

So impatiently he blurted out, "Mumma, we met Rustle! I mean I met Rustle!" He hadn't realized until this moment how excited he still was. He lowered his voice and tried to sound older, but the words rushed out before he could think. "He flew on a giant leaf and fell right into some creepers! Then a hawk attacked him, but *I* saved him with the saver's stone!" Leaf thumped his chest with pride, and more than a little arrogance. "He would 'a been stuffed in a nest except that I blinded the hawk, and it flew away, so *I* saved Rustle!" he gasped, at last taking a moment to breathe.

Fern, Burba, and Buddy stared at him in disbelief.

Mumma looked quizzical for a moment, but then frowned at Pappo, who only grinned back sheepishly and shrugged.

"You did not!" Fern sneered with a rude expression of disgust. "What a story!"

"No, Fern, it's true," stated Pappo. "Although," and he glanced at Leaf, "perhaps this telling of the adventure is a little hard to believe. Maybe if we all caught our breath first, we could hear the story again . . . a little slower. But for now, you should know that Leaf was amazing!" Pappo's eyes twinkled.

Leaf sneered at Fern. He put his hands on his hips and tried to look like Rustle.

Pappo added, "Leaf kept his head when he blinded that hawk with the saver's stone. And Rustle was lucky," added Pappo. "Otherwise, both of them might've been carried away!"

Mumma shivered. "Oh, that is too scary!"

Leaf stepped over and patted her hand in a reassuring, older Twig sort of way. "I knew just what to do, Mumma. You won't have to worry about me in the forest. I'm pretty old for my age, you know." With that, he gathered what remained of the berries and nuts. He wore a satisfied grin, along with his hunting tools the entire time.

Mumma appeared unconvinced. Her eyes glinted at Pappo, and her topknot quivered as she suppressed a remark about how careless he had been with Leaf. He ignored her.

Fern sat back on her heels. In an irritating, plaintive voice, she demanded, "Who is Rustle anyway, and why did Leaf help him? I don't believe Twigs fly. That's just nutty, so what was he really doing?" She stared at Leaf incredulously.

"Now, now," said Mumma firmly. "We'll talk about it later! It's time to clean up and eat, or the sun will go to bed before us!" With that, all but Mumma bustled about and clumsily prepared supper.

Right away, Fern picked up Burba and Buddy and plopped them into curled ivy leaf.

Excited by the prospect of eating again, the twins blew bubbles with their drool, and babbled joyfully. Sweetly, Buddy blew a rainbow-colored bubble that twinkled in the fading light. Burba watched in wonder until the bubble was the size of his brother's head. Then with an evil gleam in his eyes, Burba poked it, narrowly missing Buddy's eye. Good-natured as always, Buddy only giggled. He rocked back and forth and pulled his toes with delight. Right away, Buddy blew another huge bubble for Burba to pop.

"Enough!" Fern said sternly. She was anxious to hear about Rustle, so she shoved some berry patties in Buddy and Burba's mouths. She barely gave them time to chew before wiping their faces with a limp leaf.

"If you promise to go right to sleep right now, I'll let you have a sapsucker!" Without giving the twins a moment to respond, Fern stuck the sweet treats in their sloppy fists. "Time to go to bed now!" she growled. Briskly, she yanked them from the leaf-chairs, and started to drag them toward their hollow.

"I'll take them, Fern," Mumma said tenderly. "You rest now." She held up a finger to hush any protests from Pappo. She stood up slowly and limped across the floor. She didn't want to miss her favorite time of the day with Buddy and Burba. Mumma loved to hum lullabies until they fell asleep. Then she would sit silently nearby on her mushroom stool, while she listened to them breathe and watched them dream.

With their tiny hands in Mumma's, the twins became calm and quiet right away. She led them away to their moss beds.

Pappo sat in the center of a dark spiral on the floor. "Let me tell you a story about Rustle," he began, and then hesitated. "Although I don't know much about Rustle 'cause Rustle doesn't know much about himself!"

"Yeh, like how he can fly! Really, Leaf! He probably just jumped out of tree, and you wouldn't know the difference anyway!" Fern smirked with superiority.

"He flies on leaves, you cappynuthead!" Leaf retorted impatiently.

"Oh!" Fern look surprised. Obviously that hadn't occurred to her.

"Do you want to hear about Rustle, or not?" Pappo grumbled. He motioned to Leaf and Fern to join him there on the tree ring.

Leaf and Fern glanced at each other, plopped down at once next to Pappo, and crossed their lanky stick legs. Fern leaned forward until she could rest her elbows on her knees, and cup her chin in her palms.

Leaf felt reluctant to remove his hunting tools just yet, so he pushed the saver sideways, and braced his back against it. He tugged the rope into his lap. Casually he tossed the whistletube over his shoulder.

Fern frowned at him. By her exasperated expression, it was clear that she thought her big brother was just showing off, and that he should take off his hunting tools. But she was more curious about Rustle than irritated with Leaf, so she focused her attention on Pappo.

Pappo jiggled his mint tea a bit as he squirmed around to find the smoothest spot on the spiral. Finally, he crossed his legs, too, and leaned forward to tell his story. Warm mist from the tea gave him an eerie, ghostly expression.

"This all happened before you came into the world," Pappo nodded at Leaf. "As you know, the cold breeze that rushes across the great ice pack and down from Echo Peak brings plenty of rain to our South Forest. There used to be enough rain to reach the grasslands, and all the way over to the woods beyond. But now there are too many long seasons when the wide valley is so dry the grass crackles. Now the only trees that grow across the grasslands are close to streams."

"Yes, yes, Pappo," said Fern as she squinted her eyes in a pretense of pain at listening to Pappo's dull story.

Pappo only smiled. "Listen, Fern! One time, after a dreadfully long, dry season, there was a great fire in the grasslands. The woods across the wide valley were swept up in the firestorm, too. From the tip of the Old Seeder, Ivy and I watched the grass and trees burn all the way to the Blue Mountains. When the fire ended, all that was left was a curling, dark haze.

The next day we went to the valley's edge to look for injured creatures. But instead, Ivy found a tiny Twig babe rolled up in a red leaf, and laying in a clump of white aster blossoms. The babe could barely talk, yet he pointed to his chest, and said *Rustle* over and over, so we figured out that must be his name. He also kept pointing at the sky. He told us his paps and mamma flew up there. We kept searching the sky, but we never saw anything. It was all very strange."

Pappo shook his head sadly. "We tried to pull him from the valley edge and take him back to the Old Seeder, but he kept pointing at the sky, and refused to leave the grasslands. So we waited with him there a long while."

Pappo took a deep breath, and patted the air to reassure Fern and Leaf, who were looking terribly worried.

"Now, now. Rustle was a pretty smart Twig babe, so it wasn't long before he was more interested in following slimers into the forest, rather than sitting around. He had a knack for finding cappynuts that the chatters buried, so we all enjoyed eating those! Rustle seemed to know just where huckleberries grew, and he even knew how to find a creek. He could hear water splashing by listening for its echo. He already had more skills at his young age than some old Twigs I know!

"But still, Mumma and I kept trying to get him to come back with us to the Old Seeder. But he refused to come. One day he ran off into the trees. We heard him shout over and over that his paps and mamma and brothers are flying here, and he was supposed to wait for them. He yelled at us again and again that he was *always supposed to wait!* Finally he just disappeared into the forest."

"He stayed there all by himself?" asked Fern in disbelief. "Just a Twig babe?"

"Yes, he grew up wild. Every now and then, as the seasons flowed by, we'd stumble across him walking along a creek, or hanging from a tree branch. He was always very good at hiding. Sometimes I sensed that he watched me hunting, and that he spied on me and other Twigs. But I hardly ever saw him.

"Finally, one day he simply stepped out of a blackberry thicket, and pointed to my saver. He stayed put long enough for me to make him some hunting tools of his own. I taught him how to use 'em properly, too. After a while, he took off into the forest again. I guess he just liked to be by himself. There's nothing wrong with that!

"Rustle popped up while I hunted more and more after that day. He'd follow me around, and copy what I did. Sometimes he'd talk a little—mostly gibberish. But as the seasons came and went, whenever we ran across each other, he started to jabber plenty, and it began to make sense. Some days he'd tell me about what creature he stalked in the forest, or show me feathers he'd pulled out of a blue jay's tail. He never talked about how he ended up in our forest, though, so I never found out. I kinda' think he just doesn't really know himself, or maybe he can't remember."

With a melancholy expression, Pappo gazed out the knothole doorway at the sprays of cedar fronds tenderly brushing the bark.

Leaf listened as the fronds whispered *hush, hush, hush....*

Absentmindedly, Pappo murmured, "I think maybe, he just doesn't *want* to remember anymore."

Leaf and Fern glanced at each other, bewildered. *Why wouldn't someone want to know where they came from?*

"But what *did* happen to his paps and mamma?" Fern asked. Her orange eyes blinked rapidly with the sudden realization that Rustle's family had probably been lost in the terrible fire.

Pappo shook his head and patted Fern's hand. "I'm afraid there are no more Twigs across the grasslands, little one. How Rustle survived the fire, or if he even came from there to here...we'll never know. But there's more to the story," Pappo winked at Fern.

"One day, Rustle popped right into our haven." He waved at the doorway, and Fern and Leaf followed the motion of his hand as if they expected Rustle to jump through the knothole, and stand right before them.

"Mumma and I noticed right away that he seemed happy for some reason. He was much stronger, and had grown very clever in the forest ways. He told us he lived at the crest of the ridge now. He lived there because the breeze that blew down from Echo Peak was perfect for flying. That's when he told us all about the amazing leaf-flyers he could build. At last, Rustle found something he was really good at, and wanted to do. We were truly happy for him. After that, we never worried about him."

Leaf grinned. He understood perfectly.

Pappo continued, "Rustle visited a few more times when you were very young, Leaf. I'm sure you don't remember him."

Leaf shook his head. "No, I don't," he admitted.

"Well, I wish I saw him!" exclaimed Fern. She stared jealously at Leaf.

"Now, enough Rustle stories!" declared Pappo. "I have many more, but not tonight! It's time to tuck yourselves into your moss beds!"

Leaf clutched his strap protectively. He felt very reluctant to remove it, or take off the rope, whistle, or saver. Thinking quickly of a reason to keep them on, he asked, "Uh, Pappo...can I sleep outside tonight? You know, on that big wide branch up higher? I'll be careful, promise!"

Pappo smiled a little as he washed and put away the tea cups. He understood why Leaf wanted to sleep outside. He wanted to feel close to the day's adventures a little longer. "Yes, Leaf," he nodded, but with a stern voice he added, "but don't stay up all night gazing at the stars!"

"I wanna' sleep outside, too!" whined Fern.

Pappo silenced her with a firm glance. "Fern, to bed with you. Now!"

Before Mumma might return, and object to him sleeping outside, Leaf leapt out of the knothole. He climbed to his favorite broad branch, and nestled into a soft cocoon of cedar fronds. He stretched, yawned, and laid on the saver that was still stuck in its back loop. Leaf rolled onto his side, and shifted the saver until he was comfortable.

The air smelled musty, but the scent of rain on the cedar bark was soothing. Leaf lay quietly and listened to a quick burst of rain beating against the Old Seeder's trunk. The wind blew in fitful gusts. The mammoth tree's fragile, new cones broke off and fell away. A scratchy, odd song twisted among the branches like a gloomy lullaby. The raindrops rolled off the cedar fronds above Leaf. The soft cocoon kept him warm and dry.

When Pappo calls me to hunt tomorrow, I'll be ready, he thought sleepily. Leaf fell into slumber with a smile on his face. He dreamt of floating through a black sky on dark red leaf.

As Leaf slept, the storm that battered Thunder Peak regained its power, viciously attacked the Sharp Peaks, and crept toward the Old Seeder. Because the glacier lake was spilling into the canyon, the river now swelled to unbelievable heights. The sheer cliff walls strained to hold back the bizarre torrent. The engorged river raced toward Echo Peak and Leaf's home.

At first, only fitful, whooshing gusts blew through the Old Seeder's branches, and warned of the storm's approach. Aimless winds sucked away the mist that curled on the forest floor. The air grew cool, and then warm, and then cool again. A dank, musty scent and swirling dust filled the air. The old tree held firm against the ever increasing power of the storm's winds until at last, after one powerful gust, it shuddered.

In the narrow canyon in the Sharp Peaks, the river beat against the walls of the canyon like a rabid wolf desperate to escape its cage. It was not long before the river found a fracture in the rock. Here, a stream had strayed through the granite, wandered beside a mountain meadow, and fallen over a high cliff. It was the same waterfall that fell beside the Old Seeder.

The Rushing Waters flooded the fracture. As it reached the waterfall, an astonishing arc cascaded over the cliff. Boulders cracked and thick mist spiraled up into the air as the water smashed into the pool beneath the falls. Beside the cliff, an avalanche began a slow, menacing slide down the bluff toward the Old Seeder.

Leaf fought his nightmare. A huge rock-like fist moved toward him through the black sky. All the while, there were wild, piercing screams everywhere at once. In his dark dream, Leaf was terrified he'd be knocked from the branch, so he dug his fingers into the soggy, wet bark, desperate to hang on. A lurching motion made him dizzy, and the hopeless shrieks made him weak with fear. Leaf clawed at the bark, but he felt himself slipping, losing his grip. He fell. Lost in a sickening spin, he was sucked into a deep, black hole.

A horrific *RIP!* and *BOOM! BOOM!* jolted Leaf awake. A brilliant flash and a *CRACKLE, RIP, CRACK!* shattered a limb.

Leaf woke up. He *was* falling!

Panicked, Leaf grabbed at the branches rushing by, but again and again he lost his grip. At last he slammed sideways against one branch, and landed on the spindly end of another. Shaking and nearly senseless, he pulled himself to the wide part of the branch. He lay there, panting. Burning flashes hurt his eyes, and his leafy hair bristled up like a startled quilla's. Thunder pounded all around. The Old Seeder swayed back and forth in a weird, sucking wind that whipped its long branches into whirls.

Then in one horrible moment, a brutal gust ripped Leaf off the branch. Once again he fell, but this time he was caught up in a whirlwind—thrust aloft—floating in a huge, swirling wall filled with leaves, dirt, and splinters. Leaf tumbled head over heels in airborne somersaults until at last he was abruptly spit out. He plummeted to the earth like a boulder rolling over a cliff, and landed in the mud with a *THUMP!*

It happened so quickly, he didn't even scream. He had no idea where he was. But wherever it was, he knew he was still in danger. Beneath Leaf's hands, the earth heaved and rolled in a sickening lurch. Leaf tried to stand, but the ground slid sideways under his feet. In the darkness he saw the shadow of a birch tree falling toward him.

The last thing Leaf heard was the crash of branches as he was once again slammed into the mud.

Leaf floated in a black tunnel for a long time. When he woke up, his mouth was full of leaves. He moved his fingers, yet he could not lift his hands to his aching head. After a great effort, one hand broke free of a leafy tangle. He wiped dirt from his eyes. Inch by inch he struggled to free himself from a thick mat of shredded birch leaves, and a muddy muck. With a determined push, he sat up, weak and shaken. He felt for his saver, whistletube, rope, and strap. He had each one. But everything still felt wrong.

What is that horrible rushing noise?

Instinctively, Leaf turned to look at the waterfall. Instead of the slender falls, he saw a white, churning cloud of water billowing up.

Confused, Leaf looked up at the sky to get his bearings. All seemed normal there.

Faint stars played hide-and-seek with a pale, fading moon. Orange and pink clouds streaked playfully between them. The sun was blowing up like a shimmering, golden bubble on the horizon above the Blue Mountains. A flock of white snow geese floated effortlessly up from the valley, and spiraled in on itself like the twists of a pinwheel. It was dawn. The day seemed like any other.

But everything is different! Leaf held his head and tried to think. *What happened? There was a storm. And a whirlwind. And a landslide!* Leaf sucked in his breath as he remembered. *Pappo, Mumma, Fern, Buddy, and Burba!* In a panic, Leaf scratched his way from under the birch tree to the top of a nearby boulder. But what he saw from there made him sink down to his knees, shocked.

A flood—not just a flood but an enormous river—flowed around the Old Seeder! Leaf stared up at the cliff, and then back at the horrible sight. *It must be the Rushing Waters!*

From atop the rubble of the avalanche, Leaf stared at the Old Seeder—so far out of reach now, and surrounded by floodwaters. He felt so tiny and helpless. Leaf looked through the thick branches of the Old Seeder for his haven. At last he spotted it, and there in the knothole doorway stood Pappo waving frantically!

In an awful moment of realization, Leaf knew at once what Pappo was trying to tell him.

We're trapped!

CHAPTER ELEVEN

LEAF LEAVES

Pappo screamed to be heard above the violent sound of the Rushing Waters.

Still, Leaf could barely hear him. He concentrated to make out the words.

Pappo cupped his hands around his mouth. "Rustle.... find Rustle! Chompers! Find the chompers!"

Confused, Leaf shook his head. *Why?*

Pappo's shrieks floated over the noise of the river. "Rustle must fly! Fly to chomper dam! Chompers build dams!"

All of a sudden Leaf understood what must be done. *The chompers can build a dam and block the Rushing Waters!* Leaf jumped up and down, waved, and screamed back he understood, although he doubted Pappo heard.

At once, Leaf scrambled uphill through the splintered trees and thick mud of the landslide. He knew there was a path near the tall sugar pine tree, which still towered on top of the hill. The trail led to the ridge and its crest. But when Leaf reached the sugar pine, the path was gone! Only the rubble of the avalanche spilled into the forest's shadows.

Leaf zigzagged back and forth over shredded logs and gigantic boulders, searching for the trail. He climbed higher and higher with each traverse. The effort was difficult. The rubble was slick with mud. Sticks poked at him and branches stuck straight up instead of sideways, which made Leaf feel dizzy and disorientated. He dared not look back at the Old Seeder. He must think only of reaching Rustle as swiftly as possible.

Leaf struggled to the very top of the avalanche. He scaled gargantuan slabs of granite. The slabs had been thrown about like a freakish pebble-toss game that young Twigs played. To the right of the upheaval, towered undisturbed fir trees. They soared up silently—deathly still beside the landslide—untouched.

Leaf collected his thoughts. *I must find another trail to the crest!* Finally, after an exhausting search at the edge of rubble where it met the trees, Leaf stumbled across a deer path wandering away and uphill. It disappeared into an eerie, hushed forest.

Leaf hesitated. *Where are the birds?*

He turned to gaze once more upon the devastating sight now far below him. Leaf had a perfect view of the river cascading over the cliff. Beside the flowing waters, lay a peaceful meadow in the foothills of Echo Peak. Leaf thought how weird it was that a meadow could lay so serene by a raging river. The meadow's bright, white asters and bobbing goldenrod nodded to the Rushing Waters, as if to wave it along.

With renewed determination to find Rustle, Leaf raced off into shadows. Right away he slipped and stumbled into a puddle, and fell flat on his face. Disgusted, he rolled over on his back, spit out a mouthful of dirty water, and lay there staring up through the limbs of a towering fir. The early morning sun created gleaming starbursts in its long branches. *How beautiful!* Leaf sighed.

The water rinsed the mud from the leaves on Leaf's head. He rolled back over, pushed himself to his knees, and washed the mud from his face and body. He blinked his emerald eyes at his blurry reflection in the pool. *What was he supposed to do again? Oh, yes! Find Rustle,* Pappo had shouted.

At once, Leaf jumped up and ran along the deer path. Before long, it split into two trails, and then forked again. Leaf paused. He must continue uphill toward the crest but which path to take?

As he stood there wondering, a weird *WHIP, WHIP, WHIP* and *BRRMMMMR!* whirred from a nearby log. It sounded like tiny wings were beating frantically inside it.

Cautious of the bizarre hornet-like noise, Leaf knelt at one end of the log, and peeked in, but could see very little. Leaf moved very slowly. Giant forest hornets that Twigs called skullfaces often nested in rotting logs. *But this sounds like something else. It isn't buzzing. It's whirring. Still, is it dangerous?*

The whipping grew more frenzied. Leaf shoved aside some of the slushy clumps of moss and dead leaves. He peered deep into the shadowy log. A teeny silhouette flitted around deep in the hollow. Furiously it beat its fragile wings.

"How'd you ever get stuck in here, little hummer?" wondered Leaf aloud. At once a rush of wings flew out of the opening Leaf had made, and right past his nose! Startled, he sat back on his heels and laughed in embarrassment. *Oh, slimerspit! It's just a silly hummer!*

With an unsettling, loud *BRMMMMR! BRMMMMR!*, the hummingbird returned. It hovered over Leaf's head, and then zipped back and forth right before his nose. Fascinated, Leaf watched the hummer's fluorescent feathers shimmer in the sunlight. "Go on, now," Leaf murmured, hoping to soothe it. "You better fly home now."

But the hummingbird refused to leave its rescuer. It flew in erratic patterns in and out of the low hanging limbs, and then darted back at Leaf, and stabbed at the bright green leaves that covered his head.

"Hey!" Leaf laughed. "Go on now!" He brushed it away, and turned to study the forest paths. "So which trail should I take?" he asked the hummer. He took a step down the wider one.

At once a brilliant flash and an insistent *BRMMMR! BRMMMR!* erupted. The hummer flittered just above his nose, and then flew straight down the narrow trail.

Its feathers sparkled in the crooked sunbeams that stretched down through the high branches.

"Oh, fine then. Might as well follow you!" Leaf muttered agreeably. At once he jogged after the hummer. The tiny bird continued to dive at Leaf's head along the way. He shooed it away repeatedly, but always it returned.

The path seemed to lead nowhere. Leaf was beginning to wish he'd chosen the other trail when he felt a cool, fresh breeze on his face. He remembered Pappo's story. The one about how Rustle used the breeze from Echo Peak to fly on his flyers. He felt hopeful the hummingbird had led him to the ridge crest after all.

A bright white wall of sunlight unexpectedly appeared. Leaf glanced up, startled. The forest ended abruptly. Dark peaks towered so high that Leaf thought they would fall on top of him. On the forest edge were tall firs and on the other, a rock-strew, sheer cliff.

For the first time, Leaf saw the jagged Sharp Peaks up close. They split the horizon and stabbed the sky. Weird trees with white bark dotted the cliffs. Their ancient trunks were twisted into questioning expressions as if they wondered what Leaf could be doing on their ridge. Many scrubby trees grew in between crumbling rocks. These trees were stumpy and thin like the air they breathed. A little ways higher, the trees gave up growing altogether.

Uneasy, Leaf paused, choosing to remain in the shadows of the forest. Beyond this line of trees, and the rest of the way up to the crest, there would be few places to hide.

Leaf scanned the skies. To his relief, there were no sky hunters circling overhead searching for prey or sticks for their nest. The sun blazed in a sapphire blue sky. The harsh glare made Leaf blink and squint. He held his hand over his eyes to shield them so he could see the path winding upward to the crest. He realized he must be very careful not to slip, or the sound of the gravel might give him away. He must not draw attention to himself.

But the silly hummingbird kept fluttering around and poking at his head.

"Go on, now!" Leaf whispered. "Go find some honeysuckle! Leave me alone!"

The glowing feathers on the hummer's tiny body seemed to melt together like liquid in the sun. Its wings beat the air so fast they were just a fuzzy wedge. Its black eyes stared at Leaf intently. Growing more annoyed, Leaf batted at the hummer like it was a gnat.

"Go back to the forest, you nutty hummer! Stop following me!" Leaf muttered.

The tiny bird hovered in front of Leaf's face for a moment more. Then, with a flurry of blurry wings, it wandered forlornly off into the forest's dark shadows.

"Thank the moon!" Leaf exhaled. He turned back to study the ridge, and stared up at the imposing cliff. *Well*, he reassured himself, *all I have to do now is follow this ridge and find Rustle!*

A clatter of tumbling rocks startled Leaf. He jumped at the unexpected noise. *What made the stones fall?* he wondered, but saw nothing.

Far above Leaf, beneath a flat ledge that jutted out from the cliff, a scaly, legless creature slowly slipped into a dark crevice. Only a faint *Rsssst! Rsssst! Rsssst!* escaped from the shadow.

CHAPTER TWELVE

A LEAF FLYER

Wary and watchful, Leaf hiked up the winding, rocky trail. He chose his way slowly and carefully. He tried to fade into the shadows of large boulders as much as possible. The climb was painstaking and tedious.

At last Leaf reached a slanted, granite slab near the crest. He eased himself onto its highest point—a smooth knob which jutted out and overlooked the forest below. Leaf sat very still, trying to pretend he grew out of the gray granite, although, his emerald green hair sparkled in the sun.

Maybe my hair will look like a bush that sprouts out of this boulder! he thought.

Leaf narrowed his brilliant green eyes to slits as he searched the ridge for Rustle's coppery, leafy head. He saw only gray rocks. *Oh well,* Leaf sighed. He didn't really expect to find him that fast. It would have been too easy! He considered yelling or throwing rocks to signal Rustle. Then he thought of a better idea. He pulled the whistle from his pocket and blew a low, soft tone.

Even with such a quiet note as this, a gray nutcracker was startled. Surprised by the strange note, it jerked up its head. It had been collecting pine nuts scattered under a whitebark tree. The huge nutcracker ruffled his wings, and glared suspiciously at the green-haired Twig far above perched on a boulder. At last it *KRAAK'ed* a rude reply.

Leaf smiled. *Whistling should do the trick!* He tried to whistle a melody, but it was hard to breathe in the high, thin air. His notes came out hideously shrill and screechy, which was how he usually whistled anyway. *"Never could play this thing,"* he thought with disgust.

Horrified, the nutcracker flew off.

BRMMMMR! BRMMMMR! tickled Leaf's ear. The hummingbird was back! It flew at Leaf's nose, and stuck its long, narrow beak into his whistletube as if it suspected sweet nectar may be hidden there.

"Oh, go on, you nutty hummer!" Leaf cried, louder than he meant to.

It was then he heard a whistle drifting up from the forest. *Rustle! It's Rustle! Thank the stars!* Even in Leaf's excitement, he knew not to yell out to him. It might alert a hawk or weasel. Each would stick a Twig in its nest, or worse. Instead Leaf leapt from the ledge, and landed on a pile of loose gravel right before a dark crevice. For an instant Leaf thought he heard a quiet *Rsssssst! Rsssssst! Rsssssst!* hissing from the shadowy crack beneath the ledge.

The hummer suddenly flew at his nose, and jabbed frantically at his eyes. Irritated Leaf ducked and waved it away. At the same moment the gravel broke loose beneath his feet, and abruptly carried Leaf downhill in the middle of granite pebbles. Off balance and out of control, Leaf rode the landslide down the slope all the way to where Rustle stood waiting...and grinning.

Rustle easily dodged the loose gravel as it spilled down the ridge. With a crooked smirk he studied Leaf's descent as if he intended to offer a few valuable suggestions about riding landslides, if Leaf survived. The wispy fronds of a hemlock tree drooped around Rustle's head like a crown. His copper-colored leafy hair and eyes blended to perfection with the hemlock's reddish-brown bark. He stood with his hands on his hips. He kept one eye on the sky as he watched for sky hunters, which may have been alerted by the rocky racket. He seemed to care less whether Leaf had injured himself.

Out of breath, Leaf slid right to Rustle's feet. He sat there panting and dizzy. After a moment he stood up. His legs shook. The hummer whipped its wings around Leaf's head, and *BRMMMMR'd* loudly in his ears. He waved it away impatiently.

"Well, Leaf, where'd you get your pet, eh?" Rustle laughed. "Does it have a name? Maybe..."

Leaf interrupted him at once. "Rustle!" Leaf gasped. "Rustle, we . . ." He couldn't finish. The hummingbird beat its tiny wings against Leaf's cheek as if wishing to share its joyful life. Annoyed, Leaf waved it away again.

Rustle laughed, "Leaf, catch your breath! Sit down! This hummingbird couldn't beat its wings faster than you're breathing! The air is as hard to catch on the crest as a whisper. Sit down and breathe like me!" Rustle stuck his face near Leaf's, and slowly sucked in some deep gulps of air to demonstrate.

Dizzy and panting, Leaf forced himself to keep the same pace as Rustle. He soon felt better.

"Good!" Rustle declared. "Now, tell me, what brought you to the crest? It must be very important, eh!" Rustle grinned. His eyes opened wide as he mocked Leaf who still looked pale.

Rustle took Leaf by the shoulders, nearly lifted him off the ground, and forced him to sit on a root in the cool shade of the hemlock. He patted Leaf's back roughly, and ruffled his sloppy hair. "Now, little Twig, why are you screeching like a dizzy chatter to the sky hunters? Are you hoping for a ride to one of their nests?" Rustle's eyes twinkled.

"Oh, Rustle!" Leaf gasped at last. "There's been a terrific flood and a landslide! A river is rushing around the Old Seeder! Pappo and Mumma and Fern and Buddy and Burba are trapped and Pappo sent me to find you and he kept yelling *chompers! chompers!* 'cause you gotta' go and get a chomper to build a dam and save them all from the terrible flood!" As Leaf finished his eyes crossed. He bent over with his head between his knees, and tried not to faint. He gasped for breath, and closed his eyes, once again sick and dizzy.

"Leaf, is your family safe?" asked Rustle, now gravely concerned.

"I think so," muttered Leaf between his knees. "But they're stuck in the Old Seeder and Pappo kept yelling your name at me, and he kept yelling chompers, too. You can go do that, right? Do what he wants you to do?"

"Well, I'm not sure," Rustle murmured. He stood with one hand on his hip, and one hand on his chin. He lowered his head, and closed his eyes, thinking intensely. "I'd hav'ta fly all the way across the valley to the chomper dam. I suppose it could be done..." He thought some more. "Of course!" Rustle snapped his fingers. "I just gotta' go as fast as I can, eh? So I gotta' start from really high up! Hmmm. But I'm gonna need more weight to get it right!"

"Oh, that's crazy!" gasped Leaf. His head hung so low between his knees, it brushed the moss. "Chompers aren't gonna' help anyway. They hate Twigs. They'll stuff you in their dam! How're you gonna' get a chomper to help?"

Rustle shook his head. "I don't know, Leaf. And I sure don't want to fly over the popper fields looking for one. Poppers are pretty vicious, too. But if your Pappo needs me to..." his voice trailed away.

Leaf sat up and gazed seriously at Rustle. They stared at each other in silence.

Finally, Leaf said, "I don't know what else you can do. *I* don't know how to get them out of the Old Seeder." His eyes pleaded with Rustle for help.

A long sigh floated from Rustle like the breeze from Echo Peak. With a sharp nod, he declared, "The day isn't flowing any slower, little Twig. Off we go!"

"Where're we going'?" asked Leaf. He was surprised that Rustle used their family phrase, and with his sudden commanding attitude.

"We're gonna' fly to the chomper dam!" Rustle called out over his shoulder as he hurtled a mushroom, and jogged into the forest. He disappeared into the speckles of a shadowy sunlit path.

"*We?*" asked Leaf, stunned. "Whadda' ya mean *we?*" he shouted. He scrambled to his feet, jumped over the mushroom, and raced after Rustle's fleeting silhouette.

The hummer flitted anxiously through the trees, darting back and forth in crooked patterns, yet continued to chase after Leaf.

Leaf's shouts echoed off the cliff walls. "Whadda' ya mean *we?* Whatcha' talking about! I don't know how to fly!"

Rustle sprinted like a stag along the narrow trail, leaping high over roots, silent and fast.

Leaf stopped shouting, and stumbled along behind Rustle. He needed to breathe more than protest.

After a while Rustle led Leaf into a sunny clearing with flat stones dotted here and there. The two plopped down on one of the smoothest rocks. He nodded at an enormous hollow log nearby. "It's in there," Rustle stated flatly. "When I heard your screeching, I stuck it in there and hurried to find you. I think I can make it work for two. But I need your help fixing it up. It's only made for one."

"Uh, sure, I can help," Leaf said hesitantly. "But are you sure that you want *me* to fly on it, too?"

Rustle looked surprised. "Of course! If anything happens to me, you gotta' find the chompers! I'm sure Needles meant that you are supposed to go, too, eh?"

"Uh, I guess so," replied Leaf. "But I don't know how to fly on a leaf-flyer."

"Oh, don't worry about that. I'm gonna' stick you on it so you can't fall off, little Twig," Rustle laughed. He stood up and hurried over to the log. Gently, as if it were the fragile wings of a butterfly, he pulled a giant, crumpled red leaf out of the log and across the grass to the center of the clearing.

Leaf jumped up to take a closer look. Instantly, he was bewildered. *This is just a crumbly, old leaf! This can't be what Rustle flies on!* The leaf's stem jutted out at an odd angle and made the whole flyer rock unsteadily back and forth. Worried, Leaf glanced at Rustle.

"Pretty exceptional, eh?" said Rustle with an irritatingly smug tone. He strutted around the flyer examining it with obvious pride.

"Uh, yes, exceptional," stammered Leaf, but he felt anxious more than admiration.

"Of course, we'll need more spider webs to make sure you don't fall off," explained Rustle.

"Sure...," Leaf muttered, even more puzzled, "good idea."

Rustle strolled over to an immense cappynut tree. The trunk's wrinkled bark had twisted into a creepy-looking face like it was warning Rustle to keep his distance. The gnarled limbs looked more like they'd grab a Twig rather than welcome one. Yet, with one hand and one foot on the scarred trunk, Rustle stood ready to scale the scratchy, gray bark. Casually, he called out over his shoulder to Leaf. "Now you gotta' distract the spider so I can grab its webs."

"I gotta' distract...." Leaf mumbled, as he reluctantly searched for a spider's silhouette in the branches above. "...*THAT?*" he cried out, shocked. An enormous, black spider with two red spots on its back squatted in the middle of a far-reaching web. The long, shimmering strands were stretched tight between several branches halfway up the cappynut.

"Sure!" replied Rustle cheerfully. He snapped a dead stick off the trunk. The splinter was very sharp. "Here take this and poke it! I'll grab the webs while it's chasing you!"

Leaf's mouth dropped open.

"Go on now, Leaf!" Rustle urged. "We wanna' catch the morning breeze off Echo Peak if we're gonna' fly all the way over the popper fields! If we land in one of their burrows, they'll eat us for sure!"

Aghast, Leaf took the stick from Rustle. His hands and feet moved in slow motion like they were dripping with mud. But he remembered that this was no time to worry about spider fangs. *If Rustle needs spider webs, then I gotta' help get them!* he resolved. He clutched the stick. Grim-faced, he forced himself to climb over the grizzled face of the knothole on the trunk, and past Rustle.

The pretty hummer perched above the spider on a skinny limb, far away from the web. Its expression was grave. It stared seriously at Leaf. For once, it sat still.

"That's the way, Leaf!" Rustle chuckled. "I'll be right behind you!"

With stealthy steps, Leaf tiptoed along the length of the branch until he balanced unsteadily right below the ugly spider's web. He hoisted the stick to his shoulder.

The spider sensed that some large creature was near. Even though it could not see far, it felt the vibrations from Leaf's movements. It crouched low, ready to race across its web and seize whatever prey landed in it.

"Ready?" Leaf hissed at Rustle out of the side of his mouth.

Rustle laughed aloud. "I don't think he can hear you, you know!"

"Well, he can still figure out where I am!" Leaf retorted.

"It can probably *see* you from there, Leaf!" Rustle laughed. "You're pretty close!"

Leaf squinted at the spider, wondering if it could see him or not. He lifted the splinter high, but at once he was off-balanced by the stick's length. Quickly he gained control. He glared at Rustle, who leaned nonchalantly against the trunk watching him with amused interest. Leaf took a deep breath, and then swung as hard as he could, but his swing was wide and he missed the web.

Rustle burst out laughing.

Embarrassed, Leaf began frantically slicing the stick back and forth through the air. After one wild pass, the stick caught in the web, and a few of the strands broke! Immediately, the spider rushed toward Leaf! Its fangs dripped with blinding, poison globs. Its eyes gleamed, anticipating a very fat catch!

"Ahhh!" screamed Leaf. He scrambled backwards, but couldn't move fast enough. The spider clutched at his leafy head! Panicked, Leaf jumped! As he fell, a splintered limb caught hold of his strap. He lost his grip on the stick, and it fell useless to the ground. Leaf hung helpless in the air, flailing his arms and legs around like a helpless chick struggling to fly.

The gruesome spider spun a strand from its butt, leapt into the air, dropped by Leaf, and bounced up and down beside him. It swung back and forth. Its many eyes focused on its prey. Its eight legs swept the air making its heavy body swing closer. It seemed to be deciding whether to cast its web over Leaf, or sink its fangs into him.

Leaf stared at it in horror!

Just then—with a blur of flickering wings—the hummingbird appeared before Leaf's nose. It hovered between the spider and Leaf, and bravely jabbed at the monster.

The spider recoiled, but only briefly.

"No! No! Go away! Go away" cried Leaf, more terrified for the tiny hummingbird than for himself. He waved frantically, trying to force the hummer to fly away.

In a sudden blur of motion, Rustle seized his saver, leapt out onto the limb above the spider, and sliced the strand on which the spider dangled. It plopped harmlessly onto a pile of leaves below the tree, and promptly scuttled away. Rustle then stuck his saver into the middle of the web, and twisted it around until it was wrapped with a heavy, sticky ball.

Leaf was stunned with Rustle's speed and skill. He swung back and forth with his mouth open, speechless.

The hummer flew to a tangle of honeysuckle vines covering a nearby thicket. The battle was over. Now it was content to search for nectar.

Rustle vaulted over a knothole and dropped toward Leaf's head feet first. With his heels, he snapped the branch that had kept Leaf captive. Together, they tumbled onto the bed of leaves and moss below.

"Will it come after us?" Leaf asked. Anxiously he scanned the pile of dead leaves beneath the cappynut tree.

"Na, don't worry about it. It has enough to do just repairing its web. Come on!" Rustle yanked Leaf back to the flyer. "These will work just fine," he exclaimed. He shoved the sticky strands onto the leaf with his saver, and stretched them out from side to side. He swirled a bigger glob right in the middle.

Leaf wondered how this would help the leaf fly any better.

"Here now, Leaf," Rustle declared, "you sit right there in that webby pillow." He pointed at the glob. "That should keep you stuck on, eh? I don't think you'll fall off the leaf then. It's really sticky."

Leaf suddenly felt extremely alarmed. He imagined falling from high in the sky in a ball of tangled webs. "Yeh, I don't *think* I'll fall off," he muttered unhappily. "I won't fall far anyway." He wondered if the strands of webs would catch him if he did fall. He worried about dangling from the leaf as Rustle flew wildly through the air. With a shake of his head, the visions disappeared.

"So, how do we get it going?" Leaf asked.

"Well, we're gonna need to take the flyer up there," answered Rustle. He pointed up at the highest tip of a nearby sugar pine tree. The tree towered above them, and bristled like a gigantic pine cone against a crystal blue sky. "We're gonna hav'ta kick off from the highest branch and catch the breeze!" exclaimed Rustle.

"*Catch the breeze?*" gasped Leaf. "Slugslips and slimerspit!"

Rustle laughed. "Don't worry, Leaf. If we can't catch a breeze, we'll stick in the trees!" He grinned wickedly at his rhyme.

Leaf stared up in shock at the tip of the tree. He tried to imagine leaping off the top branch into the sky with nothing but this spindly-looking flyer beneath him! He glanced at Rustle, whose eyes sparkled with glee...or madness. *Rustle's either eaten bad mushrooms, or has a bad case of head rot*, Leaf decided at once.

But Rustle grew serious. He tugged the flyer toward the tree. "Hurry, Leaf," he urged, "we need to catch the breeze." Rustle motioned to Leaf to lift the stem. "Careful of the sharp needles in the pine tree. Don't let any of them poke holes in the leaf or we'll have to start all over!"

Just great! One more thing to worry about! Leaf hoisted the flyer above his head and warily eyed the clusters of needles that had grown so large they looked more like quilla needles.

The two Twigs climbed skillfully and fast, even with the bulky flyer between them. The flyer was light and easier to manage than Leaf had thought possible. The Twigs tugged it up higher and higher until at last they stood on the topmost branch of the sugar pine. Mesmerized at the view, Leaf and Rustle paused to gaze at the grassy valley. The beaver dam could clearly be seen stretched out before a glassy pond far away.

"We're gonna fly right over the popper fields, and land on that chomper dam!" Rustle declared confidently.

Leaf took a deep breath. He hoped Rustle didn't notice that his hands were trembling.

The slender branch on which they stood swayed back and forth. It gently bounced with their weight. A slight, cool breeze ruffled the red maple leaf flyer. It floated up gracefully.

Rustle grabbed hold of its stem to steady it. "Look! It already wants to fly!"

Leaf nodded, not trusting his voice. He was afraid it would squeak.

"Come on," exclaimed Rustle, excitedly, "hurry! The day isn't flowing any slower!"

At once Leaf felt as if Pappo stood beside him, encouraging him to try something new and scary. Leaf decided Rustle wasn't nutty, just courageous in a weird way. "Nope," Leaf agreed, "the day isn't flowing any slower!"

Rustle smiled. "Let's go, Leaf!"

Leaf plopped onto the sticky web-seat, gripped the sides of the giant leaf, and tried not to look down. He reminded himself that he always had wanted to fly.

Rustle crouched behind him, gripped the stem of the giant leaf-flyer, and balanced his lanky body over Leaf's head.

Unexpectedly the flutter of wings brushed Leaf's cheek. *BRMMMMR! BRMMMMR!* The tiny hummer fluttered right before his eyes. It seemed worried about his new friend. But as the red leaf-flyer slid off the tree's tip, the hummingbird realized it was being left behind. It hovered for just a moment more, and then darted away, zigzagging among the tree tops.

"Hang on," Rustle shouted, "here we go!"

CHAPTER THIRTEEN

POPPERS!

The leaf-flyer dropped off the tip of the sugar pine tree with a sickening lurch.

"We're off!" cried Rustle, and then to be sure they actually were, he yelled, *"Whoohooo!"* as they fell.

The air whipped Leaf's face, and his breath was sucked away! His eyes streamed tears in air that was so cold it bit his cheeks. All was a great blur, and the sky rushed by so fast it swirled into blue streaks. The next moment the flyer was pushed up from below like a giant hand had shoved them high into the sun. Then at once the flyer slipped sideways, and Leaf felt sick. He shrank down into the cradle of sticky spider webs.

Rustle stood on the back of the maple leaf. He gripped the stem with one hand to steer. With the other hand he yanked at a thick strand of webs that stretched from the tip of the leaf and alongside Leaf. The edges of the flyer flapped noisily in the brisk breeze. Rustle braced his legs on the leaf, leaned left, and yanked the webs hard to the right to correct the sideslip. The flyer responded quickly to his demands. Rustle steered the leaf-flyer with great skill. But when a gust of wind caught the edge, the flyer swirled up into a cloud, and at once he lost his bearings in the mist.

Are we flying backwards? wondered Leaf. In the gray shroud that blanketed his senses, Leaf could not tell if they were flying up or down, forward or backwards. He ducked low in his cradle.

Rustle shrieked, "Sit up, Leaf! Lean left! Left! We're slipping sideways!"

Rustle violently yanked the web-reins again. The leaf dropped down out of the cloud. They whirled in a circle just above the tree tips, and then shot off again on a steadier breeze.

"Sit up!" ordered Rustle. He kicked Leaf impatiently.

Leaf bolted upright, and the leaf-flyer responded to his rigid body right away. The flyer circled around, and suddenly the tip of the leaf pointed east. Once again they soared off toward the valley on a fast downdraft. They flew at such incredible speed Leaf could see nothing but his own flat tears. Soon the flyer's tip lifted up, and flattened out on a smooth current of air. Now they floated gently, and Leaf's vision cleared. He could see the forest behind them and far below. Strands of mist, lost from clouds, knitted the tips of trees together into a patchy quilt.

Very soon, the leaf-flyer caught up to a flock of white snow geese floating silently north. Surprised by Twigs in their midst, the leader immediately slanted its huge wings and drifted away. In the next instant, with a whisper of a thousand feathers, the entire flock tilted their wings and spun away, too, following their leader.

Leaf glanced over his shoulder and grinned.

Rustle grinned back.

We're flying! "Whooohoooo!" exclaimed Leaf breathlessly.

Rustle's shouts flew away with the wind. "It's a little slippery, but the best flyer ever!"

They dropped lower on a sloping stream of air, just above the grassy valley. Tall blades waved their sharp tips. Leaf watched patterns in the grass sweep by beneath them. They were made by the wandering treks of grassland creatures. He was fascinated. *The world looks so different from up here!*

Black noses pointed up, too. Leaf noticed only a few black spots at first, but soon there were dozens, and then hundreds as the leaf-flyer's shadow startled the prairie dogs. Little black tails shot out, and quivered in alarm. Leaf distinctly saw teeth chattering away—bright, sharp teeth! Warning whistles blasted from popper burrow to popper burrow, colony to colony, as Rustle and Leaf floated above.

Leaf began to feel very uneasy. He searched for the edge of the grasslands where the woods began, but they were flying too low to see well. The grass seemed to stretch endlessly before them. If they dropped much lower, the blades might slice right through their leaf-flyer.

"Uh...we need to get higher..." Rustle muttered.

With a sudden dizzy pitch, a gust of wind tumbled the flyer into a furious roll!

Rustle screamed, "Hang on! We're gonna' crash! Hang on!" He strained against the webs until finally they snapped! The leaf-flyer ripped in half!

Leaf grasped the spider webs desperately, but the strands tore loose. He fell through the leaf, and plummeted to the earth. He landed with a grunt and a groan still wrapped in a cocoon of webs. He sat up, dizzy and shaken. In shock, he watched the two pieces of the leaf-flyer swirl violently through the air above his head.

Still riding half of the flyer, Rustle clutched the leaf's stem with white fists. He spiraled left, and then right, and then flew upside-down. The flyer somersaulted midair, rolled over and over until at last it plunged into the ground. It smashed with a sickening crunch right next to Leaf.

Near panic, Leaf wrestled free of the tangled webs. Imagining the worst, he limped to where Rustle had been buried by the leafy wreckage. He held his breath, leaned over the crumpled flyer, and ripped apart what was left of the leaf. Rustle lay motionless. Leaf stared at him, horrified.

But then Rustle twitched. "Oh," he groaned. He shifted his legs under the mangled leaf.

"Good grasses!" cried Leaf, relieved.

Obviously in pain, Rustle rolled away from the crushed flyer. He pushed himself up to an unsteady stance, and then ignoring his own injuries, knelt to examine the mangled leaf. He tried to fit the tattered pieces together. "Well, we can make it fly again, don't'cha think, eh, Leaf?"

"Uh," Leaf stared doubtfully at the shredded flyer, "uh, no."

Rustle scowled at him. "Well, at least we're not hurt!" he said as he cradled his elbow. He grimaced. More as an afterthought than with real concern, he asked Leaf, "So you aren't hurt, are you?"

"Oh no, not me. I'm not hurt," answered Leaf even though he felt like his head was smashed flat. His ears throbbed badly, so he tugged the leaves on his head with hopes that it might stop the pain in his ears. He looked around. "So where are we?"

"Uh, oh," Rustle sucked in a sharp breath. He motioned to some nearby burrows, and whispered, "We're in a popper field! We better get out of here before they know we're around. Just do what I do, and keep quiet!"

Afraid to even blink, Leaf immediately envisioned a popper snapping him in two! *Great!* Leaf glanced around. *There isn't even a tree to climb! And with the color of this yellow grass, we'll stick out like sticks on snow!*

Rustle put his finger to his lips, drew his saver from its loop, and held it out in front of his chest. He motioned to Leaf to do the same.

With trembling hands, Leaf held his saver awkwardly in front of his skinny chest. He hoped he appeared intimidating. The Twigs crouched low in the dry grass prepared, Leaf guessed, for an attack from poppers. Dozens of high mounds of dirt surrounded them.

"Move behind me," whispered Rustle. "Step light so they won't hear us in their burrows." He nodded at the dirt piles.

Leaf noticed that Rustle stepped like a praying mantis when it crawled on a wet leaf—one high step after the other. Rustle lifted his knees so far up he brushed them against his ears. So Leaf did the same, but he really didn't know why. *This is dumb. They must have heard the leaf-flyer crash,* he thought ruefully. *If only we could see above this suffocating grass!*

Rustle marched on with painfully slow steps.

Leaf followed close behind him, but he had a creepy feeling, and it grew creepier and creepier. It felt like he was being watched! All of a sudden, a shadow flickered in the corner of his eye. Leaf spun his head around, and gasped! He stared right into the eyes of a popper! It was peeking above the edge of its burrow just a few paces away.

With a flash of bright teeth, the popper whistled an intense, angry blast, which alerted the whole colony! Dozens of poppers popped out of their burrows at once. Their penetrating stares and earless heads made them looked unreal and fierce. They clicked and whistled to one another. More and more poppers sprang from their burrows until there were so many of them that Leaf lost count. They popped up and perched on their dirt mounds, agitated and ready to attack. They waved tiny claws in fury at the Twigs.

At the same moment, Rustle and Leaf instinctively disguised themselves by twisting their arms and legs until they looked like scrawny trees. Twigs were skilled at being trees. The only problem was that there were no trees in the grasslands.

And the poppers knew it! Irritated by his poor disguise one of the poppers moved closer to Leaf and trilled angrily.

Frozen in his tree-posture, Leaf whispered out of the side of his mouth, "Rustle! Help me! What do we do now?"

Rustle looked pale, and blank-faced.

Just then a thumping noise in the grass, moved closer and closer. Rustle and Leaf stared wide-eyed at each other, wondering what sort of beast it could be, and what they should do now.

The poppers went rigid!

With a frenzied burst of bizarre chatter, a freckled-faced chipmunk leapt from the thick grass, and plopped in between Leaf and the popper who threatened him. The chipmunk, paused, took a deep breath, and then *CHRRRRRT'd!* – a screech blasted through puffy cheeks. In a blur of speckled fur and bristling tail, the chipmunk whirled between the Twigs and the poppers. He kicked in the tops of the burrows, and *CHRRRRRT'd!* over and over wildly at the nose of every popper it passed. The mad chipmunk's whiskers stuck straight out from its quivering cheeks. His tiny nose twitched as if on fire, and his eyes were glassy, glimmering flames of fury.

The poppers were so terrified they dove into their burrows in a panic! But one popper hesitated. He peered closely at the chipmunk. So the crazed chipmunk stared back at it angrily, thumped his foot, and *CHRRRRRT'd* one last time! At once the popper spun away and dove into its burrow.

Pleased, the chipmunk hopped around, thumping the matted grass over and over with its rear feet until it was sure all the prairie dogs had fled. Finally satisfied, he sat very still in the center of the popper mounds. With kind eyes, he blinked curiously at Leaf and Rustle. They were too shocked to move during the fearsome display, and were still posed like stubby trees.

From behind one of the chipmunk's ears, Feather's leafy head poked out. Her beautiful, bronze leaves fell across her rose-colored eyes. Her long, curly swan feather drooped beside her glowing smile. Breathless and excited, Feather cried out, "Twigs! You're Twigs! Oh, Twigs!"

Astonished, Leaf and Rustle glanced at each, still holding their stiff poses.

"I saw you on your whirlathing! Oh, and when you crashed! I came right away!" Feather immediately sounded concerned. "Oh, are you alright? Oh, you must be hurt! I came to help you out of the popper field. You need a ride, don't you? Oh, Twigs at last! And you crashed right here! Oh, I'm Feather and this nutty chippie is Speckles! Oh, look! Your whirlathing is all smashed up but that's all right because I can help you get away from the poppers!"

Giving up on the tree pose, Leaf and Rustle dropped their twisted arms and straightened their legs. For some reason Rustle looked insulted. He clenched his fists, and frowned.

Feather glanced at the nearby popper burrows. At once she became worried. She lowered her voice, and whispered urgently, "You better catch this ride now. Poppers don't scare for long." She smiled brightly and held out her hand to help Rustle up.

Leaf and Rustle nodded to each other, and shoved their savers into the back loops on their straps.

Rustle took a step toward Feather. With a gruff voice he said, "We didn't crash, and it's a leaf-flyer not a whir-lathing! And we didn't need any help!"

"Oh!" Feather looked surprised, and then confused, startled by Rustle's grouchy tone. Her eyes blinked fast like a hummingbird's wings in flight.

Leaf scowled at Rustle, smiled at Feather, and reached for her hand. As he did, he eyed Speckles warily, who now calmly munched a blade of grass. Feather smiled at Leaf, grasped hold of his hand, and pulled him up behind her. He grabbed hold of Feather's vine-belt, breathed with relief, and hung on tight. *She even smells good,* Leaf couldn't help thinking.

Feather reached out to Rustle again, but he ignored her hand. He took a hop, landed smartly on Speckles' rump, and firmly gripped Leaf's shoulder strap to keep from sliding off. He smirked at the back of Leaf's head as if he had ridden a chipmunk all his life.

"Well, good," said Feather hesitantly. After a pause, she added more matter-of-factly, "Hold on tight, Sky Twigs!" With a nod and a twitch of Speckles' braided leash, she urged the chipmunk to spin around. He bounded away.

As Leaf bounced along, Feather's long, bronze leaves whipped his face, and her swan feather tickled his nose. Speckles jumped over rocks and mushrooms. He changed directions abruptly, and wove a path through dense thickets. Somehow Leaf managed to hold on to Feather's belt. Mostly he tried to keep Rustle from yanking him off. Rustle hung on to Leaf's strap with such ferocity he nearly broke it.

Speckles ran fast. He scrambled over ash-filled logs, dodged lichen-covered limbs, and hopped down a moss-covered creek bed. At the end of the ride Speckles jumped into the roots of a musty-smelling cappynut tree. He whirled around in a circle, and with a shiver shook all the Twigs off his back.

Feather evidently expected this method of dismount. She sailed through the air, and landed on her feet in soft clover.

Rustle and Leaf plopped on their bottoms in a patch of pink and yellow daisies. Feeling very foolish, they plucked the delicate, sweet-scented petals from their leafy hair. They tried not to stare at Feather who was watching them curiously.

Feather stood with both hands on her hips, and her head tilted back slightly as she studied the two Twigs sprawled in the fragrant flowers. Her rosy eyes were calm with no hint of any shyness. Her hair was unusually long—bronze colored leaves that curled over her shoulders. A white swan feather stuck out of a braid tied around her head. Her birch leaf tunic was well-worn, yet its golden color was still vibrant. An ivy vine-belt twisted many times around her waist. A sharpened granite shard was stuck in it at a jaunty angle. The rock-slicer was sharpened to a deadly point.

Feather rested her hand upon the shard, and drummed her fingers as if deciding whether to pull it out and threaten them with it. An amused grin played on her lips as she waited for the two Twigs to catch their breath.

Leaf recognized at once that the cool stance of Feather was very similar to that of another overly confident, young Twig he knew. He glanced at his friend who sat beside him.

Rustle angrily plucked pink petals from his hair. His coppery eyes flashed as if he were daring Feather to help him again.

Just great, Leaf worried, a*nother Rustle.... only this one's a she!*

CHAPTER FOURTEEN

ON THE BACK OF A CHIPPIE

"Thank you," Leaf stammered gratefully. "Where are we?" He and Rustle stood up, still flicking pretty petals from their hair.

"You're in my forest, of course. Where do you want to be?" Feather replied. Her question was intense, like her eyes. A second later, as if she remembered some long ago forgotten manners, Feather added, "You're most welcome to be here, Sky Twigs."

Rustle frowned at her. "We gotta' find the chomper dam," he grumbled. "Come on, Leaf. We gotta make it by night." He started toward a deer trail.

"Chompers?" Feather looked puzzled. She jumped in front of Rustle to stop him from leaving. "You don't know where the chomper dam is? All the Twigs here know where it is!" Feather giggled at her own joke. "What kinda' Twigs are you? Where're you from anyway?" Like a Twig sprout might tease her brother to get attention, Feather pointed at the last pink petal dangling from Rustle's hair. "Are you gonna' go all pretty like that? You really look pretty, you know!" She reached toward Rustle's head to pluck the delicate petal from his copper-colored leaves.

Rustle stumbled backwards to avoid her help. Angrily he yanked the petal out himself, and threw it on the ground.

"You two sure are strange Twigs!" Feather giggled at her own private joke, again, which was only funny to her. "I don't know any Twigs stranger than you!"

"Well, you don't know much, do you, eh?" Rustle retorted.

For an instant Feather looked hurt. Then she grinned mysteriously. "Well I know more than you do. I know where the chomper dam is, and you don't." Feather crossed her arms, stubbornly planted her feet, and smirked. With a superior air, she tilted up her nose and peered at Rustle with half-closed eyes. "But it's too far to reach by night . . . if you're *walking*, that is, *eh!*"

Irritated by her tone, which sounded very much like she was mocking him, Rustle scowled at her. He straightened his strap and shifted his saver to hang crosswise properly. Without another word he nodded to Leaf to join him, and stomped to the edge of the clearing.

Leaf hesitated. He wanted to talk to Feather. He didn't understand why Rustle was being so unpleasant. They were leaving without even thanking her for saving their lives! Still, they were on an urgent mission. Leaf gave Feather a weak smile. Reluctantly he followed Rustle toward the deer path.

"Wait!" Feather commanded.

Surprised, Leaf and Rustle stopped walking.

Feather's voice sounded as if she gave orders all the time. She continued, "You seem to be in a great hurry to get lost in my forest, Sky Twigs. Perhaps I can help." Feather knelt and ripped up a stiff blade of grass. She pulled it tight between her thumbs, lifted it to her lips, and blasted a screechy, irritating, long whistle. Then she tilted her head to the side and listened.

Leaf and Rustle glanced at each other, uncertain what they were supposed to do. Rustle felt no need for

Feather or any more of her offers to help. Restless, he shuffled his feet and inched toward the woods. Leaf didn't want to go. He liked Feather, and she certainly knew how to whistle with grass blades.

A brisk *PATTER, PATTER, PATTER* and a shadow rushed up behind Rustle and Leaf. The Twigs turned to look just as a plump chipmunk exploded from the woods and leapt over their heads. The chippie's fur had weird, crooked stripes, and his wild eyes twitched. Excited, he zigzagged back and forth between Feather, Speckles, Rustle, and Leaf, hopping on stiff legs. His cheeks were stuffed so full, his eyes were nearly shut. He whirled around, and then with a *BLRRRP!* spit out four blueberries at Rustle.

Rustle ducked.

Leaf grinned.

A softly flowing shape with silvery whiskers crept up behind Leaf. A curious, moist nose nuzzled his hair. Her velvety whiskers tickled Leaf's ears, and the chippie's gentle muzzle brushed his cheek. Leaf gazed into her warm, friendly, almond-shaped eyes. He realized at once, this chipmunk had a striking similarity to Speckles. She must be his sister. Her gold freckles, sprinkled her coat from cheek to tail tip, and glowed in the sunlight. She nibbled on a strand of Leaf's hair. By her sweet manner, he knew she liked him. Leaf giggled and stroked her cheek.

Feather held out her hands, palm up, to each chipmunk. They came to her, one at a time, and pressed their damp, black noses to her hands. Then they sat back on their haunches and groomed their ears and tails.

With a loud, irritating voice, Feather lectured the three chipmunks, "In my forest, we have names for everything. You see, *my* name is Feather. Speckles' name is Speckles. And there's Claws." Feather swept her hand in the direction of Claws, who looked very confused. "And this berryblossom is Whisper. And Whisper, knows her name is Whisper, don't you, Whisper?" Feather asked as she stepped over and kissed Whisper's nose. Then, with a very serious expression, she gazed into Whisper's eyes as if passing along a horrible secret. Feather whispered loudly in the chippie's ear, "But we don't know the Sky Twigs' names, do we Whisper?" Feather whispered louder, "It's probably because they smashed, and hit their heads, and forgot they even have names!"

"We didn't smash," said Rustle, tightlipped. "We landed."

Feather threw him a skeptical glance. "You landed in a popper field? Is that what Sky Twigs do?" she asked innocently. "Looked a lot more like twirling and swirling and looping and crashing, if you ask me."

"We flew there in my flyer. We landed just where we wanted to," retorted Rustle angrily.

"We're not Sky Twigs," Leaf said quickly with a worried glance at Rustle. "I'm Leaf of the Old Seeder Twigs. And this is Rustle of the Ridge Twigs."

Rustle glowered at him.

Puzzled, Leaf stared back. He couldn't understand why his friend was so rude. Feather was just being friendly in an irritating Fern sort of way. After all, she did rescue them!

"Allo, Leaf," Feather murmured. But Feather's expression and tone had changed. She stepped closer to Rustle, and stared at him intently with a confused look on her face. "You're Rustle from a ridge, you say?" She peered into Rustle's eyes.

Uncomfortable she was so near, Rustle looked away. With a sarcastic tone, he replied, "Right, Rustle's my name. At least you got that right." With a toss of his head, he flipped his coppery leaves from his eyes. "And since you have tame chippies, we'll just ride 'em to the chomper dam then, eh?"

Feather stepped back, embarrassed. She shook her head to clear her thoughts. "Fine," she declared, "Leaf, ride Whisper. And you," she nodded brusquely at Rustle, "you get Claws, *eh!*"

Claws perked up his ears at the sound of his name and Feather's nod.

Now feeling a little uneasy with the prospect of riding the crazy chipmunk, Rustle studied the wild-eyed chippie from afar.

Leaf grinned with delight. His dainty chippie Whisper was a pretty, little creature. She appeared quite gentle.

Whisper sniffed him up and down, giving great attention to his leafy head. She took one of his leafy strands of hair in her tiny teeth. She chewed thoughtfully. "Hey, stop it!" cried Leaf, and he shooed her away.

"Whisper!" admonished Feather, "I didn't say you could eat him!"

Whisper looked contrite, and turned to offer Leaf an easy jump up. Leaf noticed a thin, glowing wheat-braid around Whisper's neck. He reached up, grasped the leash, and quickly jumped onto her shoulders. Leaf settled comfortably into her soft fur. Whisper crouched motionless, careful of her new rider. Then she shivered briskly to adjust to Leaf's light stick body.

Rustle decided to take a running jump onto Claws.

Shocked that a strange-looking, lanky Twig was racing toward him, Claws dodged Rustle's leap with a hop and a twitch. Rustle plopped into the flowers. Claws turned to stare at him with wide, rolling eyes. Then he shrugged and hopped around on stiff legs defiantly.

Ignoring the smothered laughs of Feather and Leaf, Rustle jumped up, and dusted away the blossoms. Right away, he grabbed Claws' leash, and swung his leg over his back. In spite of the chippie quivering and dancing sideways, Rustle stayed on. He did actually appear to be an experienced chippie rider. Confident now, he nudged Claws toward Feather.

"Let's go, then!" he said irritably.

Feather looked away, hiding a sly grin. Expertly, she leapt on his Speckles' back. The chippie had not left her side since throwing Leaf and Rustle into the daisies. Feather spoke a soft word into Speckles' furry ear. At once all three chippies bolted down the deer trail. Feather led the pack, Leaf was second, and Rustle followed.

Astonished and startled at the swift pace, Leaf struggled to stay on Whisper. With a hop and a leap the chipmunks bounced from the shaded woods onto a dusty path that led uphill. The trail was smothered in the mingled scents of strange beasts. Leaf tucked his head into Whisper's neck, gripped the leash tight, and concentrated on keeping his balance. He could barely see beyond Whisper's fuzzy ears as he bounced along. He wondered where they were headed.

The chippies ducked under a growth of ivy, and they were in the woods again, rushing breathlessly along on one trail after another.

Whisper was taking great care to keep Leaf on her back, even as she jumped over fallen logs and across steep gullies. Leaf kept his face buried in her neck. He breathed in Whisper's fragrant fur. She smelled of nuts and berries. Leaf chuckled at the grunts and groans he heard from Rustle riding behind him.

Rustle moaned aloud with every rut and pile of rocks Claws bounced over. Purposely wicked, Claws chose the worst way to go, and if the path became smooth, he simply leapt around like a wild whirlwind.

Leaf decided Claws had to be too excited to control even for Feather. *Rustle deserved him! He had been so rude!*

Feather glanced over her shoulder past Leaf to Rustle, who ignored her. She gave Leaf a little wink. Leaf grinned back. It was fun to see the mighty Rustle so off-balance.

The chippies started up a steep trail that traversed a bluff above a swollen stream. Once they reached the top, Feather kept them to a fast pace, and led them toward Thunder Peak's foothills. As they climbed higher and higher, Leaf felt confident enough to peek at the grasslands, which spread out across the valley far below. Once again, it appeared beautiful and peaceful. The blades swirled in rhythm with the wind. Far away, the dark Sharp Peaks bordered the sea of grass.

Now the chippies trotted through tall weeds onto a flat plateau. They hopped through a deep, rutted path sculpted by the claws of a large beast. Leaf did not recognize the marks. *There are probably many creatures in this land that I don't know*, he realized.

They raced along the dusty trail as fast as possible. It was almost as if Feather worried they might just meet the beast who had left this well-beaten path.

Leaf caught a glimpse of color in the barren land-scape. A tall, dazzling blue feather curled above a quail's head. Its stubby tail brushed patterns in the dust as the quail skipped away from the onrushing chippies. Even though it was pudgy, and burdened with its too-long, fancy head whorl, it still managed to leap into the sky, and float down from the bluff. Leaf watched it fly away into a white hot sun, and he realized it must be past midday.

Just as they rounded a large boulder, Feather pulled hard on Speckles leash to keep him from slamming into a high, log wall.

Whisper slid across the loose gravel. She skidded and braced stiff-legged, but could not stop. She slammed into the pile of logs. Immediately Leaf somersaulted over her shoulders, and landed upside-down between Whisper's belly and the wall of tree trunks.

"Ow!" Leaf's muffled voice was barely heard, buried in Whisper's fur.

Whisper hopped backwards at once. She blinked her brown eyes in sorrow at Leaf, distressed that she had smashed him.

Leaf stood bent over, and rubbed his back. Even though he couldn't help groaning in pain, he smiled at

Whisper, and patted her nose to reassure her he was fine.

With a trembling nose, Whisper nuzzled his ears and leafy head.

Behind him, Rustle had yanked Claws off the path. Now both lay on their sides in the dirt. Rustle stood up hastily. He brushed himself off briskly, embarrassed at his clumsy dismount. He nudged Claws with his foot, urging him to get up.

Claws rolled to a crouch, scowled at Rustle with weird, glaring eyes, and quivered violently to shake the dust from his fur.

Rustle coughed as he stepped out of Claws' dust cloud. He planted his feet apart, placed his fists on his hips, and examined the wooden structure before him with an exaggerated interest. "So here's the dam, then," he stated flatly.

Feather ignored them both. With Speckles close beside her, she had stepped to the edge of the gulch that lay below the dam. She stood peering over. A cracked granite slab jutted out precariously over the steep gully. Mumbling to herself, she stood on the slab, and stared down at the shredded logs, split boulders, and mud debris filling the gulch below her. With a worried expression, she looked up at the top of the dam. She studied the splintered trees that stuck far out over dam's edge. They perched there strangely. It appeared to Feather that only a slight breath might make them tumble and crash into the gulley below. And that breath might blow them over at any moment! She realized it was terribly risky to remain so near the dam. At any moment it might even crumble apart because of the weight of the waterlogged trees.

Leaf simply stared in wonder at the complex wall of logs above him. The trees had been stripped, and their trunks expertly interwoven. Each crevice was crammed with mud, grass, rocks, moss, and sticks. The dam rose to such a great height that Leaf grew dizzy looking up. *So this is the great chomper dam!*

Feather spoke softly to Speckles, who then hopped over to Claws and Whisper. He nudged them to follow. Speckles led them away from the dam to a huckleberry thicket. The three chippies sat in its shade, and groomed their dusty fur with bright pink tongues.

"We shouldn't stay here," declared Feather.

Rustle and Leaf glanced at each other.

With a louder, more confident tone, Feather continued, "Look there," she pointed up to the top of the dam.

"There was a flood, see? The dam will break soon." She gazed at Leaf and Rustle with a serious look of concern. "We should go now. It's dangerous here."

"Right," said Rustle. "You better go." Rustle stood facing her with his hands on his hips. His voice sounded like he was daring her to stay. Leaf stood between them, feeling very uneasy.

"No," said Feather, very worried now, "we should *all* go." She waved up where the trees teetered on the dam. "Just look!"

"Go then," Rustle glared at her.

"Uh, wait a moment," Leaf said, hesitantly. He smiled at Feather at the same time he frowned at Rustle, which ended up making him look weird and confused. "I, uh, we want to thank you for saving our lives in the popper field, right Rustle?" Leaf stared pointedly at Rustle. "And thank you for guiding us to the chomper dam, right Rustle? And for letting us ride Whisper and Claws, *right Rustle, eh?*" Leaf finished with a grim expression.

Rustle kicked the dirt, and muttered, "Uh, well, thanks," he looked up. "We can find our own way now." He turned dismissively as if she were only a gnat to be brushed away.

Feather stared at the back of Rustle's head, stunned with his rudeness. She put her hands on her hips, lifted up her nose in disdain, and stated, "Well, I might as well hang around and take a nap . . . just in case you need a ride back to the popper field . . . after your visit with the chompers, I mean." She paused. "Unless, of course, you're planning to ride the chompers back to your forest?" she added snidely.

Leaf saw Rustle tighten his mouth. He was obviously holding back a nasty retort.

Oh, just great, Leaf thought, exasperated with them both. *Rustle seems determined to have a fight with the only Twig around who wants to help us!*

Leaf spoke quickly before Rustle could squeeze out a sarcastic retort. "Yes, that's a good idea, Feather. Please wait for us."

Feather grinned, shook her leafy, bronze curls, and laughed. "Well, then, Leaf. I'll hang around . . . for you!" She gave one last sharp look at Rustle, and then walked over to the thicket where the chipmunks watched her with puzzled eyes. She crawled in between the dry, stiff stems, and curled up near its roots. The chippies nestled in the thicket beside her. Her leafy hair and the speckled fur of the chippies blended into the shade, and they were all lost from sight.

Rustle muttered, "Come on, Leaf!" He started climbing up the logs.

Leaf followed unhappily. He wanted to stay with Feather rather than follow after his grumpy friend. He hoped Rustle had some plan to convince the chompers to build a dam and save the Old Seeder.

Halfway up the dam, Rustle's mood lightened. He began humming, and then whistling, and then unexpectedly, he sang. None of his words were understandable, and his melody was badly out of tune. Still, Rustle's song sounded strangely happy. He paused for a moment, smiled, and whispered to Leaf, "Feather's a really good rider, isn't she?"

Leaf didn't think Rustle needed an answer, but he grunted in agreement anyway. His thoughts turned to his family, trapped in the middle of a flooded river. The same worry flowed through his mind over and over.

How long can the Old Seeder fight the Rushing Waters before it drowns, and my family is lost?

CHAPTER FIFTEEN

SLAPPER'S POND

The horrific sight sickened Leaf. Mud filled the pond. The dam was smashed with uprooted, twisted, splintered trees and cracked boulders. And there were no chompers in sight.

Time was running out.

"I think the chompers have left," murmured Leaf in despair.

"What do you want to do?" asked Rustle.

They stared blankly at each other. Then they had the same idea at the same time—the whistletube!

Rustle nodded. "Try it! Maybe there're one or two chompers still here."

Leaf tugged the whistle free, and lifted it to his lips. He hesitated. *My screeches are gonna scare the chompers to death not bring them here! This is all so hopeless anyway. But I've got to whistle something!* Leaf sighed heavily. He thought of Mumma when she sat on their porch-branch outside their haven and whistled the birds to sleep. Leaf suddenly felt so homesick he could only imagine the sad cooing of the mourning doves. So he whistled that—*hooo coo-hoo! hooo coo-hooo! hooo coo-hoo!*

The lonely coo drifted over the silent pond and up to the bluff. Sorrow-laden, it echoed back.

All of a sudden Rustle and Leaf heard a loud WHACK! It sounded like a huge paddle smacking sticky water, and it vibrated across the pond. There was a moment of silence. Then a series of WHACK! WHACK! WHACK!'s made Leaf and Rustle jump and look around nervously.

"Look!" Rustle tugged Leaf's arm. "Look there!" he urged. He pointed to the steep bluff beside the pond.

A shadow lurked at the entrance to a burrow. A huge beaver—a goliath beaver—crouched and stared at them! More goliath beavers appeared beside the first one at the edge of the gloomy burrow. With surprising speed, they slid from the burrow right to the pond's bank. Once they gathered there, they sat on their flat tails, sniffed the air, and glared at the Twigs.

"Chompers!" gasped Leaf. A moment later he added in a trembling voice, "And they're coming!"

The largest of the beavers waddled with a twisted limp over the shredded logs up to the top of the dam. Wary of the splintered branches and creaking, off-balanced trees, he moved with great caution across the badly damaged barricade.

Right away Leaf knew this chomper had to be the leader. The others followed at a respectful distance behind him, taking care to follow his path exactly. "Will he attack us? Are we safe?" Leaf muttered nervously.

Rustle answered quietly, "I don't know."

With growing apprehension, Rustle and Leaf watched the chompers clamber closer and closer. They paused at the end of the same log where the Twigs stood and gazed at them with piercing, narrow eyes.

Leaf was frightened. He stepped backwards and bumped into Rustle who roughly pushed him forward.

"You tell him," whispered Leaf over his shoulder. "You're supposed to tell him."

"Not me," Rustle whispered back. "You're the one who need his help."

To Leaf, the leader appeared alarming. The goliath chomper blew his breath out in heavy snorts. With surprising speed, he suddenly rushed toward Leaf and Rustle, but then just as suddenly, halted. Again he charged, and once again, halted. When Slapper wrinkled up his nose to snort, Leaf was shocked to see that the chomper's teeth were a wicked orange color. He gulped nervously. *This chomper is really angry,* Leaf realized. *We're standing on his dam! We should've climbed a tree! But then again, chompers would've gnawed the tree to pieces!* Leaf cringed against Rustle.

Rustle roughly pushed Leaf toward the goliath beaver. He stood close behind him, blocking any retreat.

Slapper charged again, but stopped abruptly only one step away from Leaf. He held his arms stiff as if he intended to push Leaf off his dam.

Without thinking, Leaf raised the whistletube up with both hands in front of his face to defend himself.

Rustle gripped Leaf's shoulder and murmured in his ear, "Don't worry, little Leaf. Chompers look scary, but they're very smart. He'll listen to what you have to say before he stuffs you in his dam."

Leaf glanced at him, uncertain if his friend was serious or not. He saw a tiny smile on Rustle's face, so

Leaf took a deep breath, and lowered the whistletube. He bravely faced the chomper leader.

Instead of pushing Leaf off of his dam, Slapper abruptly sat down on his flat tail. He hunched over, and stared at Leaf. His nose and whiskers wiggled furiously. His long claws clicked together.

Leaf took a deep breath. He tried to think of the right words to use. *Somehow I must make him understand we need his help before he shreds me for stuffing!* He opened his mouth to speak, but Rustle interrupted before he could utter a word.

"Hallo, great chompers!" Rustle yelled confidently from behind Leaf. "We come to you with great respect to give your great leader a message of great urgency! Needles of the Old Seeder is in great jeopardy! He has great need of your help!"

Leaf glared at Rustle. *How many times could a Twig say great in one breath?*

Slapper grunted, rose up on his hind legs, and towered above the Twigs.

Leaf and Rustle cowered and gasped. They stepped backwards, stumbled, and clung to each other. The tree trunk beneath them shifted and rolled a little.

Slapper's orange teeth snapped. His claws glinted in the sunlight. He clicked his tongue as if to order the tree to stop rolling.

Knowing the tree on which they stood might slip off the dam at any moment, Leaf and Rustle froze.

"Uh, great chomper leader," Leaf whispered. His voice squeaked and he struggled to keep his balance on the unsteady log.

"Speak up!" Rustle urged Leaf.

Leaf cleared his throat, took a deep breath, and spoke louder. "I am Leaf of the Old Seeder Twigs. My Pappo is Pappo. Uh, I mean, my Pappo is Needles. Ivy is my Mumma. Uh, Mumma...I mean Ivy...taught me how to whistle and, uh..." He patted his whistletube as if that explained anything. "So I whistled for you," he finished lamely. Leaf exhaled a low, shaky moan. "This isn't working," he muttered to Rustle.

Slapper took a step toward Leaf.

Aghast, Leaf shuffled backwards, but once again Rustle blocked his way.

Slapper stretched his neck far out until his giant nose nudged the whistletube.

Leaf pressed against Rustle, who was too worried about the rolling log beneath them to step further back.

Confused by Slapper's gesture, Leaf stared blankly at the goliath chomper's huge nose. "It's my whistletube," he stammered. He elbowed Rustle for help, but Rustle simply cringed behind Leaf. Over his shoulder, Leaf whispered, "What does he want?"

Abruptly, Slapper sat on his tail. His eyes held an attentive and expectant expression.

"Try again," urged Rustle.

Deciding he better get it all out before the tree on which they stood rolled off the dam and plunged into the gulch below, Leaf spread out his hands before him. "Oh great leader, please help us! The Old Seeder is flooded..." Leaf waved his hands toward the devastation all around them, "like here. My family is trapped in the Old Seeder!" Leaf pointed in the direction of Echo Peak, which loomed on the far horizon like a blindingly bright, frozen sentinel. He clasped his hands together, fought back an onset of unexpected tears, and cried out, "Please cross the valley, and save my family from the Rushing Waters!" He waved once more at the battered dam. "Please build a dam to block the flood and save the Old Seeder!"

Slapper sat silent, and stared at Leaf.

Leaf stared back. He could think of nothing else to say.

After a moment, Slapper grunted and turned around as if to dismiss the Twigs. He slipped down the side of the dam, clambered over muddied logs, and padded around the marshy edge of the pond. Immediately, Patty, Splash, and Splatter followed. Birchbite and Clacker glanced at one another. Without further hesitation they joined Slapper, too.

"No! Not that way!" Leaf cried out.

Rustle was too stunned to say anything.

"Go that way!" Leaf pointed at the grasslands. "You're going the wrong way! Across the valley! No, no! Come back! Please help!" Unable to keep his balance any longer, Leaf crumpled on the log.

Rustle patted the bunch of leaves on Leaf's head sympathetically. "Oh, forget 'em," Rustle consoled Leaf. "They're just leaving their old broken dam. They hav'ta go make a new pond now. They don't care about your haven."

In despair, Leaf watched the goliath chompers waddle away. His hope to rescue his family dissolved into unexpected tears.

"Come on, Leaf," comforted Rustle. "We'll find a way to help your family. Let's get you back home."

"But what can we do, Rustle?" Leaf asked with little hope in his voice.

"Well, we'll think of something," Rustle nodded firmly. "Maybe, we can make a leaf boat, eh? Or something like that!"

With a skeptical glance at Rustle, Leaf stood up, and dusted himself off. He felt too numb to speak. Rustle guided him over the shaky logs to the edge of the dam where they had climbed up. Leaf blinked back tears as he started down. He fumbled for a good handhold. He felt that he was moving very slowly—*almost like Fern,* he thought—*like he was stuck in mud.*

Rustle dropped down swiftly and expertly from log to log. He paused only long enough to wait impatiently for Leaf to catch up.

Feather slept in the thicket far below, and waited for their return.

Rustle smiled at the thought.

CHAPTER SIXTEEN

THE RED LEAF TWIGS

"Come on, Leaf!" Rustle called out to hurry his companion along. "You better get down before moonrise or a screecher will find you!"

Leaf nodded, worried at the thought. There wasn't much sun left to light the day. He was climbing down as fast as he could, but his legs felt as sluggish as a slimer's.

"I'm hurrying!" retorted Leaf. He tried to keep his voice from quivering. Leaf looked up at glowing clouds racing by in the dim light. A pink, twilight haze lit their edges.

"Hurry up, Leaf! You could go faster, you know!" Rustle would have already dropped to the ground if he hadn't paused to encourage Leaf every few feet. But now he was finally at the end of his patience. "Twigsnaps and slimerspit!" he blurted out. "Move it, eh!" Completely exasperated, Rustle gave up. He slid all the way to the ground and hopped from the last log to the loose gravel. He planted his feet, stood with his hands on his hips, and skeptically watched Leaf's clumsy descent. At last Rustle shouted, "You'd never know you live in the tallest tree in the forest, Leaf!"

"I'm not used to climbing down chomper dams!" Leaf shouted back. "Especially ones with trees hanging over the top!" Once more he glanced fearfully up at the large tree trunks teetering over the edge of the dam. They threatened to fall on top of him at any moment. He shuddered and concentrated on his handholds. Finally, he dropped to the gravel beside Rustle. His legs were very wobbly, and his hands hurt from gripping sticks and clumps of grass that had been stuffed in between the logs. He breathed a sigh of relief.

"Whew! That was hard!" Rustle teased his friend.

Leaf scowled.

Rustle reached out and tousled Leaf's hair. "Don't worry. You won't hav'ta do that again!" Dust rose up from the emerald leaves on Leaf's head. Rustle laughed. Then, with a hopeful look in his eyes, he sauntered casually over to the thicket where Feather had disappeared. He peeked in between the dry stems to spy on her as she lay sleeping.

Speckles, Whisper, and Claws had awakened earlier, and were now busy stuffing themselves with berries. They had so many in their cheeks, their eyes were squeezed into brown slivers, and their cheeks were as swollen as toad bellies. Warily they watched Rustle with defensive expressions and squinty eyes. They did not alert Feather.

Rustle reassured them with a whisper, "Don't worry little chippies. I don't want your berries."

The chipmunks spun around at once and scurried from the thicket in search of a hiding place to spit out their berry stash.

Rustle had stepped over so quietly and murmured so low to the chipmunks, Feather had not stirred from her nap. He crouched among the stems, listened to her snoring softly, and studied her face with a curious expression on his. At last Rustle reached down, and gently shook her shoulder. "Wake up, Feather." He spoke in a low tone. "We're going to need your help after all."

Feather sat up, stretched, and fluffed up her swan feather. She yawned deeply—making a weird noise sort of like a loon—and then she brushed the dust vigorously from her leafy, bronze hair. At last she blinked at Rustle as if she didn't recognize him. *Strange*, she thought, *he sounds so kind.* Feather rubbed her eyes, and looked at him again to be sure it really *was* him. Still puzzled, she looked back and forth from Leaf to Rustle.

"Did you find the chompers?" she asked hesitantly.

"Yes, but they're not gonna help us," Leaf answered, grimfaced. He plopped down in the thicket beside her. "We gotta' do it ourselves!"

"Oh," replied Feather, even more confused now by Leaf's declaration. Clearly she missed something somewhere.

"Come on," said Rustle. He reached out his hand to help her out of the thicket. "I'll explain it all to you. But first we need to find a tall tree. We have to scout a quicker route back through the popper fields and across the valley."

"There's a white pine just over there that's sort of tall." Feather pointed to a squatty, lopsided, whitebark pine tree. She accepted Rustle's hand, still mystified by his sudden consideration. Obviously something had changed his mind about her. "It's as tall as any tree around here," she added apologetically.

Rustle not only pulled her out, but he also refused to let go of her hand. He tugged her along beside him toward the scrubby pine. Strangely cheerful, Rustle chattered on, friendly and relaxed, "Do you think we can find a safe path through the popper fields? Bet we could figure a way across, if only we can get high enough to spot a trail. We need a good lookout. I'll bet there's a way right through the middle of those poppers, eh? We'll hav'ta trek it by night, of course. That's when the poppers sleep! I bet the grass is so tall we can even hide from the sky hunters, don't 'cha think? That's not even gonna' be a worry either, eh? Now I know it's a long way across but crossing the grasslands at night is a great idea, right? That'll work, eh?" He smiled and nodded knowingly.

Feather glanced back at Leaf, wondering if something was wrong with Rustle.

Leaf just shrugged, completely perplexed, too.

The three Twigs soon reached the crooked whitebark pine tree. Rustle and Leaf studied its wrinkled, pale bark, and stunted height. The sad-looking pine was barely as tall as the lowest limbs of the Old Seeder although its trunk was just as deeply furrowed. The bark twisted in braids around the trunk making the climb up as easy as stepping up stairs. Rustle pulled Feather up to a long, wandering limb, and yanked her down beside him.

Leaf climbed higher until he perched on the very tip of the ancient tree. From this height, he noticed how small the trees were in Feather's woods compared to his forest. In between the stumpy trees, blackened trunks shot up randomly like spears. This forest had suffered a terrible fire. Leaf realized it must have been the fire that Rustle escaped. Even so, pretty patches of color caught his eye. Tiny violet and pink flowers, drifting dandelion puffs, and the flutters of small, blue butterflies livened up the bleak landscape.

Speckles, Whisper, and Claws climbed into the whitebark pine's lower limbs, tucked their tails around them, yawned, and fell asleep at once with their cheeks pressed against the sweet-scented bark.

Feather perched in a cluster of smooth, purple cones. She wrapped her graceful arms around her knees, and stared up at a solitary star that had just appeared in the sky. She murmured an old twilight verse, "Starlight twinkle, starlight glow, tell me what the forest knows."

Rustle crouched nearby between two brittle stems that slanted down at odd angles. From the scant height of the pine he searched for a fast route from the bluff where they sat, down to the valley, and back across the grasslands to the south forest. Thoughtfully, he gazed at the wind-swept grass, which rippled with the evening breeze and tickled the sky. Any passageway through the popper burrows was hidden from view. *Still,* Rustle thought, *Feather's not afraid of the popper fields. She might get us through.*

Leaf watched Rustle speak earnestly to Feather. They pointed at the valley, nodded, and pointed more. Finally, they sat silent, and stared at the swaying grass.

The sun sat on the dark Sharp Peaks, and refused to surrender to the blue twilight.

Rustle and Feather began to speak again, but somehow their voices sounded different. They spoke in rhythm like the rippling grass, which swayed back and forth, each taking a turn, one speaking softly, and then the other. Their words drifted up to Leaf.

Rustle said something about his family being lost in a terrible fire. Feather told him about losing her family, too, in a firestorm. Rustle said he didn't remember very much. Feather said she grew up with chipmunks. Leaf heard Rustle say "ridge and Pappo" many times. Feather murmured something about being alone. Leaf watched Rustle lean his head closer to Feather's. Their voices sank lower.

Leaf shrugged and decided he'd rather watch the sun slip behind the Sharp Peaks than eavesdrop on their conversation.

Beautiful streams of yellow flowed into orange rivers in the west sky. Scarlet splashed their curling tips. The fiery colors showered the mountain peaks until at last only a few sprinkles of pink clouds were left to farewell the day. The sun sank behind the Sharp Peaks, and sucked all the fantastic colors down with it.

Far below, at the edge of the valley, Leaf watched in astonishment as two black-tailed poppers stood on tip-toe and sweetly kissed each other good night. Then they kissed their neighboring poppers, and their neighbors' neighbors. Leaf grinned. He considered telling Rustle he had discovered a new plan to cross the popper fields. They could kiss their way across! After a while the poppers disappeared into their burrows for the night, just as Rustle had said they would.

The limb below swayed as Rustle scooted closer to Feather. He rested a hand on the pine cones between them to keep his balance. The wandering limb on which they sat embraced them with its curling bark. They spoke gently, silhouetted by the evening's dark blue, velvet light.

Leaf heard Feather's voice drifting up, clear and distinct, like a skylark's melody.

"I don't remember all of it, just some things here and there. I know we had a very long too-hot season with no rain. Do you remember any of it at all?"

Rustle shrugged and shook his head.

"I remember your family, Rustle," Feather murmured. Her voice carried a disapproving note. "All branches of the Wide Valley Twigs knew about the Red Leaf Twigs!"

"Why?" Rustle sounded worried.

"Well," Feather hesitated, "your family was full of...."

Rustle flinched, ready to be embarrassed.

Feather noticed Rustle's concern so she finished her observation a little lamely, "...full of *remark-ability*!"

Rustle looked relieved.

"Do you remember them at all—any of your Red Leaf brothers?"

With a sad expression, Rustle shook his head. A few coppery leaves fell over his eyes.

"Well, you had five brothers. Their names were Pounce, Jumpfrog, Twitter, Wrinkle, and Spinner. They were all wild Twigs just like you! I think your mum ran away, because you were all so dreadful!" Feather teased.

Rustle grinned, and his eyes twinkled mischievously.

"You were the youngest, the littlest—very tiny, but awfully cute!" For some reason Feather paused and blushed. She continued, "Your older brothers hunted all of the time, but not for food. They just enjoyed trapping any creature they could. I had to rescue chatters, chippies, stickytoes, toolers, and whatever else they hunted all the time! They also threw blueberries, raspberries, and blackberries at just about anything that crawled or flew. For a while they even attacked big beasts like chompers with quilla spears until your papps made them stop."

"Did I do that, too?" wondered Rustle.

"Oh, no, Rustle," Feather reassured him, "you were just a tiny sprout, and crawled around with berries on your bib!"

Rustle frowned at the image.

Hastily, Feather changed the subject. "Well anyway, it was a weird too-hot season all across the Wide Valley. My papps warned us all the time that the seasons were changing—too hot in the warm season and too cold in the season of ice. There were terrific winds and storms like no Twig had ever seen before. The warm season came on so quickly that when the tiny chicks hatched too early, the blossoms weren't blooming and the crawlies weren't crawling. The mums could not find enough food. So the tiny chicks died of hunger.

"The creatures of the forest fought over what little food there was. The cappynuts that the chippies and chatters buried were green and sour because they could not wait for them to ripen. So the poor creatures became sick.

"*The Twig world is changing,* Papps warned us all the time *and we must be prepared to survive!*

"Oh, there was so little water that season. The river looked like a skinny, blue feather pressed into the dry, cracked dirt. We even felt sorry for the chompers. They were usually the only ones that had water when it was so dry, but even their magnificent pond was disappearing. Papps told us that they were so forlorn. Even the ducks flew away from their tiny pool of water."

Rustle and Feather sat silent for a moment.

With a lighter tone of voice, Feather continued, "But, you know, Rustle, papps made it sound so serious and scary that I just didn't really believe him. I just stopped listening." Feather brushed a strand of bronze leaves from her eyes and tucked it away behind her ear. "Really I was too young to care about it anyway—too busy playing with the silly creatures in the forest like the chippies." Feather smiled. "I fed them berry treats whenever they came to our tree home. We lived in a beautiful, tall silver leaf tree not far from your red leaf tree. My two little sisters, Lark and Swift, were tiny, pretty babes, and so, so sweet! Feather caught her breath, unable to speak for a moment. Sparkling tears clung to her bronze eyelashes. She blinked them away.

"You don't have to speak of it!" Rustle cried out, distressed for her.

Feather shook her head and frowned. "It's been so long since I really thought about that awful day. It's hard to remember. If only the smoke in my head would let me think..." she concentrated. "But I must remember now. You should know what happened to your family, and to you."

A sharp intake of breath betrayed Rustle's long-buried feeling—the feeling of wanting to know what happened to him.

Feather's eyes squinted shut as she sat thinking. At last she went on. "It was so hot that day. Even though there were dark, twisting balls of clouds, there was still no rain. It was then that it happened."

Feather paused. She tightened her mouth, and spoke with calm resolve, "We were asleep in our haven. For some reason, I woke up and listened to my sisters dream-talking. My papps snored so loud, my mum punched his arm to make him stop!" Unexpectedly Feather chuckled a little.

"Anyway, there was a great flash outside and crackling. Our knothole lit up brighter than day. The crackles sounded like they were tearing apart our tree's branches. My sisters screamed, but I never made a sound. For some reason, all I can remember is my papps' bald head popping in and out of our knothole. He kept yelling, *Hurry! Hurry! We must escape!*

"So I jumped through our knothole to the branch outside. The air was gray and smelled like smoke. Through the haze I watched red flames race right up your red leaf tree, Rustle. All of your brothers jumped to the tall, furry-looking tree that grew right beside your home. I could see your papps carrying you in his arms like a crawlyball. You were all rolled up in a red leaf. He leapt to the furry tree, and started climbing!"

"Anyway, the fire circled our tree, too. Papps and mum soaked moss packs and smothered my sisters' heads with them. While I waited for them to cover my head, I watched your papps climb higher and higher, always with you held tight in his arms. Red flames crawled right up the trunk up behind him."

Feather placed her hand on Rustle's.

"When your papps couldn't climb any higher, he hung off a limb, and threw you as hard as he could right into the smoke and flames!"

Rustle gasped. So did Leaf.

"Did I die?" asked Rustle without thinking.

Surprised, Feather stared at Rustle with a puzzled look. She stifled a chuckle and waved her hand. "No, no, of course not!"

"Whew!" exhaled Rustle, "for a moment there, I wasn't sure!" He grinned sheepishly at Feather and said, "Of course I knew I didn't."

Leaf snorted in disbelief.

Feather laughed. "Listen! You were caught by the firestorm's wind, and blown up so high that you just disappeared into the black sky! Gone! Just like that!" She snapped her fingers. Feather expression grew serious. She took Rustle's hand in hers. "Your papps tried to save your life, Rustle, and he did! You must have floated on the wind all the way across the Wide Valley!"

"But my family?" Rustle asked, although he already suspected the answer she would give.

"I didn't see any more, Rustle. My papps pushed me right off the limb. I fell on the moss in the roots. All I heard was my papps screaming, *Run, run! Run through the fire! Run for the river! We'll follow behind you! Don't wait for us!* I was so terrified I jumped right through the circle of fire around our tree. I ran faster than I ever had in my life, and never looked back." Feather paused again, and then as if to explain a shameful memory, she spoke softly. "You see, I could run faster than anyone in my family. So I made it all the way to the river before anyone else."

In despair, Feather shrugged her shoulders. "When I reached the river's edge, I realized that I was alone. Ash and smoke swirled all around me, and hot cinders fell and sizzled on the ground. I coughed and choked in the thick smoke. But still I ran back into the fire to find my family. Right away I was lost in the smoke. I remember screaming for papps and mum, and then I tripped and fell. I lay on the ground and tried so hard just to breathe!"

Rustle brushed Feather's cheek with the back of his curled fingers, and then held her trembling hands.

Feather gave him a little smile. "All at once two panicked chippies ran straight out of the smoke and hopped right over my head! For some reason, one of them stopped, turned around, and looked back at me. The other chippie stopped then, too, but she simply crouched and trembled with fear! The first chippie hopped back, and pushed his nose in my face as if to tell me *get up—get up!* I grabbed his neck and pulled myself up onto his back. We all raced away together. The chippie carried me to the river bank, and we hid in a deep burrow there until the fire had passed. The two chippies and I survived, but I never saw my family again.

As if in answer to a questioning look from Rustle, Feather smiled and said, "Yes, the chippie that carried me to the river is my Speckles! And his sister is Whisper." She smiled at Speckles, who was fast asleep on a thick branch below her. He was stretched out on his back, and his freckled, fuzzy cheeks blew softy in and out as he snored. "We have never parted since then," Feather added.

"I'm so sorry about your family," murmured Rustle.

"And I'm sorry about yours, too, Rustle. It was all so awful. I had nearly forgotten. But I'm very glad you came," she said. "I thought all the Twigs had been lost in the fire. I thought I was the only one left"

As Leaf listened to Feather's tragic story, he felt so sad. *How horrible is would be to lose everything in a fire! It would be like...like losing everything in a flood!* He searched the horizon, wishing that he could see the Old Seeder's familiar, towering tip.

An intense, full moon hovered ominously above the Blue Mountains in the east. It floated up into an indigo sky. The glistening stars grew brighter. All the scurrying creatures of the dark knew they must now be extra careful. Hunters were even more deadly in a bright night.

From his high perch in the whitebark pine, Leaf studied the valley. A late breeze from Echo Peak twirled the grass tips into curls. Like the waves of a lake forced into a quiet cove, the grass flowed back and forth, and back again on top of itself. And like water in a cove, creatures moved below the waving tips, hidden from view.

The poppers are asleep, worried Leaf, *but what else is in the grasslands?* He shivered.

CHAPTER SEVENTEEN

SCREECHER!

*W*e should go, thought Leaf. *The night is flowing fast.*

Rustle and Feather sat even closer together now as they silently watched the moon glow.

"Hey," Leaf called out. "We need to get across the valley. It's getting dark."

Feather looked up and smiled sweetly. "Hey, Leaf, do you feel like riding Whisper all night? I could tie you on if you get sleepy!"

"Sure," urged Leaf impatiently. "Let's go!"

The three Twigs dropped through the limbs of the whitebark pine. As Feather passed the branch where

Speckles napped, she kissed him on his nose to wake him. He stretched and yawned.

Nearby, Whisper woke at once, sat up, and began grooming her already glossy whiskers.

Claws saw Feather kiss Speckles, and wanting none of it, scampered down the tree. He curled up under a red-leaf bush, and gave a warning, cross-eyed glance at Feather. Then he buried his head under his tail to continue his nap!

Feather laughed as she dropped to the ground, walked over to Claws, and poked him with her foot until he finally sat up, sleepy and grumpy. "You get to ride Claws again, Rustle!" she called out, giggling.

"Looking forward to it!" he grinned back. Rustle glanced once more at the valley before he swung to the lowest branch of the tree, and dropped to the ground. His expression became serious.

The vibrant colors of the day took on an uncanny, colorless hue now that the evening was upon them. The moon's light bled the colors away. The green leaves and orange berries on the thickets became a flat gray. The leafy hair of the Twigs took on a silvery hue. The granite boulders became dark shadows dotting the ridge. A purple silhouette of an owl floated across the moon, and the white tips of a fox's ears brushed the tall stalks of the goldenrod. Hunters searched the grasslands for easy prey tonight.

Leaf noticed the spots on Speckles' back were shining in the moonlight. He suddenly realized that Whisper's spots glowed white, too. Leaf frowned. A chippie with bright speckles in a grassy field in the moonlight didn't seem like such a good idea after all.

"Rustle," Leaf whispered. "This is a really bad idea. The chippies will not be safe. Feather will not be safe. Sky hunters see best in the dark, and tonight the moon is very bright. Screechers will hunt us from above, and swift-tails will run us down in the grass. This ride is too dangerous!"

Nearby, Feather listened to Leaf's worried whisper. She spoke up at once. "Don't worry, Leaf. Speckles, Whisper, and Claws have rested. And they are very fast." She placed her hand on Leaf's arm to reassure him. "Trust me. The chippies will carry us safely across."

Leaf nodded although he still felt very worried. He tightened his shoulder strap, balanced his saver across his back, flung his whistletube over his shoulder, and knotted his rope until it felt secure. Leaf stroked

Whisper's neck, and whispered in her ear, "So, you're ready to go then, berryblossom?"

Whisper kissed Leaf's cheek with a wet nose and a tiny pink tongue. She gazed at him with warm, comforting eyes.

Leaf was already very fond of the gentle chippie. He ran his hand over Whisper's spotted back, thoughtfully. He stooped over, scooped up a handful of dirt, and tossed it on her coat, hoping to hide her freckles.

Instantly Whisper quivered. A dust cloud rose up all around. Leaf sneezed again and again. Whisper's spots sparkled once again in the brilliant moonlight. She gazed reproachfully at Leaf. Her eyes told him that she did not care to have dirt sprinkled on her beautiful fur, no matter what he was worried about.

With a resigned sigh Leaf grabbed Whisper's braided leash, and pulled himself up on her shoulders. He felt sick with fear for all the chippies, but tried to look calm.

Feather kissed Speckles on both of his cheeks, lovingly tugged his ears, and jumped lightly onto his shoulders. With a relaxed, expert grip she held his thin, golden braid.

Rustle gave a terse warning glare at Claws, who simply twitched his whiskers, and gave him an impatient grimace back. In one motion, Rustle hopped onto the skittish chippie's back, grabbed the rope-braid firmly with one hand, and gripped a bunch of fur with the other.

Claws promptly tossed him off.

Leaf and Feather burst out laughing.

Frowning, Rustle dusted himself off and scowled at Claws. He turned and pretended to study the scuffle marks in the dirt.

Claws eyed him warily until a gnat buzzed in his ear and distracted him.

Taking advantage of the opportunity, Rustle leapt on Claws back faster than a fly might dodge a slap. But this time he did not to yank the chippie's fur. Claws seemed resigned to carry Rustle for a while. Rustle nodded confidently to Feather.

Feather smiled. She turned to take the lead down the gravel-strewn bluff. As Speckles took a hop downhill, Feather whispered over her shoulder, "Keep quiet from now on. I'll lead the way. If something happens, let your chippie guide you. They see and hear better than we do!" She kicked Speckles gently, nudging him into a quick descent of the steep slope.

With stiff legs Speckles braced against the slope, and kept himself from sliding too fast on the loose gravel. Soon he slid onto a narrow trail that traversed the cliff all the way down to the valley.

Whisper followed close behind Speckles. Patiently she endured a continual barrage of tumbling pebbles set loose by Claws above her. Finally, Whisper and Claws hopped onto the trail, too. Rustle, Feather, and Leaf nervously watched the sky for hunters. There were few places to hide on this barren path.

Quickly and silently, Feather guided them downhill along the zigzagging route. Very soon they left the rocks, and bounded into the sparse cover of the grass. Speckles hesitated by a popper burrow as if unsure whether or not the poppers really did sleep at night. Feather urged him past it with a whisper in his ear and a gentle tug on his braided leash. Reassured by her touch, Speckles threaded a path through the first of the many popper burrows.

Second in line, Leaf peeked over Whisper's ears just in time to see Feather and Speckles disappear into the grass. *Here we go*, he thought. *May the moon guide us safely home!*

For a long time, Whisper and Claws followed Speckles so closely that they stepped on each other's tails. So the chippies held their tails up stiff and bristly in defense.

Rustle leaned forward and murmured a polite thank you in Claws' ear for the ride. The skittish chipmunk appeared alert, yet calm for once. Claws tilted his ears back toward Rustle to catch his every word.

Soon the Twigs and chippies reached the middle of the valley, and moved through even taller grass. Leaf tried to protect Whisper from the prickly blades that brushed against her fur, and scratched his legs. Leaf caught a brief glimpse of twinkling stars before the grass closed in completely and smothered their padding steps. Yet he still did not feel safe. *From above, we must look like a huge, spotted snake slinking through the popper field!* Whisper's ears twitched back and forth right in front of Leaf's eyes, but Leaf was worried about what he *couldn't* see. He peered deep into the trembling grass, but saw nothing.

They travelled quickly.

If I were guiding us through the valley, I would lead us around in circles all night! We would be lost for sure! He wondered how Feather could possible find the way across.

With a surprising abruptness Feather's head popped up out of the grass in front of Leaf. Her head bounced up and down at the same height as the grass tips.

Startled beyond words, Leaf stared up at the bizarre sight. It took a moment before he realized that Feather must be balancing on Speckles' shoulders! She ducked down under the cover of the grass. *So that's how she is finding the way! She's standing on tiptoe on her chippie!* Now Leaf respected her even more. He considered his own skill on a chippie with dismay. *I can barely hang on!* He held on tight to Whisper's rope, and buried his face in her soft fur.

Then in one heart-stopping, ghastly moment, a *SCREEEEEE!* sliced through the night.

Frozen in fear, everyone looked up as a shadow raced over them, swirled around, and then raced back.

"Screecher!" Rustle screamed. His shriek pierced the night sky just as loudly as the owl's had that spotted them. "Screecher!" He jerked at Claws' leash frantically, and kicked the chippie with his heels to make him run, but instead Claws skidded sideways. Rustle somersaulted off the chippie's back into a popper mound. He yanked his saver from its loop. "Run!" he screamed to Leaf and Feather. "Run!"

Yet Rustle didn't run. Instead he hopped up and down like an angry chatter. He waved his saver above his head to catch the screech owl's attention, and lure the sky hunter to him alone, and away from his companions.

Terrified, Claws tried to hop away, but stumbled over his leash. He crumpled into a quivering heap, and pressed against the side of a popper burrow.

At once Whisper whirled around, and pounced on top of the burrow in a frantic attempt to shield Claws. At the same instant, she flipped Leaf into the dirt behind her.

Speckles spun around, rushed back through the grass, and skidded up to the burrow. He threw all his weight against Whisper, and knocked her from atop the burrow in an effort to protect her. Then he crouched over the helpless, trembling Claws, and glared at the owl.

All the while, Feather was hanging onto Speckles' fur, trying desperately to remain on his back. She yelled furiously at Rustle, "No, Rustle! No! Ride the chippies! Stay on the chippies! They are fast!"

But it was too late. The screecher now had all three chipmunks in sight.

Claws flattened himself against the ground, and covered his eyes with his tiny hands. Whisper and Speckles stood over him protectively.

Feather slid from Speckles' back, and planted herself in front of the chippies. She waved her rock-slicer in the air, and watched the screecher fly back and forth. In between the owl's passes she glared at Rustle angrily.

Rustle gave up hopping around, pushed Speckles off the burrow, and jumped on top. He raised his saver defiantly at the owl, which floated silently over them in ever-tightening circles. He shouted, "Not tonight, screecher! Not tonight!"

With trembling hands, Leaf yanked out his saver, crouched beside Whisper, and watched the screecher ready itself to attack. Black, outstretched wings soared across the full moon. Fierce and unblinking, its round, golden eyes floated eerily in the dark, closer and closer. Its powerful claws scratched the night sky, and greedily grasped at the chippies.

With a skillful movement Rustle began twirling his saver in a circle above his head. With his other hand, he untangled the rope from around his waist and tied it to one end of his saver. Then Rustle twirled the long stick higher by holding the end the rope. It circled faster and faster until it was only a flat, shiny blur reflecting the moon's bright light. The stick *WHIRRRED!* like a weird, sinister beast.

Startled, the screecher pulled its sharp claws into its belly, and passed over again. But then it dipped its wing, spun around, and returned for a closer inspection. It hovered just above the spinning saver, confused by the sight and sound of a shimmering disc. It searched for the prey, which had been within its grasp just a moment before, but could not see it.

Rustle whirled his saver above them all, steady and sure.

The screech owl hung there suspended against the moonlight. It beat its wings and scratched the air. Its angry eyes searched beneath the flat, silver, humming circle. *SCREEEEEE*! sliced through the night sky again and again. At last, the screecher gave up, tilted its wings, and soared off into the dark sky. It would seek prey that was less bewildering somewhere else tonight.

"It's gone!" Leaf cried. "You did it, Rustle!" He knelt beside Claws to comfort him. Whisper gave her frightened friend many tiny licks. Speckles nudged Claws with his nose, and then kicked him with his back foot to try and make him stand up, and act less embarrassing.

Claws peeked out from between his fingers. At last, he popped up, and alertly looked around. Then he hopped about on stiff legs and trilled annoying, high-pitched barks in short bursts. He barked over and over as if he were now ready to fight whatever had threatened them.

"It's gone," giggled Leaf. "You're safe now."

Claws sat down, and smugly licked his toes as if he alone had chased the owl away.

Feather tucked her rock shard in her belt, glanced sideways at Rustle, and rolled her eyes. "Yeh, thank the moon Rustle was here!" she commented dryly. "Or who knows what would've happened!"

Rustle planted his saver in the dirt. An overly confident grin lit up his face. "I sure chased that screecher away, eh?"

"Well, *that* was wonderful!" A very tiny smile flickered over Feather's face, but at once she frowned. "Next time let the chippies run!"

"Oh, right. I'm sorry," Rustle said surprised with Feather's no-nonsense tone of voice. Self-consciously, he swung his saver over his shoulder and tucked it away in his strap's back loop. He kicked the dirt clods, glanced at Feather, and then up at the moon. "Uh, well, we should go on now, don't ya' think? The screecher might return."

Leaf looked up nervously.

The brilliant, full moon looked back.

CHAPTER EIGHTEEN

SLAPPER LEADS THE WAY

Slapper padded with purpose. He led the band of beavers up the ravine toward Thunder Peak. Only an occasional grunt and quiet slap of flat tails betrayed their struggle through the awful destruction of the evening before.

Shattered boulders, suffocating mud, and uprooted, splintered trees were stuffed into the steep canyon. The violent pounding of the outburst had fractured the sheer granite cliffs, and great, gray slabs had collapsed into the ravine. Fortunately, the avalanche had blocked the river from continuing its rampage toward Slapper's pond. The raging river was turned back into its own canyon. Nonetheless the brief outburst did plenty of damage. Nothing that lived in the ravine survived the sudden crush. And never again would a cheerful stream tumble over its rocks to a peaceful pond below.

The beavers waddled along. Their slick fur reflected the brilliant moon's glow. They struggled over the broken slabs of granite that had broken away during the avalanche until at last they heard the thunderous roar of water. One by one they crept through the crevice in the cliff to the ledge overhanging the canyon beyond.

When Slapper stepped through he blinked in disbelief. The amazing ice dam was destroyed! And nearly all of the pine trees along the edge of the river had been sucked into the floodwaters and shredded to pieces. But the yellow cedar from which Slapper fell long ago still leaned out over the river. Its powerful roots continued to grip the huge boulders on the river's embankment. The tree still stretched over the rapids just like a bobcat might lean over a pond with one paw raised, ready to snatch a fish.

Slapper led the others to the roots of the yellow cedar. He climbed on its trunk, and waddled around an enormous knothole. He crawled far out over the river, and crouched among the odd, jutting branches. He reached the end of a slippery limb, and sat on his flat tail in a cluster of cones. Slapper balanced just above the swirling, white tips of the engorged, icy river.

Nervous but determined, Patty, Splatter, Splash, Birchbite, and Clacker followed Slapper. The turbulent waters roared just below them, and enveloped the beavers in a freezing mist. Patty nuzzled Slapper's back to let him know she was near.

Slapper gazed at the mesmerizing rhythm of the rapids. *I am strong. I am the leader.*

Patty sat patiently waiting for Slapper's decision. On the outstretched limb behind Patty sat Splash and Splatter, huddled together and afraid. They blew frosty, heavy breaths, shivered, and pressed against each other. Nearer to the great tree's trunk, Birchbite and Clacker sat with their tails planted flat underneath them, and their hands cupped over their bellies. Alert and calm, they watched Slapper and waited.

Slapper looked over his shoulder at his goliath mate, daughters, and the bachelors. *Are they strong enough? Will they follow?*

Patty gazed at Slapper, her eyes filled with love and loyalty. She did not understand why Slapper had led them here, but she would never leave his side. There was no uncertainty in her expression. She answered

Slapper's question silently. *I am strong. I will follow.* Patty grunted to encourage her daughters. *You are strong...stronger than me. You must follow, too.*

Splash and Splatter grew silent. But the next moment they blew out warm breathy puffs, and nodded briskly.

Insistent grunts erupted from Birchbite and Clacker to be sure Slapper heard their pledge. *We will not be left behind!*

Splatter looked down. With a quick sideways wriggle, he dropped into the Rushing Waters, and at once was swept away. One by one, Patty, Splash, Splatter, Birchbite, and Clacker plopped into the river. A long line of brown heads bounced and bobbed among swirling, white tips as the bitterly cold water sucked them into the canyon.

With the shock of the freezing water, Splatter's nightmares rushed back. At once he remembered being slammed against giant boulders in the rapids. He remembered choking, coughing, and terrible pain. There was a horrifying, thunderous roar, and a sensation of floating through darkness until somehow he was shoved through a narrow crevice in a cliff face. He vaguely remembered being carried along by a swift-flowing, deep stream. He had tumbled over the edge of a high cliff in the midst of a waterfall. Then there were hazy memories of floating there in a quiet pond under an enormous cappynut tree.

After that, his pain softened into a bed of fluffy moss, and there was a scent of sweet cedar fronds around his head. He heard a gentle hush like a soothing hum, or perhaps it was soft whistling. A melody sang over and over. There were words—*Needles, Ivy, the Old Seeder, Needles, Ivy, the Old Seeder.* The murmurs sounded as if they wished to tell him something important. Then there was the haunting coo of a mourning dove from a carved whistletube.

The Twig pup on my dam made the same coo with the same whistletube!

Now, floating in the freezing water, he clearly remembered the Twigs, *Needles and Ivy,* and how they had tried to mend his horribly broken legs. For days, the two Twigs had sat patiently beside him. They had cared for him, even while he snapped and clawed at them viciously.

Slapper remembered again the moment that he woke up. The pain had grown less overwhelming. But he had been so afraid. His legs were bound with sticks and flaxen wraps, so he chewed them off right away.

The scent of mint hung heavy in the air and suffocated him. Bizarre trees stretched their thick, green branches over him, and he felt he was a captive. So he struggled from the strange nest where he had been stuffed. He knew the two Twigs must be close by, and he also knew Twigs were treacherous. So Slapper had crawled away and escaped the towering trees and smelly nest. And over time all the nightmares and memories of the two Twigs had faded away.

But when Slapper heard the Twig whistle the dove's call on the dam, he heard the soft words, *'Needles and Ivy'* murmured again. He remembered the Twigs who had tried to mend his legs, and had saved his life. He realized the young Twig on his dam must be their pup. And he also understood from the frantic sounds the Twig pup made that the place to which he had been swept so long ago—*the Old Seeder*—was in jeopardy. Slapper knew that somehow, he must help *Needles and Ivy* and *the Old Seeder! And he knew how to find them! Follow the river!*

Now the rushing currents clutched at him with grip more deadly than they had before, yet Slapper was unafraid. Even though he once again choked, coughed, and fought for air, he was determined to stay afloat, and find the crevice in the canyon wall that led to the stream, and the Twigs who had saved his life so long ago.

The swollen river carried the beavers over giant boulders that stuck up from under the water. Slapper was swept away from Patty, Splash, Splatter, Birchbite, and Clacker. The white tips scattered the beavers like minnows slapped by a beaver's tail. They scraped against the steep granite walls, but the beavers were strong. With powerful webbed strokes, they paddled to reach each other. With fierce jaws and teeth, they gripped each other's flat tails. United in a tight circle, they became a raft that was buoyed up on the white tips of the rapids.

With a sudden swirl, their beaver-tail raft was sucked into an even faster current. A thundering pulse throbbed through the water, and echoed off the granite walls. A heavy mist curled up in ominous waves, and filled the canyon until it spilled over the cliffs. Then at once the mist lifted, and the Rushing Waters disappeared before them.

In horror Slapper and Patty stared at each other. *A waterfall!* And they were being pushed right over the edge! With every instinct to survive pulsing through their bodies, the beavers paddled furiously against the current, but their raft rushed closer and closer toward the edge!

At that very moment—in a sudden confusing tangle of twisted beaver bodies—they slammed onto a huge slab in the middle of the river. The giant rock rose up at the very spot where the river dropped over the cliff. It jutted up so high that it split the waterfall in half!

Desperately, Slapper scratched at the wet rock until he was on top of its slippery surface. He twisted around and bit Patty's neck. With a great heave, he pulled her up beside him. Birchbite and Clacker shoved Splash and Splatter up with one great push. Once Splash and Splatter were safe, the bachelors clawed their way up behind them. At last the beavers huddled together on the rock. The river swirled around the giant slab, and threatened to suck them over the falls. The beavers pressed against each other. The thunderous roar of the mighty waterfall overwhelmed them.

Slapper forced himself to breathe in a steady rhythm. He carefully made his way to the tip of the rock that hung out over the cliff. White spray filled the air and obscured his vision. But when the mist cleared for a moment, Slapper peeked over. At once he felt dizzy and sick. Crystal clear water cascaded over the cliff in heavy waves, and plunged far below until it disappeared into a fantastic, crashing chaos. Slapper swayed as he stared down. *How could I have survived this fall so long ago?*

In an instant Patty was beside him. She braced her body against Slapper's, nuzzled his cheek, and nodded encouragement. But she did not dare look over the edge at the watery turmoil far below.

Slapper looked away from the terrible sight, and breathed in deep, even gulps. Then he gazed at his daughters and the bachelors. Their eyes studied his every move, trusting him to keep them safe. Slapper shook the freezing water from his pelt, and nodded brusquely. Ignoring the terror of the falls, he studied the steep walls of the canyon. Then he examined the currents, and how the water flowed past.

Splash, Splatter, Birchbite, and Clacker waited patiently for Slapper to signal what they must do.

After a long while, Slapper looked at Patty. Only to her, would he show his true feelings, his despair.

But Patty already knew.

They were trapped!

CHAPTER NINETEEN

SLAPPER'S TALE

"Stay away from the door!" ordered Mumma in a frightened voice.

"But it's closed!" retorted Fern.

"Now!" Mumma responded with a waggle of her finger and a shiver of her topknot.

Reluctantly, Fern pulled herself away from the view out of the tiny window in their knothole doorway. She wandered to the moss blanket spread on the floor in the middle of their haven.

Mumma lay crooked and stuffed within the deep pillows of the large chair. "The door stays closed and you stay away from it! And keep Burba and Buddy away from it, too!"

With a scowl, Fern caught hold of Burba's tiny arm, and for the twentieth time dragged his wriggling body onto the blanket.

Pappo was on edge, too. Their door kept creaking. Even though he had carved it to fit perfectly in the knothole, the Old Seeder now shifted back and forth constantly against the push of the floodwaters. Every so often, the door made a *CAAWK!* noise like an irritated crow. Pappo sprang up again to check the door's tight fit. He worried that the flood might twist the trunk so hard that the knothole would warp, and the door might pop right out.

Fern had been kept busy plugging the small knotholes in the haven with thick clumps of moss. Mumma worried that the ancient tree would topple over and be pulled into the powerful floodwaters. If that happened, their lives depended on somehow keeping the freezing water out. So Fern had stuffed wet balls of moss in every knothole in every hollow. All around them long, green strands crept down the wood. It looked like dark, slimy roots were sprouting from the inside of the old tree.

Now Pappo pulled open the door and stared out at the bluff above the Old Seeder. He had opened it a hundred times already that day, and searched where Leaf had disappeared into the forest. Each time Pappo had shoved the door shut with a disappointed expression. Now as before, he opened the door, glanced out, but did not see Leaf. This time he quickly slammed the door shut, whirled around, and glared at a tiny twin drooling on the floor in front of him.

Burba kept trying to crawl between his legs and reach the porch branch outside. Pappo crossed his arms, frowned at the stubborn twin, and stood guard in front of the door. Burba blinked innocently, blew a spit bubble, and then somersaulted back to the blanket where Buddy and Fern sat.

Time crawled by. There seemed to be little to do.

The twins bowed their heads together, and concentrated on ripping threads from the moss blanket. Fern braided them into long, strands. Buddy and Burba decided it would be interesting to stuff the braids in their mouths, slowly pull them out, and then stuff them back in again. They giggled louder and louder with each pull.

Fern grimaced with disgust as she took the soggy braids away from the twins and wiped their slobbery faces and hands with a limp leaf. She glanced hopefully at Pappo. "Can't we have one knothole open? It's so stuffy!"

Pappo's expression softened. He plopped down on the blanket. "Let's sit together." He motioned for Fern and the twins to scoot in closer, which they were happy to do. Pappo cupped an elbow in his palm, and tapped his chin absentmindedly with a skinny, knotted finger. "I'll tell you a story about...," Pappo considered his choices.

Fern, Burba, and Buddy watched him with hopeful expressions.

Pappo started to speak.

With a worried frown, Fern interrupted him, "As long as it's not a story with a lesson!"

Pappo chuckled.

Mumma smiled wisely. She propped herself up on one elbow, and shooed Fern's objection away with a limp leaf. "You three could use a lesson or two!" she said with a grin. "Make it a long lesson, Pappo!"

Pappo grinned at Mumma.

The twins glanced at each other, not sure if the story would be exciting, or if they were being tricked into taking a nap. In any case, they tugged the corners of the blanket around them, and snuggled close together, ready for Pappo's story.

At once sulky, Fern threw herself on her back, tucked her arms under her head, and crossed one leg over the other. She stared dismally at a dark, swirling knothole in the hollow's ceiling above her.

Mumma adjusted her moss packs, which kept sliding from her head. Losing patience, she untied her golden topknot. Her crumpled leaves fell around her face, and gave her a frightening, alarmed bobcat sort of appearance. She mashed the cool packs on her head, and held them there, trying to keep her hands along with her thoughts occupied.

"Wanna' hear a story about a chomper?" Pappo asked innocently.

"Oooh," gasped Buddy and Burba.

"Well, that sounds pretty scary, Pappo," stated Fern matter-of-factly. "I don't think the twins are old enough to hear a story about chompers yet."

"Well, maybe you're right, Fern," answered Pappo.

The twins glowered at Fern.

"But this is a true story," Pappo continued, "and it's about a great big chomper that fell right over the cliff in our waterfall."

"Really?" asked Fern, although she tried to not appear too interested.

Pappo smiled and winked at Mumma who smiled back. "Now you know that chompers build the most excellent dams, and that their ponds are very, very important. Their ponds create havens and food for lots and lots of creatures, right?"

Fern rolled her eyes. This was going to be a boring lesson story, after all. She turned away.

"When the seasons are too hot and dry, the chompers are the only ones with water 'cause they store it up! And when the seasons are too rainy, their dams stop the floods."

"Oh, Pappo," exclaimed Fern as she glanced over her shoulder, "what about the great big chomper? Tell us about him!"

Pappo frowned at her. "Well, all right. Now you also know that chompers are *very* scary. In fact, Twigs stay far away from chompers. They love to shred up sticks, rip apart trees, and bury whole logs underwater just so they can eat them when they get hungry."

The twin's eyes grew large. They were very impressed.

"So a wise Twig never goes near a chomper," Pappo declared. He waggled his finger in the air to make his point. "Anyway, so when Mumma told me she saw one slide over the cliff, and drop down in our waterfall, I just told her to keep away from it. But we decided to go look for it anyway and see if it was floating in our pond."

Fern could no longer hide her interest in the story. She rolled over on her belly, cupped her chin in her hands, and stared at Pappo.

The twins fought over who should have most of the blanket. At last giving up the battle, they smashed their tiny bodies together, and wrapped themselves up to their noses. Their wide eyes peeked anxiously out at Pappo.

Mumma lay back on her pillow, lost in the memories of that time long ago.

Pappo continued, "Well, it turned out to be an *enormous* chomper! And he looked just like he was dead!"

"Well, *was* he dead then?" asked Fern impatiently.

"Well," Pappo went on, determined to draw his story out as long as possible, "as I said, this huge chomper came tumbling over the waterfall all the way down into our little pool. He bobbed up and down in there awhile, and then he sort of floated over to the shallow edge. There he lay, just floating around and bumping against the rocks, sorta' dead-like."

"Yeh, yeh, but he wasn't," urged Fern, hoping Pappo would get the point quicker.

Pappo chuckled. "Nope, he wasn't. I stood on a rock and poked him with my saver."

"He was very brave," Mumma added softly.

Fern rolled her eyes.

"So, I poked him," Pappo went on, "and he kinda' groaned and rolled over."

"Ooooh!" gasped the twins.

"Then he grunted!" exclaimed Pappo louder, relishing the moment.

"Ooooooh!" gasped Buddy and Burba again.

"And then he coughed!" cried Pappo.

"*Oh, go on!*" complained Fern.

Pappo laughed. "Well, this chomper was pretty big, but even then we could tell he was still not more than a few seasons old. His legs were broken up really bad. We decided to help him. We whistled for help from all the branches of Twigs around here. They came right away. We all took our ropes, and shoved them under his arms with our savers. We were very careful to watch his weird, orange teeth all the time! But this chomper was hurt so bad, he never woke up. He just groaned and whimpered all the time. The Cappynut Twigs jumped on his chest and tied our ropes together. Then we tossed the other end of our ropes over the low branch of that cappynut tree by the waterfall pool, you know the one?"

Buddy and Fern nodded their heads, now completely absorbed in Pappo's every word. Burba's eyes glowed as he tried to understand how a chomper could be lifted out of the pool by Twigs, ropes, and sticks.

"We tied the other end of the ropes to a big log. As soon as we rolled that log into the pool, that chomper was lifted right on up out of the water! All we had to do then was swing him over to the roots of the cappynut! We cut the ropes, and he dropped right down on top of some soft moss!"

Delighted, Burba clapped his hands, awed by the clever engineering the Twigs had accomplished. Fern and Buddy glanced at him, irritated that he'd slowed down Pappo's story even more. They waited impatiently for a more interesting part to the story.

Pappo winked at Burba. "So then we wrapped his broken legs with sticks, flaxen straps, and ivy vines. We found plants to shove in his mouth, and we dribbled water on his nose, so he'd lick it. We sat beside him a long time. We'd only speak in whispers so as not to disturb him, but still he had scary night dreams. We watched over him many, many days.

"Finally, his poor legs healed up some, but still he never really woke up. Sometimes while he slept he'd snap and grunt at us like he was mad! Other times he'd claw the air like he was drowning! When he was like that, Ivy whistled her songs to calm his dreams."

Mumma added softly, "There were a few times that I thought his eyes open just a little. It seemed like he was staring at the carvings on my whistletube." She shrugged. "But maybe I only imagined it."

Mumma and Pappo glanced at one another. Even though this had happened long ago, they both remembered it very well.

Pappo went on. "Well anyway, one day we woke up from a nap, and that chomper was gone—vanished— just like that!" Pappo snapped his fingers. The twins jumped. Pappo grinned.

"Oh!" cried Fern. "So is that why you sent Leaf to the chomper dam? Do you think Leaf can find that chomper and he'll help us? Do you think he'll come back with Leaf and build a dam and block the river?"

Burba scrunched up his nose, drooled, and nodded. He had already figured this out.

"Well, Fern," Pappo answered thoughtfully, "Actually, I don't think he knew where he was, or that we were trying to help him. I was just hoping...." Pappo's voice trailed away. His eyes turned to Mumma's, full of unspoken worries.

Mumma's voice was firm and sure. "He'll remember us, Needles. And he'll help us. Leaf will bring him here, I'm sure of it."

"Yes, Ivy," Pappo agreed, although he sounded less convinced, "maybe that chomper will remember us after all."

CHAPTER TWENTY

GRASSLANDS

Speckles stretched up on tiptoe as Feather balanced on his head once more. The grass grew so tall in the middle of the valley that Feather could no longer see which way to go.

"Speckles stand up taller," whispered Feather. The chippie stretched onto the very tips of his toes. His tail struck straight out like a prickly quilla's, and his arms spun in circles at his side in a desperate attempt to keep his balance while he lifted Feather just a little higher so she could see above the grass tips.

Ever wary, Rustle and Claws crouched on one side of Speckles. Nervously Leaf and Whisper squatted low on the other side. They peered in opposite directions into the thick grass. Leaf and Rustle held their savers across their chests, ready for danger. All waited for Feather to decide which way to go.

Ever since the horrible screecher attack, Leaf noticed they had moved into grass that grew much taller than along the valley's edge. Now Feather could not see above the tips at all. Leaf had the sinking feeling that they had crossed their own trail again and again. As he watched Feather stretch on tiptoe, search left and right, to the left, and then back right again, he was sure of it. They were lost!

With a disappointed sigh, Feather slid from Speckles' head, over his shoulders, and stood beside him with one arm draped over his neck, completely discouraged.

Far above them the moon slid through an ever brightening sky. Its midnight luster faded with the rising sun. To the east, pale pink and orange streaks wandered about in confusion.

Distracted and worried, Feather kissed and patted Speckles while she considered how she might find the way through the towering grass.

Claws sniffed Rustle's sloppy, leafy hair. He was hungry. With a quick, sneaky bite, he ripped off a coppery leaf, and hopped off to enjoy the treat. Rustle scowled and rubbed his head.

Grateful for her calm and patient nature, Leaf hugged Whisper as she daintily nibbled one tiny, new leaf sprouting from his ear.

They all stood silent, and wondered what to do next. The tips of the grass swayed above their heads in the morning breeze.

Unexpectedly, Rustle looked up, excited. "The breeze!" he said urgently. He waved his hand above his head. "The dawn breeze blows away from Echo Peak. We need to go that way!" He pointed in the opposite direction that the grass tips were bending. "We must ride into the breeze!"

"Right!" exclaimed Feather. "Let's go!"

At once they hopped on the chippies and plunged into the grass. They zigzagged among the popper burrows, urging the chippies to cross the valley before the poppers greeted the day. After a long jog Feather slowed to a brisk walk to rest the chippies. She yanked out her curly feather from her headband and, once again, balanced atop Speckles' head. She stuck the feather up as high as she could reach. It fluffed up and blew briskly in the light wind. With a satisfied smirk, she slipped back down onto Speckles' shoulders.

"The breeze is blowing stronger. We must be closer to the forest," she whispered over her shoulder to Leaf. He whispered the good news back to Rustle, who nodded silently.

At that very moment, Speckles burst into a loud, chatter. He braked to a stiff-legged stop, nearly tossing Feather over his head. Surprised and unprepared for the jolt, Feather smashed her face into Speckles' neck, flipped off his shoulders, spun around upside down, and hung there, staring at his toes.

Whisper tried desperately to stop, but instead slammed sideways into Speckles. Leaf flew up, and then plopped hard in the dirt—his feet in the air, and his legs tangled up in Whisper's braided leash. Nose to nose, Whisper and Leaf stared at each other in astonishment.

Prepared for the unexpected as usual, Claws reacted in just enough time to leap right onto Whisper's rump, but Rustle was caught by surprise. He somersaulted over Claws' ears, into the tall grass, and disappeared. Claws immediately panicked. He rolled off of Whisper, slammed against the ground, and promptly tucked himself into a quivering ball.

"What's wrong, Speckles?" Feather's voice trailed away.

A light footfall caught her attention.

Still hanging upside-down, she looked around. Feather gazed into the soft blue eyes of a tiny swift fox kit. It appeared just as confused as Feather. Instantly relieved, Feather chuckled and dropped from Speckles' neck to the smashed grass. She held out her palm in greeting, "Hi, sweet kit! What'cha doin'?"

Leaf untangled his legs from Whisper's braid. Laughing with delight, he knelt beside Feather, "Allo, you teeny thing. What are you doing wandering around out here by yourself?"

The fox kit took a startled step backwards, and froze with one paw lifted above the grass. The kit's muzzle had two dark patches on each side, and its coat was so fuzzy the fading moonlight cast a glow through its fluffy fur. Since it already looked so much like a cat, Feather and Leaf half-expected it to mew. Instead the kit's curiosity gave way to a surprising bravado. It wrinkled its tiny nose and muzzle into a puffy snarl. Its eyes squinted menacingly. Its oversized, pointed ears leaned forward, stiff and threatening, which threw the kit off balance.

The fox kit's hair bristled out like a bobcat's. And like a cat, it had already decided that the Twigs were more play than prey.

But before the kit could twitch its whiskers, there was a swish of rustling blades. The swift fox kit's mum emerged from the grass. With a startled expression she stepped protectively over her kit. With one paw she shoved the kit further under her belly. Then she lowered her head, curled her lips above her fangs, and growled wickedly. Her tail flicked a warning. Her eyes burned in fury!

Horrified, Feather, Speckles, Leaf, and Whisper pressed together in a ball of Twigs and chippies. In their midst, Claws ducked his head under his hands, and trembled in fear.

The fox mum hesitated. Three plump chipmunks lay in a tangled clump right before her. Prey had been scarce in the parched grasslands. Because she was so small, her prey had to be even smaller. She often stalked bobos and even crawlies when she was desperate for food, but now an unexpected, fat meal lay crumpled right before her. She grinned, licked her lips, and opened her mouth wide to suck in the sweet scent of the chippies. With a brisk scoop of her paw, the fox mum shoved her kit out from between her legs. *Such perfect prey for my kit to practice hunting!*

Aghast, Leaf and Feather instinctively threw their arms out wide to defend Speckles, Whisper, and Claws even though the tiny kit was no larger than a fluffy duckling.

Excited by the game, the fox kit crouched, bunched up its back legs, dug its teeny claws into the grass, and readied itself to pounce!

All of a sudden a chilling shriek burst out over their heads!

The leaves on Leaf's head curled in horror! Feather covered her ears with clenched fists, shrank onto the ground, and yanked Leaf down beside her! Speckles and Whisper jumped on top of Claws, and they shivered together in one speckled bundle! Claws moaned, terror-stricken, from beneath the chippie pile!

The wild scream sounded as if a crazed badger had claimed its prey!

Stunned, the fox mum scanned the grass around her for the badger that was staking its claim on the chip-munks. The grass rustled nearby.

A blood-curdling snarl warned the fox once more to back off!

With painfully slow steps, the fox mum moved backwards. She never took her eyes off of the spot where the grass had rustled. Knowing enough not to fight with a badger over food, the swift fox mum quickly seized its kit by the scruff of its neck, whirled around, and dashed into the popper field.

Rustle stepped out from where the grass had rustled, and the scream of the badger had burst out. "Whew!" Rustle exhaled and laughed. "Leaf, Feather, get up. It's just me!" He reached down and pulled Feather and Leaf to their feet. "It was me!" he reassured them again. He patted Speckles and Whisper. Then he nudged Claws with his foot. "Get up!"

Feather's eyes flew open wide with surprise. She threw her arms around Rustle and hugged him tight. "That was great!" she exclaimed. The swan feather that was stuck in her headband fell over his eyes.

Bewildered and embarrassed, a crooked grin crept across Rustle's face. He blew puffs at the feather to keep it from tickling his nose.

"Excellent!" cried Leaf. "Can you teach me to scream like that? That was terrific!"

"Uh, sure, no problem" Rustle stammered as he disentangled himself from Feather. He looked sideways at her, and then at his toes.

Feather clapped her hands. "Yes, that was excellent!" Leaf joined in her applause.

Excited by the commotion, Whisper and Speckles hopped around the Twigs on stiff legs. They bristled out their tails, and jerked them back and forth to warn any beasts, which might still be lurking in the grass, that two very scary chippies were on alert. Claws grew dizzy watching Speckles and Whisper bounce. He fell over backwards.

Gently Feather sat Claws up, and kissed him right between his eyes. She patted the air to calm down Speckles and Whisper. Her slender hands waved back and forth in the air like butterfly wings. At last, the chipmunks settled down, and pressed their noses to Feather's palms. She stroked their necks and murmured in their fuzzy ears. With skilled hands, Feather adjusted the chippies' braids to hang properly.

"Are the chippies all right?" asked Leaf, especially worried for Claws.

"Well," Feather replied, "They are tired and hungry, just like us. But they'll make it to the edge of the forest. Then we must all rest and eat. Hopefully there will be shelter there, and maybe we can find some food."

"Don't worry, Feather," Rustle said with a confident, light-hearted air, "there will be a safe place to rest and plenty of food too. Come on, now. The day isn't flowing any slower! Let's go!" For some odd reason, he gave Claws a quick hug before he leapt onto his back. Too weary to protest, Claws hopped sideways with a half-hearted buck. Then unexpectedly, he sat down. Rustle patted Claws' neck and muttered something that sounded strangely like encouragement.

Feeling like an expert chippie rider, Leaf jumped on Whisper. He urged her to follow Feather and Speckles who had already disappeared into the tall grass.

Together, facing into the early morning breeze once again, they all headed off toward Echo Peak.

"Come on, then," Feather's voice drifted back, "the wind isn't blowing any slower!"

CHAPTER TWENTY-ONE

A DESPERATE DROP

The pale, merciless, full moon disappeared over the edge of the canyon. The sky grew light blue, and wavered through the thick mist of the powerful waterfall. With the coming daylight, the sheer walls of the canyon revealed their colors. There were wide bands of burnt orange bordering sparkling shades of grays. Crooked greens lay atop thin purples, and wandered in broad stripes up, and then down, and then up again. The colors were squeezed together from seasons long before the ice dam froze. It was the mighty glacier itself that had carved the canyon, and exposed its colors. But now, melted by a warmer world, the glacier retreated far up

Thunder Peak. It left the ice dam to block the lake. But then, seemingly in spite, it burst the dam.

The beavers gazed up at a glistening rainbow arching through the billowing mist. They shivered from cold and fear. Pressed together for warmth on the great granite slab, they watched in hopeless fascination as the endless flow of water plunged over the cliff.

Slapper and Patty tried to calm their frightened daughters. Patty licked their wet fur to warm them while Slapper grunted softly. Bravely, Birchbite and Clacker had sat up all night to guard against the river. Finally, they lowered themselves onto their hands, and leaned against Splash and Splatter, who gratefully nuzzled them.

Once again, as he had done many times during the night, Slapper searched the river upstream. If only they were strong enough to swim against the current they could make it to a ledge or a crevice. Once there, they could find a trail—a way up out of the canyon. But he dared not risk it. He glanced at his daughters, and caught Patty's cautious glance. His mate and daughters did not have his strength. Slapper searched again anyway.

What was that? Slapper sat up. His back became rigid. He blinked. Did he just see what he thought he saw? He snorted the mist from before his eyes, stood as high as he dared, and stared upriver. Alerted, Patty, Birchbite, Splash, Clacker, and Splatter stood straight up beside him. All of them saw it, too!

Tree branches! Enormous tree branches poked up above the river's surface. Clumps of soggy cedar fronds waved to the beavers, and leisurely spun around in a circle.

In a clatter of excited chatter, Patty, Splash, and Splatter looked back and forth from Slapper to the floating tree. Birchbite and Clacker simply tilted up their chins and looked intently at Slapper, waiting for his command.

Slapper studied the tree's oncoming branches with keen precision. At the same moment, he recognized the crooked yellow cedar—the same tree from which they dropped into the river the evening before. The cedar's roots had surrendered to the weight of its top-heavy, slanted trunk. At last, it had fallen into the river, and now drifted waterlogged, but still floating.

As the tree caught the mighty waterfall's tug, it picked up speed. It bounced up violently, riding high on the rapids' white tips. The huge tree was thrust along by the powerful current of the falls. It floated directly toward the slab in the middle of the river—and them!

At once, Slapper bit the air with a hammering, loud *CLACK*! They must do as he orders, and they must do it quickly if they were to survive. Slapper nudged the beavers to the very edge of the waterline. They crouched on the granite slab just where the river split into two. They waited—poised to leap to the heavy, slippery trunk rushing right at them.

The tree spun closer, faster, and then with sudden, breathtaking speed was sucked into the waterfall's grip. Its topmost fronds drooped in a tangled, matted mass. Its lower branches were splintered and poked above the water like quills of porcupines. The spear-like limbs threatened to stab the beavers, and the matted fronds to strangle them.

The beavers flattened their tails on the rock, hoping to gain more power to leap high and far in the thin, cold air.

For one heart-stopping moment, the log spun away from the slab, but just as quick it whirled back. It floated nearer, on the fast current that ran alongside the slab.

Slapper whistled one urgent blast, and at once the beavers jumped onto the yellow cedar. They scratched and clawed their way through the branches to reach the thick trunk. The tree's topmost limbs slammed onto the slab, and with a great lurch, it slid up and over the rock. The tree was pushed relentlessly up onto the slab by the power of the water until half of it jutted out over the waterfall. It lay stuck there, dipping up and down— half of it on the rock, half over the falls. Unbalanced, it teetered like a see-saw over the cliff.

Gripping the slippery bark with teeth and claws, Slapper crawled to the knothole. With a piercing whistle, he commanded Splash, Splatter, Birchbite, and Clacker to dive into the hollow trunk. One by one they dove through the knothole.

But where's Patty? Slapper desperately searched for his mate. Then he spotted her! Patty was clinging to a drooping limb that stretched out over the falls! She clutched the bark with her claws, and stared at Slapper. Hopelessness filled her eyes.

In a heartbeat, Slapper raced along the trunk until he was parallel to Patty's branch. Willing great strength into his crooked legs, he launched himself through the air, and landed on the branch nearest Patty. In one motion he reached out, caught her neck with his teeth, and yanked her to him just as her claws lost their grip on the limb. With incredible strength he pulled her all the way back to the knothole. Furiously he shoved her swollen body through the knothole. He stuffed her deep into the hollow trunk where Splash, Splatter, Birchbite, and Clacker huddled together. There was just enough room left in the trunk for Slapper, but it was too late!

The tree slipped and lost its balance on the slab. Its topmost branches suddenly dipped down at a sickening angle. Its roots burst up high out of the water!

Horrified, Slapper gripped the bark, unable to dive into the hollow trunk. He clutched desperately as the yellow cedar slid over the edge of the cliff. He heard terrified clacking and shrill whistling from inside the hollow trunk. Patty pleaded for him to dive through the knothole, but Slapper knew he dared not let go, or he would fall into the blast of the falls.

The tree was sucked into a white, crashing chaos! Slapper held on!

All that could be seen of the goliath leader as he disappeared into the white spray was his huge, flat tail. He had slapped it over the knothole to protect the others stuffed inside. It was a desperate attempt to keep them alive!

CHAPTER TWENTY-TWO

SKULLFACES!

D*on't move,* Leaf told himself in his dream. *Stay asleep.* But his empty belly rumbled again like stones tumbling down a hill. At the sound, Rustle stirred in his sleep. Leaf opened his eyes. Now fully awake, he propped himself up on one elbow. He peered through the filtered light of hanging moss to the woods beyond.

At dawn's light, the band of Twigs and chippies reached the edge of the South Forest. Sleepy and exhausted, they had stumbled into the roots of a huge cappynut tree, dropped onto the moss, and fallen into a deep slumber.

Beyond the tree's roots, and not very far away, the chipmunks scurried busily among tiny, blue periwinkles that twinkled in the morning sun. Speckles, Whisper, and Claws scooped up scattered nuts and sweet huckleberries as fast as they could stuff them in their mouths. Their fuzzy cheeks were so full the chippies nearly toppled over. One by one they scurried over to a heap of rocks, and popped in and out of the cracks. It was a futile attempt to hide their treasures from each other. Every once in a while, in a fit of greed, they bounced stiff-legged at each other, and burst into angry chatters if another came too close to their stockpile.

Silly chippies, Leaf laughed quietly, *there's plenty of food in the forest!* At last Leaf crawled from the roots, stiff and bruised. He stretched in the warm sun—yawning as loud as a hoot owl's call. Suddenly, Feather appeared beside him, and yawned a huge yawn that sounded a lot like the crazy call of a loon. It startled him so much he jumped.

"Oh, it's only you!" Leaf said, relieved.

"Good morning, Leaf." Feather grinned. "Do you have anything to eat? I'm starving!" She stared at the berries the chipmunks were spitting into their secret, rocky holes. Casting defensive glares at the Twigs, the chippies tried to guard their berries, and at the same time stuff their cheeks with fallen pine cone seeds.

"Sure," he replied. He pulled out a crushed berrycake from the pocket on his strap. "Uh, I'm afraid I fell on it . . . many times."

Feather stared bleakly at the smashed, day-old berrycake, and considered whether or not she was really that hungry.

"I'll take one!" announced Rustle from behind them. Immediately he reached over Leaf's shoulder to grab it. With a quick flick of her fingers, Feather knocked his hand aside.

"Wait," Feather commanded. "I have an idea." In the next moment, she studied the ground as she circled the moss-drenched cappynut tree under which they stood.

Since Feather seemed preoccupied, Rustle rolled his eyes at Leaf, snatched the mashed berrycake from his hand, and shoved it in his mouth before Feather could turn and see him do it.

"Here," Feather declared. She reached into a patch of green grass. "This will do." She lifted up an old, hollow cappynut shell. It had lost its cap and was splintered on its top edge. "Look," she exclaimed, pleased, "it even has a handle!"

Leaf and Rustle exchanged glances, wondering if the other thought that Feather was truly weird, too. They shrugged.

Feather rinsed out the shell with some water from Leaf's cappynut shell and hooked the handle over her belt. Then she whistled a low signal to Speckles, Claws, and Whisper. They stopped grazing, and quickly stashed the rest of their treasure in the rocks. Then they sat and stared at Feather, their ears rigid and alert. She lifted one finger to her lips to hush them, and with her other hand pointed up at a tree limb high above her head. The chippies looked up. Fat, fuzzy, black and yellow striped bees hummed in the rays of sun. They zigzagged back and forth attending to a large beehive.

"Honeybuzzers!" she whispered.

Rustle and Leaf stared at her, astonished. Stealing honey was never a good idea. Honeybuzzers guarded their beehive fiercely. They could be aggressive and dangerous when defending their honey.

But without any hesitation, the chipmunks set to work. They scampered all over the meadow and bit off fluffy, white tips of dandelions. They filled their cheeks so full with the feathery stems they could barely see beyond their whiskers.

Feather scrambled up the cappynut tree and out onto the same limb where the beehive hung. The entire way, she skillfully hid amid the leaves and clusters of cappynuts. Feather crept more slowly as she crawled closer to the hive. The bees busied themselves with their work, completely unaware a honey thief lurked nearby.

Claws, Whisper, and Speckles climbed further up the trunk, and onto a limb just above the large beehive.

Worried and bemused, Rustle and Leaf watched the chippies crouch on the branch as if ready to leap into the air.

Then Feather's fingers appeared from a bunch of leaves, and with a brisk *POP!* snapped!

At the signal an explosion of shimmering dandelion fluff was spit out by the chippies. The shiny puffs shivered and glittered in the sunlight as they swirled on a light breeze around the beehive.

At first the honeybuzzer guards hovered in confusion, but then they attacked the fluff! With an enraged *HMMMRRMM!* they dove at the puffs with such fury the beehive was left completely unguarded!

With a flash of her sparkly slicer, Feather sliced through the hive, and yanked out a large comb dripping with honey. She shoved it into the cappynut shell she had hooked onto her belt. Swiftly she dropped from limb to limb, followed closely by Speckles, Whisper, and Claws. Above her, the bee guards continued to attack the dandelion fluff with vicious rage.

"Amazing!" cried Rustle. "Perfect!"

"That was great!" praised Leaf.

Feather grinned. "Thank you, thank you. All I needed was the courage of chippies!" She licked her honey-covered fingers. "Now, gather some of those blossoms over there, and we'll have honeysuckle juice and a honey feast!"

Rustle and Leaf grinned with delight as they rushed off to collect the blossoms. Soon the honeycomb was broken up, and a sticky piece given to each chippie and Twig.

Rustle tried to shove a huge piece of his honeycomb in his mouth at once, but ended up dribbling the honey all over his face in the process.

Claws was so excited he tried to gulp his piece all at once, but it stuck in his throat. His eyes bulged out and his nose turned white.

Alarmed, Rustle slapped the chippie's back until Claws gulped and sucked in a huge breath of air. Rustle broke off a tiny piece of his own honey comb. "Here, you nutty chippie," he soothed Claws. "Only eat a little bit at a time."

Claws daintily nibbled the piece for just a moment. Then overcome with excitement again, he shoved Rustle to the grass, sat on top of him, and licked his face clean of honey. Rustle chuckled and tried to dodge Claws' tiny, pink tongue.

Feather and Leaf glanced at each other and exchanged smiles. Rustle's tenderness for the weird chippie didn't really surprise them. Rustle was a little odd himself.

Finally Rustle was able to push the chippie off of his chest. With one hand he held Claws at arms length and with the other hand offered a tiny piece of honeycomb. When Claws was finished with that one, Rustle gave him another.

The honeysuckle blossoms were soon sucked dry. Honey still stuck to the Twigs' cheeks and fingers, but they felt too lazy to wash it off. They all lounged on the moss below the cappynut tree, rested and full.

Suddenly Leaf felt very uneasy. "What's that?" he asked. He tilted his head and frowned as he listened. A loud, heavy buzz moved toward the clearing. "Watch out!" he cried, "a skullface!"

In a low, urgent voice Rustle murmured, "It's after the honeysuckle!" He motioned to the blossoms scattered on the ground around them. "There's more skullfaces over there!" Rustle crouched down. He pointed to a pair of poisonous, white-face hornets hovering above the honeysuckle vine. "Stay still! Don't let them see you!"

The clearing filled with a swarm of skullfaces. Hornets inspected the rock pile where the chippies had hidden their sweet berries. Their dark eyes peered from behind a creepy, white, skull-like mask. The hornets' stingers dripped an evil poison, ready to stab a victim over and over. Their legs hung heavily from their black bodies as they searched the small meadow. Actually it was the honeybee hive that had drawn them here. For white-faced hornets killed buzzers, and fed their plump bodies to young skullfaces waiting back at their nest.

"Quick! Wash off the honeysuckle juice!" whispered Feather urgently.

Speckles, Claws, and Whisper sat wide-eyed beside her, frozen in fear, their cheeks smeared with honey.

"Oh, no," Feather moaned, "the chippies smell sweet!" She grabbed Rustle's water shell and splashed the last of the water all over the chippies' faces. But the water only made the dribbles of honey sparkle in the sun. More fearful for her dear friends than herself, she clapped her hands and whistled sharply. With a swish of stiff tails, they bolted. Becoming a fast, freckled blur of chippies, they disappeared into the forest.

"Great," Rustle groaned, and rolled his eyes, "let's hope the skullfaces didn't see *that!*" He tried to lick the honeysuckle nectar from his fingers, but it was too sticky.

Cautiously the Twigs stepped backwards until they could hide in the tree roots.

A couple of the skullfaces flew up and inspected the honeybees' hive. But the fearless honeybuzzers swarmed in a dark mass—a frenzy of fat, golden globs with stingers, which for the moment, drove the skullfaces away. The frustrated hornets searched for an easier hive to attack. They hovered over the cappynut shell that Feather had dipped in the honey hive, but it had been licked clean. Only the scent remained. More and more hornets collected under the lowest branches near where Feather, Rustle, and Leaf hid in the roots. The Twigs smelled very attractive to them.

Leaf moved his hand slowly to grab his saver from his strap's back loop.

"No," whispered Feather, "if you anger them we won't have any chance at all!"

Rustle nodded his agreement nervously.

Leaf tugged his saver free anyway, and frowned at Rustle's warning wave. In painfully slow motion, Leaf stepped out from the roots into the sunlight, and jammed the saver into the dirt between his feet. He slanted the tall stick back and forth until the gemstone, which was tied in a knothole at the top, caught a single ray of sun. As soon as the light struck the stone, it flashed and burned into a nearby tree trunk. At once the bark smoldered. Leaf aimed the scorching beam at a clump of dead leaves near his toes.

Instantly Rustle realized Leaf's plan. He crawled on his hands and knees from the roots to gather dry sticks and grass. Rustle piled the debris on the leaves already being scorched.

Soon a long, wavering wisp of white smoke curled up from the pile. Next, flickers of blue and yellow flames danced brightly. Then the tiny flames burst from under the leaves into a startling hot fire.

Leaf knelt to steady the saver.

Rustle quickly tossed a strip of damp moss over the flames. At once, a smoky haze drifted over his feet, and began to rise around them.

Diligently, Rustle continued to feed the fire, and at the same time coax the smoke from the moss. Leaf concentrated on keeping the hot sunbeam aimed at the heap. Feather crawled closer to Leaf, and gently blew on the flames to make them burn hotter.

Soon the smoke lay over the clearing like a milky-white fog. It curled up into higher and higher waves until a thick pool of choking smoke swirled above Leaf's head. Rustle, Leaf, and Feather held blossoms over their faces, and blinked back tears.

Confused by the smoke, some skullfaces became tangled in branches, and others flew straight into tree trunks. Bewildered and smothered by the suffocating fog, some bounced off each other. Others crashed into the rock pile, and crawled helplessly around. Finally the skullface leader signaled its deadly swarm to turn back into the forest. Bruised and confused, they zigzagged sluggishly away.

Rustle tried to stomp out the smoldering pile of leaves and moss while Leaf and Feather coughed and waved their arms around until the smoke melted into the blue sky.

"Slimerspit!" Feather exclaimed to Leaf in admiration. "How'd you do that?"

Leaf shrugged as if it were nothing at all. "Oh, all Twigs know how to do that. They just use their saver stones!" said Leaf proudly.

"Oh," murmured Feather. Strangely, she looked away as if she were ashamed of something. She kicked a tuft of grass, crossed her arms, and muttered under her breath, "Well, *I'm* a Twig, and *I* don't know how."

Right away Leaf knew he had said something wrong but he didn't know what. He looked at Rustle for help, but Rustle only glared at him. Feeling very uncomfortable, Leaf decided he'd be better off whacking the still smoldering piles of leaves than facing either of them again. So he beat the pile with strips of moss.

With surprising gentleness, Rustle tugged at Feather's arm to get her attention. "Of course you don't know how," he said cheerfully, "you don't have a saver! But that's no problem," Rustle patted his chest. "I'll make you one!"

Feather looked at him hopefully.

Happy he had her attention, Rustle chattered on, "I'll make one for you as soon as we get to the Old Seeder. There's some excellent wood there. I prefer ashwood or cappynut myself, but you can choose what you like. And I'll get the most perfect creek stone to stick in the top, too! Now let me think where to find it." Rustle sauntered away, his voice sinking into mutters as he discussed the complex subject with himself.

Feather looked questioningly at Leaf who rolled his eyes and shrugged.

Rustle spotted a small, blue butterfly on a tall, purple-colored flower. He leaned over and absent-mindedly spoke seriously to it while it fluttered around his nose. As if sorting out his thoughts, he mumbled louder, "Let's see, now. Feather's stone should be a bright, pretty, rosy shade like the color of her eyes, eh?"

The butterfly settled on a white aster to listen. Slowly it closed and opened its wings.

"And it must be really sparkling, too, eh? It has to sparkle a lot just like her eyes do when she laughs." Rustle sensed a light step behind him. He froze, and then whirled around to see if he'd been heard. His eyes locked on Feather's warm gaze.

Hesitantly, Feather stepped up to Rustle, blinked her pretty, rosy-colored eyes sweetly at him, and murmured, "Thanks." Her smile sparkled, just like Rustle said.

Embarrassed beyond belief, Rustle stumbled backwards, tripped over a pine cone, lost his balance, and abruptly sat down. He nearly squashed the blue butterfly, which fluttered panic-stricken into a stalk of goldenrod. Now covered with gold pollen, it zigzagged over the blue periwinkles, seeking refuge somewhere in the meadow.

Ignoring Feather, Rustle jumped up and walked stiffly to where Leaf was trying to ignore them both and smother the fire with moss. Rustle stomped on the wispy strands of smoke with his bare foot, forgetting that underneath the moss the cinders were hot. Now in pain, he stifled his cries and hopped around until his foot cooled down. After that, he walked to the edge of the meadow and simply stared at the treetops.

Leaf and Feather grinned at one another. Silently they gathered water in the cappynut shells from a nearby creek. Feather whistled for the chippies. Speckles, Whisper, and Claws bounded cheerfully from the forest. She adjusted their braided leashes, and gave them all kisses and hugs.

When Rustle walked back through the meadow, Leaf and Feather noticed at once that he had grown serious. His expression was odd and worried.

Rustle asked Feather, "Can the chippies carry us again? All day?"

"I'll see," she answered right away. Feather walked to Speckles, stroked his cheek, and spoke softly in his ear. Then she nodded her head as if to encourage him.

Leaf thought, *if Speckles is willing, Whisper and Claws will be too.*

Rustle and Leaf watched anxiously.

Feather turned and smiled.

Whisper, Speckles, and Claws merrily chattered their teeth, waved their hands, and clicked their bright, pink tongues.

"They're ready to go!" Feather called out. "Come on!"

Leaf ran to Whisper, gave her a brief, secret kiss on her cheek, and jumped on her back. Rustle walked over to Claws, patted him between his eyes, and swung his leg over the chippie's back confidently. Feather leapt lightly onto Speckles' shoulders and leaned down to pet the swirling fur along his neck.

"Do you know where we are?" Leaf asked Rustle, wondering if they were lost.

"Oh, I haven't been in this part of the forest before, that's all," Rustle answered casually. "But don't worry, Leaf. We just need to climb up through the Sharp Peaks and take the crest trail. I didn't figure on climbing all the way to the crest, but it'll be a sure trek from then on, eh?" Rustle realized at once that Leaf felt discouraged, so he added, "I'll bet we'll see the Old Seeder by night fall! Come on, now. The day isn't flowing any slower!"

"Right," Leaf said quietly. He had hoped that they were closer to his home. Worried about his family, he stared up at the Sharp Peaks. Their dark cliffs hid the canyon—and the violent Rushing Waters.

Feather sensed Leaf's disappointment, and added, "That's right, Leaf! The sun's not shining any brighter!"

In spite of his pessimistic mood, Leaf could not help but grin. Feather always twisted his family's old saying into her own words.

Taking the lead, Rustle made a quick check of his companions. He nodded. "To the crest then, eh?" Without another word, he led them into the foothills of the Sharp Peaks.

The straight, towering fir trees, drooping hemlock branches, and thick, heavy fronds of the cedar trees overwhelmed Feather. She had never seen or imagined such huge, mammoth trees existed. In awe, she gazed up until she grew dizzy.

Before long, they plunged into the darkest part of the forest. Even the highest tips of the Sharp Peaks were now hidden from view. Thickly shrouded limbs stretched out to interweave their fronds, leaves, and needles. A deep green pallor was cast upon the forest floor. The Twigs and chipmunks were nearly invisible. They faded perfectly into the flickering shadows below the ancient trees.

Yet as they passed a barren blackberry thicket, an old rabbit mum urgently thumped the earth in warning.

Startled, Whisper jumped sideways.

As he calmed Whisper's fearful, jerky steps, Leaf wondered about Rustle's strange expression in the meadow. *What was he worried about?*

CHAPTER TWENTY-THREE

DANGER ON THE CREST

All morning the narrow trail led them up. The dark forest now lay far below. The Twigs trudged in front of the chippies—leading them by their golden braids. All stumbled on the steep, rock-strewn slopes of the ridge.

Only haphazard stands of grizzled whitebark pine trees grew here. In contrast to their weirdly twisted, misshapen bark, their cone clusters scented the thin air with a sweet fragrance. All around the white trees, gray-feathered nutcrackers floated down from the sky on white-tipped wings. With sharp, black beaks they wrenched open the purple cones, stuffed the nutty seeds in their throats, and zigzagged back to their secret hiding places. Skillfully they buried the seeds deep in the earth. At once, they flew off to harvest more.

Speckles, Whisper, and Claws slipped on the loose gravel, and watched the skies uneasily. There were few trees where chippies could hide. Above, there was too much sky. Too much blue emptiness stretched over them in every direction. It was creepy and threatening.

A lazy red-tailed hawk circled so high it looked like a winged speck. Yet it saw everything. Coldly, it calculated whether or not to attack these oddly-shaped shadows plodding uphill. Their silhouettes were neither creature nor tree. The meshed movements of the Twigs and chipmunks did not look like prey, so after a while the hawk tilted its wings, and spiraled away.

Rustle slowed their exhausting uphill march as they neared the crest. The sun burned hot. He dropped Claws' braid, and it dragged between the chippie's paws. Rustle paced back and forth nervously across the slope of the mountain as if worried about an attack. But rather than watch the sky, he peered into the shadows between the boulders. After a while he paused in the shade of a huge, gray slab that jutted out from the cliff. He stared at the crevice at its base, and then motioned to the others to join him there. Still, Rustle did not relax his guard. He began to pace once more.

Feather and Leaf glanced at each other as they watched Rustle grow more anxious. They also felt uneasy, but they didn't know why. And Rustle just ignored them. Yet they all needed to rest, and the shade looked cool. It was so hot Leaf felt shriveled and brittle. The giant slab looked familiar, but he was too tired to think about it.

With an unusually strained voice, Rustle told them, "This is a good spot to rest for a while." Although he sounded doubtful that it truly was.

Feather and Leaf gratefully plopped down beneath the slab. The uphill hike had been difficult. The trail traversed the ridge for the most part, but sometimes they had to hike straight up. It was then they would slip on loose gravel, slide backwards, and bump into each other.

Speckles, Claws, and Whisper scratched the dry dirt, searching for seeds or juicy shoots of grass. They often glanced up, nervous, distracted, and worried about danger that might dive at them from the sky. Whisper found a stash of dark, nutty seeds. She chirped for the other two chippies to join her in her feast.

But danger did not always come from the sky. In the cool earth, deep below the boulder where the Twigs rested, two gray rattlesnakes lay asleep in their den. Their diamonds on their scales meshed into one pattern as the snakes pressed together. The rattlers had felt the movements above through vibrations in the earth. The warm scent of chipmunks slipped unexpectedly into their den. At once awake and excited, their pink, forked tongues licked and smelled the air. They uncurled their long, thick bodies, and crawled over one another toward a winding tunnel that led to a thin crack below the huge, granite slab above. Still too cold to move fast, the rattlers slid slowly through the dark.

Feather and Leaf lounged beneath the slab in the cool shade. Rustle stood guard nearby. Gratefully, they all quenched their thirst. Feather set a cappynut shell full of water on the ground for the chipmunks. Speckles, Whisper, and Claws had stuffed their bellies with seeds, and now searched among jagged rocks for more treats.

Leaf leaned back against a narrow crack at the base of the boulder. "Hey, this place looks familiar," puzzled Leaf. "Isn't this where I found you, Rustle?"

Rustle looked down the slope and spotted the white-bark pine where he had tried to leap on the nutcracker and fly away. "You're right, Leaf!" he answered. "I heard your whistle..."

The next instant teeny, fluttering wings and a glowing body flittered and hovered in front of Leaf's face. *BRMMMMR! BRMMMMR!* pulsed around his ears.

"Hey, look here," Leaf called out happily. "It's the little hummer who followed me from the forest when I left to find you, Rustle!"

"Well, that's lucky, eh! Leaf has a hummer!" declared Rustle.

"Really?" asked Feather, "His own hummer? That is lucky! So then, what's her name?" she wondered.

"Pester, if you ask me, eh," retorted Rustle.

"Of course that isn't her name!" Feather said reproachfully. "Leaf probably gave her a wonderful name! I'll bet her name is Shine or Shimmer or something like that, right Leaf?"

"Uh, right," mumbled Leaf as he batted at the hummer. "It's Shimmer."

"See, I told you!" laughed Feather.

Rustle and Feather grinned as they watched the teeny bird dart back and forth. It fluttered in and out of Leaf's bright-green, leafy hair, and poked its sharp beak in his ear. Then it whipped its wings at his eyes all the time humming a loud *BRMMMMR! BRMMMMR!*

Leaf ducked, and waved it away. "What'cha doing?" he asked, confused.

"I think she's trying to tell you something!" Feather giggled. "What'cha want, Shimmer?"

The hummingbird pecked at Leaf's nose, flew away, but then rushed back. It pecked his nose again, fluttered up a short distance, and then dove at Leaf's head as if it were stabbing a nectar-filled blossom. Suddenly it stretched its wings out wide to halt its dive in midair. It hovered directly in front of Leaf's nose, and peered intently into his eyes.

A slithering shadow moved in the dark crevice behind Leaf's back.

As if desperate to tell Leaf something, Shimmer finally perched on Leaf's nose and jabbed him right between his eyes.

"Watch it!" cried Leaf. He batted Shimmer away, but the hummingbird refused to leave. Disgusted and irritated, Leaf stood up to defend himself better. He took a step away from the crack behind him.

The first rattlesnake silently glided out from the crevice into the bright sun. It narrowed its golden eyes into a slit, and rose up to balance its flat head on a legless body. The rattler paused to gather the hot rays just behind Leaf. A moment later, the second rattlesnake slithered out, and lay flat. It stretched its scaly belly over the hot rocks to warm itself.

"Watch it!" shouted Rustle. "Rockcrawlers!"

Shimmer zigzagged away, panicked.

A chilling *Rsssttt! Rssssttt! Rsssttt!* erupted! The snakes curled into defensive coils. Their rattling tails whirred an evil *Rssstttt! Rssstttt!*

Before Leaf could catch his breath, Rustle yanked him away from the snakes. At the same moment, he grabbed Feather's arm and dragged her across the dirt toward a large rock. He crouched behind the boulder, and forced Leaf and Feather to duck down, too.

Horrified, Feather screamed a warning to the chippies, "Run! Run!"

Speckles and Claws looked up. At once they bolted downhill and jumped into a crooked pine tree.

Whisper leapt away but was brutally yanked back onto the ground. Her braided leash, which had hung loosely from her neck, snagged on a jagged rock. It trapped her with a tight and tangled noose around her neck! Whisper tried to run, but the leash yanked her back to the ground. Desperately she kicked at the deadly knot with her back legs, but it only choked her more violently. She was trapped!

Immediately, the rockcrawlers slithered near the terrified chippie—one on each side. They sat swaying their heads in unison as if they were sharing a wicked chuckle together. The rattlers looked away only to hiss and spit at the Twigs, warning them to stay back. *Rssssttt! Sssssppptt!* They gazed greedily at Whisper. *So easy a prey! So easy to kill! Rsssssttt!* She struggled helplessly before them.

Speckles realized Whisper could not free herself. In one heartbeat, he sprang from the tree, raced to her side, and threw himself between Whisper and rattlers.

In his haste to follow Speckles, Claws somersaulted off the branch, and slid clumsily over the loose gravel. He reached Whisper a moment later and braced his shoulder against Speckles. Bravely, the chippies pressed their bodies together to form a shield for Whisper. Claws scratched the air furiously with his tiny claws, clattered his teeth, and shrieked angrily.

Terrified into weakness, Whisper no longer had the strength to fight her leash. She cowered behind Speckles and Claws and trembled uncontrollably.

Leaf stared at the horrible scene, shocked.

The weaving rockcrawlers grinned. *One had suddenly become three! A feast of chippies! Rssssttt!*

Feather screamed and tried to leap from behind the boulder to defend her chipmunks. Rustle struggled to hold onto Feather. He shook her violently by the shoulders and shouted something over and over.

Leaf heard Rustle yelling but he couldn't understand him because of Feather's screams. *What? What is Rustle hollering about?*

With a sharp breath, Leaf and Feather suddenly stared at each other. At once they understood Rustle's words.

They all moved quickly.

Rustle and Leaf leapt onto the rock, swiftly unwound their ropes, fashioned large, floppy loops, and swirled them slowly in the air. The loops grew wider and wider.

Feather whistled sharply to Claws and Speckles to leave Whisper. They only glared at her angrily. Feather whistled again and again, insisting that they come. At last, reluctant and confused, Claws and Speckles heeded Feather's signal. They tore themselves from their stance defending Whisper, and raced to Feather's side.

Abandoned, Whisper buried her head between her hands. Frightened beyond tears, she curled into a tight, fuzzy ball.

Surprised at the sudden departure, the rattlers watched the chippies run away. Furious now that two of the chipmunks had so easily escaped, the rockcrawlers spun their heads back around and prepared to strike Whisper. Their mouths opened wide. Their fangs uncurled and dripped their lethal poison. *Rsssttt! Rsssttt!*

Instantly, Leaf and Rustle threw their ropes. In a long, sickening moment the loops drifted through the air as if wisps of slender clouds. They floated gracefully toward their targets, the rockcrawlers' heads, and landed perfectly!

With a quick swipe and slicing movement of her hand, Feather told Speckles and Claws what to do. At once the chippies dashed toward the snakes, seized the ends of the ropes in their teeth, and dragged the rockcrawlers down the ridge toward the whitebark pine. *Rsssttt! Rsssttt!* faded into the breeze.

Feather rushed to Whisper. She knelt gently beside her, and swiftly loosened the choking braid from her neck. She kissed Whisper's dry nose and stroked her shivering ears.

Just as quickly, Leaf knelt beside Whisper and gazed into her eyes. With trembling hands, Leaf held hers. Whisper licked him with her tiny, pink tongue.

A moment later, Speckles and Claws returned dragging the ropes, and grinning. The rattlers were gone.

Rustle joined them. In a burst of joyfulness, Claws wrapped his fuzzy arms around Rustle, and he and Claws tumbled over backwards. Speckles chirped and offered whisker tickles to Whisper, Feather, and Leaf while Rustle tried to disentangle himself from Claws' happy hug.

BRMMMMR! BRMMMMR!

The glowing, blurry wings of Shimmer flitted in between the chippies and Twigs. Merrily, she bounced from leafy head to tufted ear, humming her laugh blissfully.

Leaf giggled. "Why you silly little hummer!" he exclaimed. "You were trying to save us, weren't you?" Shimmer landed briefly on Leaf's nose. Softly she swept a wing over his cheek. For one very special, breathless, and motionless moment, Shimmer sat still. Leaf stared into her dark, intense eyes. Her brilliantly colored feathers sparkled in the sun. Then with a flutter and a flash, Shimmer flew up and away toward the forest.

Leaf blinked. The tiny hummer had been so annoying just the day before. Now he realized she had been guarding him on the crest. He held his hands over his eyes to try and spot the pretty hummingbird in the hot crystal sky, but he could not. Leaf sighed. He wondered if he would ever see Shimmer again.

His gaze fell to the forest far below. It gleamed with so many different colors and textures—fuzzy emeralds, velvety greens, leafy hazels, and misty blues. Still, even as hard as he tried, he did not see the feathery tip of his home, the Old Seeder. The jagged cliffs along the crest rose up, and blocked his view.

Feather and Rustle motioned to him. It was time to go.

Leaf nodded. He felt so homesick.

Whisper hopped over, and gently kissed his ear as if she understood why he felt sad.

When I left, it was so simple. Find Rustle. Find the chompers. Build a dam. But it wasn't that simple at all. And now, what can I do?

With her never-ending enthusiasm, Feather hopped onto Speckles, and looked over at Leaf. She smiled encouragingly. "Come on, Sky Twig! The day isn't glowing any hotter!"

Leaf groaned. *She'll never get that saying right!* he decided, and grinned.

CHAPTER TWENTY-FOUR

THE MIGHTY DAM

Leaf, Rustle, Feather, and the chippies followed the ridge trail down into the forest until at last they stumbled from the shadows of the lofty firs. The path led them to the bluff above the avalanche. Horrified, they halted and stared in stunned silence at the sight of the Rushing Waters crashing over the cliff and beating furiously against the massive trunk of the Old Seeder.

The river had already sliced a sickening cut in the forest floor. Curled waves of mud had become its embankments. The rolling foothills of Echo Peak fought against the flooded stream's new course, and pushed the river toward the valley. Once there, it swamped the grasslands, and drowned any popper too slow to leave its burrow.

From the towering height of the bluff, Leaf stretched on tiptoe and searched for his family in the Old Seeder, but he could not see them or his haven's grizzled knothole. He hung his head, worried and sad.

CRACK! CRACK! CRACK! The noise of wood snapping echoed off the cliff. *CRACK! CRACK! CRACK!* The distinct sound of splitting tree trunks rang out over the crash of the falls.

Leaf jerked his head up at once.

"There!" shouted Feather and Rustle in unison. "Look there!" they pointed at the top of the falls.

A lone, dark silhouette of a goliath beaver stood high on a boulder in the middle of the river just before the foaming water tumbled over the cliff.

At once dizzy, Leaf squeezed his eyes tight. *Did I see what I thought I saw?* Leaf took a deep breath, slowly opened his eyes, and in disbelief squinted to see through the mist of the waterfall.

From the top of the falls, Slapper stood up on his crooked legs, and waved to the Twigs.

Leaf pointed excitedly at him, and then at huge logs floating in a dark mass further upriver. "Look there! There! They're building a dam!"

Patty, Birchbite, Splash, Clacker, and Splatter tugged enormous tree trunks stripped of their limbs across the meadow, and rolled them into the river. They dove in after them and wrestled the trunks relentlessly in the swift current until each log slammed into another, and was wedged into granite crevices underwater. The dam grew thicker and taller. Slapper dove in to guide the colony's work with expert precision and skillful engineering. The beavers constructed a wall of logs stuffed with rocks and mud. The log pile grew higher and thicker until slowly and surely, the mighty dam began to choke the Rushing Waters.

From their vantage point atop the avalanche, the Twigs could easily see the beavers push more logs into the river. With amazing power the beavers swam against the fast current, and maneuvered the logs into a thick barricade. In awe, Leaf watched the dam grow, the river swirl back upon itself, and at last spill into the high mountain meadow beside it. A large, spreading pond formed. At the meadow's far end the water became a river once again, and rushed off on a new course behind Echo Peak.

Patty and Slapper inspected the strength of the dam from every angle, above and below. Slapper had allowed one slender stream to continue as it always had, spilling over the cliff by the giant cappynut tree and the Old Seeder. The waterfall was once again just a silvery strand in the vast green forest.

When the roar of the Rushing Waters began to disappear, Pappo stepped through their haven's knothole and onto the porch-branch outside. In astonishment he looked down through the cedar's branches. The river was gone!

Leaf spotted him at once, and from atop the bluff, he yelled and jumped up and down to get his attention.

Pappo saw him and yelled back. He waved excitedly, and called for Mumma, Fern, Buddy, and Burba to join him on the branch. The twins bounced out, and then up and down wildly. Fern hung desperately onto their skinny arms, frightened they might fall. Their familiar, jubilant shouts echoed to up to the bluff and off the sheer cliff walls.

Leaf and Rustle waved and laughed with relief and joy.

Hastily Leaf led Whisper down the slippery heap of the avalanche to the wide mudflow that encircled the Old Seeder. Unable to reach the tree trunk because of the thick, sticky mud, he simply stood below the tree, and waved to his family, who were quickly sliding down from limb to limb.

Rustle and Feather trailed behind, stepping carefully through the broken limbs until they stopped beside Leaf. With his usual quick thinking, Rustle unwound his rope, looped it over a splintered sapling, and tossed his rope to a low hanging limb of the cedar tree. He easily maneuvered the thin log to lie across the mud. It stretched perfectly from Leaf to the Old Seeder's trunk. Grinning smugly, Rustle swept his arm out over the slender branch, gallantly inviting Leaf to cross over to his family.

With a great, happy, bounding leap Leaf sprang over to where his family stood waiting. At once a flurry of stick arms embraced him. Leaf laughed and untangled himself from their suffocating hugs. He kissed Buddy and Burba on top of their heads, and didn't even mind that their drool dripped all over his knees. He even hugged Fern, and for once she actually hugged him back.

Mumma held her side as she gently smoothed out Leaf's unkempt hair. She murmured, "Welcome home, little Leaf."

From across the mud flow, Whisper watched the melee with great concern. To her, it looked as if Leaf were being attacked by strange Twigs. Whisper's eyelashes blinked rapidly, her whiskers trembled, and her fuzzy ears lay flat against her spotted head.

Leaf glanced over. Immediately he sprinted across the branch-bridge to comfort her. Fern, Buddy, and Burba played 'follow the Leaf' and followed him across. Hesitantly they encircled Whisper, and with amazement gazed at the pretty, graceful chippie.

"This is Whisper!" Leaf proudly introduced her. He stroked her tufted ears and patted her spotted shoulders. "Whisper, this is Fern, Burba, and Buddy."

Whisper pushed her nose very close to each of the tiny Twigs' noses, and blinked curiously. Just to show how special she was—in case they didn't already know— Whisper groomed her whiskers and claws until they shimmered.

"Oh!" cried Fern and the twins in wonder. Cautiously, they patted her spots. Daintily, she nuzzled their hair.

Pappo led Mumma over the branch.

As Leaf helped her step off the little bridge he cried out, "I'm home! I found Rustle and the chompers!"

"So we see!" laughed Pappo. "They were here before you, Leaf! And I see you brought a new Twig to our forest, too!"

Rustle and Feather grinned, and good-naturedly stepped up beside Leaf. They were immediately followed by Speckles and Claws.

With big grins, Pappo and Mumma hugged Rustle. "Thank you, Rustle!" Then they each grasped Feather's hands. "Welcome, dear one! Our haven is always yours! Thank you both for helping to bring our Leaf back to us, and saving our home!"

A long shadow fell over the Twigs. Startled, they all looked up at the cliff.

High on a boulder beside the waterfall, Slapper stood up, and waved to Needles and Ivy far below. A red sky framed his silhouette for the sun was setting behind the Sharp Peaks. In the fiery glow, and standing so high above the Twigs, Slapper truly appeared to be a goliath beaver. With one more brisk wave he abruptly left.

Slapper had a lot of work to do. He needed to strengthen the dam, and inspect the pond. He and Patty wanted to build a new lodge. She was already deciding where. The newborn kits would soon arrive. Splash and Birchbite were off looking for a burrow to make their own. Splatter and Clacker were exploring the pond's far bank for a spot to build their lodge. Slapper knew they would return soon and together, help build each other's homes. Slapper paused to gaze appreciatively at his new surroundings. This place was truly beautiful. He would live here now...close to his friends...the Twigs.

As the sun set behind the Sharp Peaks, it swelled into an explosion of crimson streaks, which burst into sparkles that celebrated the end of the day. It lingered for a moment more, and then the sun slipped away— leaving only a thin, wavy ribbon of orange as a keepsake.

CHAPTER TWENTY-FIVE

THE OLD SEEDER

The chirping of pale green frogs greeted the cool twilight. They squatted on the cedar's soft, red bark and waited for teeny gnats which, if unlucky, would be rapidly whipped into the frogs' flat, pink mouths.

Leaf and Rustle stood atop a wave of mud that curled around the trunk of the ancient cedar tree. The mud had piled up so high their leafy hair brushed the fronds of a low branch. Sadly they gazed at the scattered debris tossed senselessly about by the flood.

Shattered saplings and tangled thickets stuck out of the distorted roots like weird whiskers. Uprooted honeysuckle bushes that had been tossed high up into trees now hung from the limbs, their red berries out of reach of the confused deer. Braids of grass, vines, and flowers crisscrossed the shallow creek that now trickled where the river had once rushed.

From the tree trunk above Rustle and Leaf, a large, gray squirrel poked its head out of its musty-smelling knothole, and glared suspiciously at them. With a bossy chatter, it zigzagged down the trunk to the ground. It hopped back and forth from mud bank to mud bank on either side of the creek as it searched intently for its stash of cappynuts.

Rustle and Leaf glanced at each other. They couldn't help but be a little amused at the squirrel's hopeless quest. It was such an irritating creature.

"Guess we'll need to toss that chatter a few cappynuts now and then," Leaf chuckled.

Rustle stood with his hands on his hips, a familiar pose to Leaf. But now a braided leash slid through one hand. It looped over the fuzzy neck of Claws who stood beside him trying hard to be patient and not squirm too much.

Claws tugged gently at the braid, and twitched his whiskers until they blurred into a fat-looking mustache. Rustle reached out to stroke the moist nose of his chippie friend, and murmured, "Soon, Claws, soon."

Leaf grinned at Rustle's gentle tone.

"Feather and I are returning to the crest," Rustle told Leaf. "There're some leaf-flyers of mine up there that Feather would like to see."

Leaf smiled knowingly. "I'll bet she'd like to find a giant tree up there, too, so she can live near you, eh."

Rustle's laugh was a little self-conscious. "Well maybe so. But seriously, Leaf, I've been thinking about it. Now I know I can build a flyer that carries two Twigs so I can't wait to try it out again!"

Unexpectedly the memory of the sickening drop from the treetop, and the biting rush of cool mist made Leaf feel dizzy. For a brief moment he felt alarm for Feather, but then he breathed deep, and warned Rustle, "Just be careful up so high in the sky, my friend!"

Feather strolled up. Speckles followed, dragging her leash behind her. The chippie hopped anxiously about to avoid the worst of the soggy, mud pits. "So what are you two Sky Twigs up to?" Feather teased.

On a sudden impulse Leaf hugged her and at once choked up. He blinked away a few tears. "Thank you, Feather, for your help!" he managed to mutter. "I am always your friend!"

"And I am yours!" Feather exclaimed sincerely, and disentangled herself from Leaf's emotional embrace. "Can we bring you something back from the crest? Maybe you'd like a rock crawler egg?" she joked.

Leaf grinned. "No thanks!" he declared.

Feather giggled, "Well, maybe not then."

"But will you look for Shimmer?" he asked a little wistfully. "Maybe leave a pile of thistle seeds for her on the rocks?"

"Of course, Leaf. We'll watch out for her." Feather glanced at Claws who had begun to fidget and chew on Rustle's hair impatiently. "Go on, now, Leaf. We need our sleep tonight. Dream sweet dreams, little friend. We'll see you again soon, I'm sure."

Leaf nodded, and with another grateful glance at Rustle and Feather, he left the two standing close to one another.

"Fare well!" Rustle called after him.

"Yes, you too," Leaf called back. "Fare well!"

Now feeling a little sad, Leaf climbed up to where his Pappo sat relaxing on the broad porch-branch outside their knothole.

More tree frogs crawled out from the ragged furrows in the cedar bark. They politely took turns flattering each other's chirps. The forest pathways wandered into dark, velvety shadows where silent creatures padded along, unseen.

"Is Whisper staying here with you then, Leaf?" asked Pappo.

"Feather thinks she should stay. I guess Whisper likes me," answered Leaf, looking very pleased. "It's up to her, but I hope she wants to live in the Old Seeder. She already found her own knothole. She's sleeping down there." He pointed to a small knothole not far below them.

"Wonderful!" Pappo said sincerely. "She's very special, and seems very fond of you!" Pappo smiled and chewed on the root of a grass blade.

Lost in thought, Leaf hung his legs off the side of the branch and rhythmically tapped his heels against the bark. He stared at the grasslands glowing in the moon light.

Between the Old Seeder and the valley lay tangled trees, bizarre mud piles, and gleaming pools of water abandoned by the Rushing Waters. The scars of the flood and the avalanche appeared grotesque at night.

Leaf noticed that few birds had perched in the cedar limbs, and he suspected many of the forest creatures would not return at all.

Still, I'm finally home—and safe.

Leaf puzzled over the strange feeling that made him feel sad and uneasy ever since he had returned home. Something was missing. Missing, or maybe just lost. *If only I could figure out what was wrong.*

Sensing his troubled mood, Pappo gazed at his young son, a question in his eyes.

With a deep sigh, Leaf murmured, "It's going to take a long time for the Old Seeder to be the same, won't it, Pappo?"

Pappo paused, and then answered with a firm, even tone of voice, "Leaf, the Old Seeder will never be the same."

Leaf blinked, surprised at Pappo's blunt response. *Do I already know this? Is this why I feel so awful?*

Pappo continued. "It will never be the same, Leaf, but we can hope it will become stronger. Let's hope the dam is well cared for by our chomper friends, and they keep the Rushing Waters far away from our old tree's roots."

Leaf glanced at the muddied roots far below. It would be another long season before the mats of velvet moss and puffy mushrooms offered some comfort beneath the Old Seeder again. He sighed. "Yes. We'll hope for that."

Leaf considered his new chomper friends that were now building a lodge in the deep, meadow pond they had created. He was certain they would keep the dam strong. Leaf wriggled his toes and bounced his legs a little, and then stated in a very determined voice, "The chompers will never let the dam weaken and fail. I know."

Pappo grinned, clapped his hands together, and said emphatically, "I think you're right!"

Leaf nodded with certainty, "They saved us just like you thought they would!"

Pappo put his arm around Leaf. "I'm proud of you, Leaf," he said warmly. "You were very brave. *You* saved us and our home."

Leaf shrugged and shook his head. "Oh no, Pappo, I wasn't brave at all. Rustle, Feather, the chippies, and the chompers were brave. *They* saved us."

Pappo took Leaf's chin, and turned his face so that he could look into his son's large, emerald eyes.

"Leaf," Pappo declared, "it was you."

Leaf sat silent. He tried to remember if he actually felt brave at any time in the past few days.

"Listen!" Pappo tilted his head as if hearing a secret. He looked up through the fern-like sprays of the ancient tree. "*Listen!*"

Leaf listened. He heard the sweep of soft fronds brushing against the sweetly scented cedar bark. Younger branches ruffled their new leaves tenderly. Older limbs swayed and creaked in the evening breeze.

Pappo whispered softly, "*Listen*, Leaf. The Old Seeder is thanking you!"

Leaf listened, and smiled.

Beaver dams are powerful solutions
for droughts and floods.
'Chompers' create havens for wildlife,
and are a natural counter-balance
to extremes of climate change
in our wetlands and forests.
Be a champion of beavers!
Encourage their work!

More Twig Stories by Jo Marshall

Leaf & the Sky of Fire

Leaf & the Long Ice

Leaf & Echo Peak

www.twigstories.com

Leaf & the Sky of Fire

In a far north forest, young Twigs are hopelessly trapped by gruesome bark beetles! Protected only by loyal salamanders & a weird chameleon, the Twigs have no way out of their dying forest. When Leaf, a daring South Forest Twig, attempts a foolhardy rescue, none imagine they all risk even greater peril! Now they are chased by barkbiters and fire!

Leaf & the Long Ice

Excited by stories of summer snow, Leaf's brothers, Buddy and Burba, ride a giant moth to the perilous, shrinking glacier of Echo Peak! But melting ice & blue tubes are more than the twins bargained for! A scary hermit & courageous goats are Leaf's only hope to save the twins!

Leaf & Echo Peak

Rumblings in Echo Peak warn of a coming explosion! Twigs must escape when Echo Peak wakes up but all the forest paths are precarious. Many follow Leaf & courageous marmots down into a creepy prehistoric lava tube, but deadly bats & vicious moles block their way! Where can Twigs hide when a volcano erupts?

About the Author

Jo Marshall is the author of Twig Stories: *Leaf & the Sky of Fire, Leaf & the Rushing Waters, Leaf & the Long Ice,* and *Leaf & Echo Peak.* Jo lives within sight of two active volcanoes and the Pacific Northwest rainforests, which remind her daily of shrinking glaciers, vanishing forests, and impacts on endangered wildlife. Jo is a member of the Society of Environmental Journalists, the Pacific Northwest Writers Association, the Society of Children's Book Writers and Illustrators, and many environmental nonprofit groups. In 1986, while living in West Berlin, Jo earned a B.A. in German Language and Literature from the University of Maryland, Europe. She resides in Snohomish, Washington with her husband, son, daughter, and many odd but loving creatures.

About the Artist

D.W. MURRAY is an award-winning Disney and Universal Pictures artist whose screen credits include *Mulan, Tarzan, Lilo & Stitch, Brother Bear,* and *Curious George.* An award recipient of the prestigious New York Society of Illustrators Gallery, his talent is also recognized by the 2004 Gold Aurora Award. He has written numerous screenplays, pitched story concepts to Roy Disney, and to the producers of *Touched By An Angel.* He is a former scriptwriter for *Big Ideas* and the colorful children's animated series *3-2-1 Penguins.*

D.W. Murray is the author of the thrilling fantasy novels, *Majesty -The Sorcerer and the Saint, Majesty and the Dragon's Throne,* which are compared to the Chronicles of Narnia. His recent release, *Restroshock,* is available on Kindle He resides with his family in Florida.

Find out more about D.W. Murray on his website, www.dwmurraybooks.com.

"The environmental messages contained in this highly entertaining series of stories are certainly important and are told in a way that will engage children everywhere.

The educational value of these books cannot be underestimated especially at a time when we desperately need to create a culture that is committed to protecting our natural wonders."

Dr. David Edwards
Manager of Education
The British Columbia Wildlife Park

"As someone who has worked to both protect an endangered species and engage young people in the environmental issues that will shape their future, I've learned that education through entertainment is a powerful force for positive change. Today's youth can be leaders tomorrow AND today if only they are given the tools to become aware, inspired, and engaged.

The Twig book series powerfully accomplishes each of these needs, all the while reaching young people on their level with fun, family-friendly entertainment.

I have no doubt that, thanks to this book series, countless children will develop a passion for our natural world and all living things that require it to survive. And for each young person who becomes inspired to care for our shared environment, not only will we foster a more caring society in the future, we will create a new cohort of leaders who will be agents of change today."

D. Simon Jackson, Founder and Chairman
Spirit Bear Youth Coalition
Executive Producer
The Spirit Bear CGI Movie
www.spiritbearyouth.org

About *Leaf & the Sky of Fire...*

"*This book is a wonderful read. The story and art-work are impeccably crafted and weave a fascinating tale that will help introduce children to the magic and majesty of the natural world. Importantly, it imparts a strong appreciation of the intricacies and interactions that occur in nature. As a child, it was just such books that helped instill within me a desire to understand nature, and ultimately, to work in conservation. This book teaches in the best way possible – by igniting curiosity and building connections with the one thing that truly supports us all- our home, Earth.*"

Dr. Diana L. Six, Professor
Ecosystem and Conservation Sciences
Integrated Forest Entomology/Pathology
University of Montana

About Leaf & the Sky of Fire...

"This epic story tells a colorful tale of stick creatures that live in trees and protect forests against harmful organisms and issues associated with climate change.

As a bark beetle biologist, I can relate to the difficulties in reducing tree mortality caused by bark beetles and invasive insects. Young readers interested in the natural world and preserving our forests will enjoy this engaging story."

Dr. Richard W. Hofstetter
Forest Entomology Professor
School of Forestry
Northern Arizona University

About Leaf & the Sky of Fire...

"In her Twig Stories, Jo Marshall has created a world that skillfully blends fantasy and reality in a way that is appealing to children of all ages. Anyone who cares about the environment and relishes a good story will become enthralled with Leaf, Moon and the rest of the Twigs.

Ms. Marshall has created a cast of imaginary creatures that live in an all too real world of environmental threats. Set in the Pacific Northwest in a woodland environment, these stories beckon children with their gentle, playful characters who find themselves in truly frightening circumstances. In Leaf and the Sky of Fire, the threat is bark beetles given power by the strength of global warming and climate change. As an educator, I look forward to keeping a copy of this delightful book in my classroom library as an inspiration to future stewards of our planet."

Rose Sudmeier, Sixth Grade Teacher
Snohomish, Washington

www.twigstories.com

61241166R00222

Made in the USA
Lexington, KY
04 March 2017